His he[...]
sire wash[...]
"Dear God, Em, I love you." Crushing her to his chest, he kissed her.

Heat engulfed him. This kiss was nothing like those they had shared in the past. Whatever door had opened had released her passion. She opened her mouth to his kiss, drawing his tongue deep inside and caressing it. Her hands slid deliciously up his chest to circle his neck and thread his hair. She arched into his embrace as though she were starving for his touch.

Happiness bubbled to the surface, the first he had known in months. Convention no longer mattered. He must have Emily for the rest of his life.

But even as his fingers slipped beneath her bodice to tease excited breasts, the last vestige of conscience urged patience. *Wait! Do it right! Protect her reputation.*

Emily moaned, reminding him that unless he stopped immediately, they would both be dishonored. He pulled his hand away from her soft flesh, seizing one last kiss. So rapturous was her response that his thudding heart drowned the soft sound of approaching feet. . . .

**Winner of *Romantic Times*
Reviewer's Choice Award for
Best First Regency for *The Rake's Rainbow***

SIGNET REGENCY ROMANCE
Coming in June 1998

Emily Hendrickson
A Chance Encounter

Rita Boucher
Lord of Illusions

Sandra Heath
The Faun's Folly

1-800-253-6476
ORDER DIRECTLY
WITH VISA OR MASTERCARD

The Second Lady Emily

Allison Lane

A SIGNET BOOK

SIGNET
Published by the Penguin Group
Penguin Putnam Inc., 375 Hudson Street,
New York, New York 10014, U.S.A.
Penguin Books Ltd, 27 Wrights Lane,
London W8 5TZ, England
Penguin Books Australia Ltd, Ringwood,
Victoria, Australia
Penguin Books Canada Ltd, 10 Alcorn Avenue,
Toronto, Ontario, Canada M4V 3B2
Penguin Books (N.Z.) Ltd, 182-190 Wairau Road,
Auckland 10, New Zealand

Penguin Books Ltd, Registered Offices:
Harmondsworth, Middlesex, England

First published by Signet, an imprint of Dutton Signet,
a member of Penguin Putnam Inc.

First Printing, May, 1998
10 9 8 7 6 5 4 3 2 1

Copyright © Susan Ann Pace, 1998
All rights reserved

REGISTERED TRADEMARK—MARCA REGISTRADA

Printed in the United States of America

Without limiting the rights under copyright reserved above, no part of this publication may be reproduced, stored in or introduced into a retrieval system, or transmitted, in any form, or by any means (electronic, mechanical, photocopying, recording, or otherwise), without the prior written permission of both the copyright owner and the above publisher of this book.

PUBLISHER'S NOTE
This is a work of fiction. Names, characters, places, and incidents either are the product of the author's imagination or are used fictitiously, and any resemblance to actual persons, living or dead, events, or locales is entirely coincidental.

BOOKS ARE AVAILABLE AT QUANTITY DISCOUNTS WHEN USED TO PROMOTE PRODUCTS OR SERVICES. FOR INFORMATION PLEASE WRITE TO PREMIUM MARKETING DIVISION, PENGUIN PUTNAM INC., 375 HUDSON STREET, NEW YORK, NEW YORK 10014.

If you purchased this book without a cover you should be aware that this book is stolen property. It was reported as "unsold and destroyed" to the publisher and neither the author nor the publisher has received any payment for this "stripped book."

*Greater love hath no man than this,
that he lay down his life for his friends.*

—JOHN 15:13

Prologue

December 24, 1812

Andrew Villiers, Sixth Marquess of Broadbanks, slumped deeper into his wingback chair, staring at the glass of port in his right hand. Firelight flashed through the wine like rubies, recalling the necklace he had once dreamed of placing around his wife's creamy throat. His fingers tightened.

Emily.

She had been gone six months, five days, two hours, and—he squinted at the clock—seven minutes. The exact time of death was engraved on his heart. He had held her most of that last day, tears streaming unheeded down his face as her life slipped away, her final words sighing his name. If not for the duty he owed his title, he would have joined her.

He glanced across the drawing room to where his marchioness stitched one of her hideous seat covers. Not that he cared what they looked like. Even loathing no longer moved him—for the covers, for his wife, for himself and the insanity that had brought him to this pass. But hatred wouldn't come. Fog had finally deadened the last of his feelings.

Draining his glass, he poured another.

The year had brought little but death—of family and friends, of honor and virtue, of heart, soul, and mind. His brother Randolph, gone at four-and-twenty; his father, whom he sorely missed despite their frequent disagreements; and sweet Emily, tragically dead at eighteen, a victim of his own dishonor. If only he had wed her out of hand! She would still live and he could have avoided this travesty of a marriage.

He drank deeply, searching for the relief that only wine could bring.

Fay.

An unexpected flicker of emotion stabbed through the mind-numbing haze. Abhorrence. She was evil incarnate, a pox on the face of humanity, Eden's snake, Satan's handmaiden. But he would soon get rid of her. If the child was a boy, very soon. The image of Fay lying dead had often tempted him. He was already doomed to hell, so murdering his wife would make no difference. But he couldn't do it. Death was too quick, too clean. Her crimes could only be avenged with a lingering, pain-wracked demise—which showed how far he had drifted from honor.

He owned an ancient keep in the Scottish highlands. Enough of it was habitable to house her and the servants who would guard her. Recent repairs had made the walls secure enough to prevent any escape. Banishment would be far more satisfying than mere death. He shivered as a forgotten remnant of conscience surfaced. Who would have thought that he could grow so harsh? But no one who really knew Fay would condemn him.

The decision lightened his heart. Perhaps he was emerging from the shock of the past year. Or perhaps wresting this small control of his life raised a flicker of hope for the future. *Please let the child be a boy!*

He poured more wine, noting that his hand remained steady. And just as well. He must attend services in another hour. It was the only reason he remained in the drawing room. How different this marriage was from the one he had envisioned. If only—

Again he stared at his glass. The coals shifted, freeing a burst of flame. Emily's beloved face hovered before his damp eyes. She had been too young to die. Too sweet. Too innocent. Too incredibly lovely. How could a righteous God have called her away? Why did either of them deserve such punishment? Not even Randolph . . . But he refused to recall that.

Hardwick paused in the doorway. Lord Broadbanks stared into the fire, even more morose than usual. Her ladyship looked up and frowned.

THE SECOND LADY EMILY

"Surely the coachman did not mistake the time," she snapped, with a scathing look at the clock.

He ignored her. "Mr. Stevens requests a word, my lord," he reported, naming the estate steward. "He is in the study."

Broadbanks gave no sign that he had heard.

"Send him in here," ordered Lady Broadbanks.

Her husband didn't move.

"At once, my lady," the butler agreed helplessly, suppressing a sigh. Lady Broadbanks had taken advantage of his lordship's growing distraction to meddle in estate affairs, a situation none of the servants approved. But they had no power to remedy it. She had already turned out several who had dared criticize her. After summoning the steward, he remained near the open doorway, hoping there was something he could do to help, though he knew there was not.

Mr. Stevens halted just inside the room, his shoulders imperceptibly sagging as his eyes took in the scene.

"What is it, Stevens?" asked Lady Broadbanks.

"Jeremy Fallon just returned from Dover, my lord," he reported, addressing his employer despite the man's distraction. "A woman and child are sheltering in one of the caves on Chalk Down. It's no place for man or beast, my lord. We'll have snow by morning if my knee is any prophet. She'll freeze out there. As will the babe."

"What class of woman are we discussing?" demanded the marchioness.

Stevens sighed. "A gypsy lass," he admitted reluctantly. "With an infant."

Lady Broadbanks drew herself up in furious hauteur. "A thieving gypsy! And unwed, I'll be bound. Intolerable! Evict her at once. And make sure she knows never to trespass again. I'll not have such trash on my land."

"She needs shelter," said Stevens, a plea obvious in his voice and in the look he threw at Broadbanks.

"Then send her to the workhouse," she snapped. "We want no lawless vagabonds here."

"My lord?"

In the hall, Hardwick cringed. Stevens was risking his position by questioning her ladyship's orders. Appealing to his lordship never worked. Broadbanks was firmly under the thumb of his shrewish wife, and there was little the servants could do about it.

Broadbanks lifted his head and frowned. Even the dullest observer could see that he had heard nothing of the exchange.

"How dare he insult me by ignoring a direct order?" hissed Lady Broadbanks before he could question Stevens's business.

"Do it," said Broadbanks wearily.

The clock chimed twelve as the Marquess of Broadbanks stumbled across the hall. January the first. A new year. It had to be better than the old one.

A series of raps exploded through the air. He had barely identified them when Hardwick appeared, still pulling on his coat. Someone was demanding admittance, but who would be calling at this hour? The roads were impassable.

"Murderers!" screeched a voice the moment Hardwick pulled open the door. Several rocks bounced into the hall. Others lay on the porch. "Heartless monsters!"

Broadbanks squinted to bring the scene into focus. A gypsy stood on the drive, her face swathed in a scarf, colored skirts and shawls billowing as she hurled another rock. This one smashed against the balustrade.

"You killed my husband! You killed my son!" she hissed, shaking the bundle of rags clutched to her bosom. "Murderers!" The word ended in a wracking cough. "Arrogant beasts! You set yourselves up as models of propriety, yet callously destroy everything I have."

The charges reverberated in his head, though he had to strain to hear as her voice grew weaker, her breathing more labored.

"But you will pay, *Gorgio*. I am Rom, gifted with the sight." She drew herself taller, her voice now filled with power. "Cursed you are and cursed you will be, you and all who bear the name of Broadbanks. Your women will prove barren, as will your shortened days. Wealth will drain from your fingers like water through sand. You will be as nothing." Spitting at her feet, she collapsed.

"My God!" gasped Hardwick, abandoning his butler's demeanor as he raced to her side.

Broadbanks followed more slowly. While Hardwick tended the gypsy, he hesitantly unwrapped her bundle. Inside was the frozen body of a malnourished boy.

Hardwick pulled the scarf from the gypsy's face and gasped. "She's little more than a child."

Pity filled Broadbanks's heart. "Poor thing. Get her inside and summon Dr. Harvey."

"It's too late. She's dead."

Leaning closer, he stared into a face still twisted with hatred. Her curse rang in his ears. He shivered.

The snow was thickening. "See that they are buried," he ordered dully. "Quietly."

"At once, my lord."

But as he turned back to the house, he knew that any attempt to suppress the story would fail. A footman and saucer-eyed maid stared from the front door. Two grooms watched from the drive. He sighed. Another death to usher in the new year. Not a propitious omen.

Two days later, Lady Broadbanks birthed a stillborn son.

Chapter One

June 12, 1998

She was the Marchioness of Broadbanks.

Or was she? Cherlynn Cardington stared at the telephone. Surely Mr. Carstairs would call back to admit that it was a joke, or someone would jump out of the closet to announce that she was on a hidden camera show. It couldn't be real. Bidding on lot 4753 had been a lark, for God's sake, a way to thumb her nose at the haughty, blue-blooded Cardingtons whose horror of anything unconventional was surpassed only by their pride at tracing their lineage back to an eighteenth-century baron. But she had never been serious.

Shakily pulling a half-bottle of wine from the hotel's refrigerator, she gulped the contents. It doubtless cost a fortune, but she needed to relax and think. Would a title make any real difference in her life?

A quick circuit of her tiny hotel room convinced her that it wouldn't—except to attract the attention that might get her manuscripts out of publishers' slush piles faster. But that would only speed up her rejection letters.

She shrugged, dropping the empty bottle in the trash. What was done was done. She might as well get used to being the Marchioness of Broadbanks, no matter how odd it sounded. And a benefit might turn up one day. In the meantime, there was no harm in it. But it was weird.

Bidding had been the last thing on her mind when she'd gone to Christie's. Her only goal had been to soak up some atmosphere that she could use in a book. Not until she was leaving did she spot the list of titles to be auctioned the following week. Advance bids were welcome. The Cardingtons' scorn of her breeding had always annoyed her, their snobbery triggering more than one fight with Willard. In an inexplicable fit of pique, she had placed a junk bid on a marquessate, knowing that she stood no chance of winning. The cheapest title ever sold had gone for seven thousand dollars. But at least she could fantasize for a week about outranking Willard Cardington III.

Where had the urge come from? She shivered. It had swept over her with the force of an obsession. Yet such pointless mockery was so unlike her that she'd forgotten all about the bid by the time she returned to her hotel.

Now it had won. Once she paid her ten pounds, she would be, by courtesy only, of course, the Marchioness of Broadbanks. Insanity. How low had the aristocracy sunk if a marquess could not even raise cash by selling his title?

Shrugging aside the question, she returned to her laptop, adding to her notes on the Victoria and Albert Museum. Though she had a near-photographic memory, she always kept records, fearing that she would forget the one fact she might someday need. The curator had let her examine several Regency gowns that were not on formal display. They had been fascinating, yet she couldn't keep her mind on business. Not until filling an entire screen did she realize that her hands had slipped up the keyboard, producing twelve lines of gibberish. Deleting the paragraph, she tried again. Five minutes later, she noted that a detailed description of an 1811 court gown now rested in her file on men's clothing. Obviously, she wasn't going to accomplish anything useful until she had exhausted the subject of the auction.

She snapped her computer shut.

Why had the Marquess of Broadbanks sold his title? If he needed money, he would hardly have accepted ten pounds for it. She must have been the only bidder—which itself made no sense. An earl's minor barony had recently sold for over a hundred thousand dollars.

Icy fingers played dirges on her spine.

She tried pacing again, but the room was too cramped. If only there was someone who could answer her questions! But London contained not a single acquaintance. Whatever friends she had once possessed would have written her off after two years of silence. Willard was the closest she could claim to family, but he was the last person she could call.

THE SECOND LADY EMILY

The realization hurt. Usually she ignored her loneliness, but at the moment that was impossible. She had no family, no friends, no husband. She had failed at work, at marriage, at living. She wasn't even a decent writer. Placing second in one obscure contest hardly constituted a career. She would have been better off using her divorce settlement to start over instead of blowing thousands of dollars on a research trip for a book she would never see in print. And now she had purchased a title that was of no possible use.

Willard was right. She was an incompetent idiot who withdrew into a fantasy world to escape facing reality.

The shock of the phone call was nothing compared to her morning visit to Christie's. A sleepless night set the stage for a surreal day. By noon, turmoil had swept away her earlier numbness and left her reeling.

She had arrived at the auction house the moment its doors opened. Mr. Carstairs was waiting. He accepted her credit card, then whisked her to Buckingham Palace, explaining his purpose as they drove. Even getting caught behind a traffic accident gave him time for only the basics.

Because her bid had not been serious, she hadn't read the catalog description. Lot 4753 included more than just the marquessate. Broadbanks had dumped every honor he possessed. Not only was she a marchioness, she was also Countess of Thurston, Viscountess Harrisford, Viscountess Montescu, Lady Ashburn, Lady Wexford, Lady Rainfield, and Lady Cameron. All were real and included full honors. She was now a British citizen with a seat in the House of Lords.

"But—" she choked on this last piece of news.

"I know that it has never been done before," interrupted Mr. Carstairs. "But those were the terms agreed to by Her Majesty, the Prime Minister, and Parliament."

"But—"

"Surely you are not reneging on the sale." Ice dripped from every word.

"Of course not, but—"

The car drew to a halt. A Coldstream Guard opened the door, his face expressionless beneath the bearskin hat, his scarlet coat blazing in the morning sun. Two others opened the palace doors.

"Curtsy, if you can," ordered Carstairs as they followed a secretary along miles of corridors. "She knows you are American, but try to remember protocol. Speak only in response to a question. Do not sit without an invitation. You cannot turn your back on royalty, so when she dismisses you, back out. Once she confirms your rank, you will be a British peer, but you will still be several degrees below Her Majesty."

She nearly laughed—from hysteria rather than humor. She wanted to tell him that she understood the hierarchy of British titles and honors, but she could not recall a single one. Her brain had gone into hibernation within minutes of reaching Christie's and threatened to die altogether now that she was approaching the Queen. Black dots danced before her eyes as a uniformed footman opened another ornate door.

The meeting with Queen Elizabeth passed in a fog, leaving little behind in memory. It was far worse than her first encounter with Willard's family, for terror left her as tongue-tied as the most humble of awestruck supplicants. Mortification would come later. She looked like a bag lady in a cotton T-shirt, peasant skirt, and running shoes—the first clothes her hand had touched once she had given up on sleep. A blast of wind outside Christie's had turned her frizzy brown hair into a flyaway rat's nest. Even her make-up was smeared.

But she curtsied and mumbled an inane reply to the Queen's question about her visit to London. Her Majesty seemed warmer in person than on the news, actually beaming at her newest subject. Not until Cherlynn had been turned over to a secretary and escorted to an antechamber did she begin to register her surroundings. The room was little different than the office she had once shared on Capitol Hill, though its furnishings were of wood rather than steel.

"Tell me about yourself, Miss Cardington," he began, pulling papers and a pen from a drawer.

"Mrs.," she automatically corrected, then grimaced. "I

suppose I should drop the Cardington. I refuse to presume any connection to that family. Miss Edwards will do."

"You are a widow?"

"Divorced. As of two weeks ago."

He made a note. "Why are you visiting London?"

"Research. I am writing a book."

"Ah. You are an author. Do you write under your own name?"

"Probably, but I need to find a publisher first."

He frowned, tapping the pen fretfully on the desktop. "Have you another job in the meantime?"

"Not yet. My most recent was a stint at McDonald's while the divorce was in progress. Before my marriage I worked as an aide for a Congressional committee."

"Ahh." He perked up. "Government service." The pen scratched busily. "Which committee?"

"The House Committee on the Environment. I was one of the lowest aides." And given only the shit jobs no one else had wanted. Even when she had uncovered the information that convinced Congress to narrowly defeat a bill that would have destroyed priceless wetlands, she had received none of the credit. It would have been better if she had. Willard's father had been intensely interested in that bill, though he had remained in the shadows as a silent partner of the development company that had wanted to turn the marsh into a resort and condominium complex. If Willard had known of her involvement, they never would have wed, to the benefit of both.

"It matters not," said the secretary, breaking into her memories. He pulled out another sheaf of forms and began filling in blanks.

"What are you doing?" She had tried to understand what was happening, but everyone she met today left her with new questions. She hadn't dared ask anything of the Queen, and Carstairs seemed to have disappeared, but perhaps this secretary, whose name she hadn't caught, would help.

He glanced up, sympathy softening his eyes. "Her Majesty requires just cause for bestowing a hereditary title. Even though this is a transfer of existing honors, protocol must be observed. But rewarding government service has long been done."

"Even if the government is not Britain's?" she had to ask.

"America is an ally. It is not entirely without precedent."

"I don't understand." She sighed in frustration. "I thought title sales raised money but conferred no legal status on the buyer."

"That is generally the case," he agreed, "but both Harold Villiers and Her Majesty preferred to divest him of everything—honors, privileges, and duties. Parliament concurred."

She wanted to ask why, but his words raised a more pressing question. "Duties?"

"You must take your seat in Parliament, my lady. And you must revise your will, designating an heir until such time as you produce one—or do you already have children?"

"No," she said weakly, blinking away tears as the full tragedy of the last year swept over her.

"How about siblings, cousins, or other relatives?"

"None," she confirmed, again swept by loneliness.

"Unfortunate, but time will rectify that," he murmured. For some reason, his words sounded false, though he couldn't know that the doctors put her chances of conceiving again at practically zero. "The title is hereditary, entailed to your oldest child. Parliament modified the articles of patent to include daughters in the succession and to permit a deed of transfer to a designated heir should you fail to produce one naturally."

He continued to outline the duties of a peer of England, but Cherlynn was no longer listening. All this talk of heirs was unsettling. Those icy fingers were again parading down her spine. It sounded like she needed a lawyer. At this rate, her ten-pound purchase was likely to eat up her entire divorce settlement.

"Whom will you name as your heir?" he finally asked.

"I must think," she said with a sigh. "I know no one here. Unless I designate Her Majesty."

Horror flashed across his face. "That is the one thing you cannot do," he said firmly. "The letters of patent require that you formally designate an heir, but that heir cannot be a member of the royal family."

"How about you?"

"I must respectfully decline. Surely there is someone you can name. He or she need not be a British citizen. The patent confers full citizenship on any title holder."

"Very well." His voice was fading in and out. She should have eaten breakfast, but a sleepless night spent mulling unanswerable questions had destroyed her appetite. Now her empty stomach churned and low blood sugar left her lightheaded. "Will you need a copy of the will once it is complete?"

"You misunderstand, my lady. You will be signing your will before you leave this room. You may, of course, modify it in the future." He pressed a buzzer. A sober gentleman of vast age entered. "May I present Sir Anthony Wiggins? He is a noted solicitor who will assist you in every way possible." Before she could respond, he had slipped out.

Five hours later, Cherlynn fled to the safety of her hotel room and shuddered. What had she gotten herself into? Sir Anthony had answered no questions and volunteered no information. He listed her assets—the principal one being her new array of titles—and demanded she name an heir. He didn't care who, as long as she could provide enough identification to allow contact if necessary. She finally named an aide to the Committee on the Environment, and stipulated that everything but the titles go to her alma mater. The exercise was morbid in the extreme, but even that could not explain her growing uneasiness.

Fishy odors emanated from every aspect of this case. Her Majesty had seemed almost jovial, welcoming an insignificant American into the British peerage with the enthusiasm a new saint would receive at the Pearly Gates. And not just any American, but a female who had failed at everything she had attempted in twenty-six years. Why? Even at the close of the twentieth century, when high taxes had reduced most lords to genteel poverty, when ancestral homes had been turned over to the National Trust, and when political power rested solely in the House of Commons, the peerage remained aristocratic to the bone, clinging to the arrogance and protocol of past centuries and disdaining their social inferiors. Yet the Queen and a marquess had conspired to elevate a foreign nobody to those exalted ranks, apparently with the full connivance of the British government.

For God's sake, why?

Word of her new rank had spread like wildfire. Sir Anthony had spirited her out of the palace via a rear entrance, but reporters accosted the car as it left the grounds. More waited at her hotel. Feeling like a combination rock star and celebrity criminal, she ran the gauntlet as quickly as possible, shielding her face and responding to none of their shouted questions. Upon reaching her room, she snapped several orders into the phone, then collapsed.

What now? Reporters never gave up. If anything, her evasions would encourage them to new heights. Any hope of sightseeing or research was out of the question. Even returning to the States would change nothing. Perhaps she could invert her itinerary and tour the countryside, but even that would require a bodyguard to keep reporters at bay. Granting interviews to the press was impossible. She could not explain why she had purchased the title. She had not the slightest idea what she would do next. And she had no wish to see her face blazing from millions of television screens where Willard could see how ridiculous she was.

"Damn!" Her brows snapped together. He was still influencing her behavior. If not for him, she wouldn't be in this fix.

"Room service," a voice murmured from the hall, accompanied by a discreet knock.

She hesitated. She had ordered dinner and several newspapers, but had not expected such speedy delivery. Leaving the chain in position, she peered outside. The white-jacketed man appeared to be genuine.

"Dinner, my lady," he intoned when she opened the door. His deference stood in sharp contrast to the slow and sullen service she had received for the past week. Rank still commanded privilege, she decided as he bowed himself out, leaving a three-course meal and eleven newspapers on the table.

Shock riveted her eyes to the lead story.

AMERICAN BUYS CURSED TITLE

(London) A daring young American today tempted fate in a magnanimous bid to save the monarchy from extinction. Miss Cherlynn Edwards of Cambridge, Massachusetts, agreed to take on the curse that for two centuries has exterminated branch after branch of the once-powerful Villiers family. Seventy-eight-year-old Harold Villiers, last survivor of the clan, expressed appreciation for the selfless act that will prevent the title from reverting to the crown when he passes on.

"Oh, my God!" Cherlynn scrabbled through her briefcase for the packet of letters she had purchased three days earlier. No wonder they had seemed familiar. She had forgotten her silly bid long before she found them, but all fifteen mentioned the Marquess of Broadbanks. Each was addressed to Lady Debenham and signed by Lady Travis. She had recognized the recipient's name. Lady Debenham had been an influential society hostess for much of the early nineteenth century—and a well-informed gossip.

She carefully unfolded the last one, dated March 1818, and scrutinized the faded writing on the recrossed page.

It is with Great Sadness that I must report the Death of the seventh Marquess of Broadbanks, who slipped unobserved from the cliffs near Broadbanks Hall at sunset yesterday evening, coming to Grief on the rocks below. His parting revives the old Scandals, as must be expected. To die in one's Prime always causes Talk. And more. Each new Tragedy adds Credence to tales of the Gypsy's Curse which have circulated these six years past. It would seem quite Potent, having already carried off Four Victims—miscarriage by the sixth marchioness only two days after she called the Curse onto the House; death by Suicide of the sixth marquess; miscarriage by the seventh marchioness two days later, despite having earlier produced a healthy boy and two girls; and now the death of the seventh marquess. Young Franklin is but four years old, an Endearing Boy already quite solemn over his new duties. Will he live to secure the Succession? One must hope that the sixth marchioness suf-

fers Greatly in her Banishment, for she has brought Unmeasured Grief to a Noble House.

Her skin crawling, Cherlynn returned to the newspaper. It was a tabloid, which cast doubt on its wilder conjectures, but even the bare facts were chilling enough. Since 1812, no Marquess of Broadbanks had sired a child. The five marchionesses who were increasing when their husbands acceded to the title had all miscarried. No marquess had died of natural causes. None had lived more than three years after achieving the title, though many were young when it passed into their hands. In 186 years, 71 men had held the title. Harold Villiers, 76th Marquess of Broadbanks, was the last Villiers, his branch having split from the family tree over four hundred years earlier. Few in Britain scoffed at the Broadbanks Curse. No aristocrat claimed disbelief. Until this morning, Broadbanks's death would have transferred the title to the crown. With the monarchy already on shaky ground, the Queen didn't want it.

And so they had found a pigeon willing to bid without doing a moment of research, a pigeon who was now the seventy-seventh Broadbanks.

"Damn!" She had just bought herself a death sentence. Hurling the paper across the room, she succumbed to icy tremors. But she had only herself to blame. Christie's catalog had mentioned all eight titles as well as the startling information that the purchase would include full privileges and citizenship. Yet she had not read it—undoubtedly the only potential bidder in the entire world who had not. Why else had she won?

There had to be a way out. Pacing intensified her restlessness, so she sprawled across the bed, burrowing under a quilt to counteract her continued shivering. She would have to draft a new will, of course. Foisting a curse onto Beth was unfair. Willard would make a better heir.

But that was no solution. She wouldn't be around to see him suffer, and nothing would induce her to meekly accept an early demise. Thus she must find a way to break the curse.

Morning brought newspapers that made her question her

conclusions. The previous stack had contained mostly tabloids. But allowing sensationalists to stampede her was ridiculous. More sober papers like the *Times* did not mention any curse, though they referred to the many tragedies that had beset the Villiers family. Surely she was intelligent enough to accept death without needing a villain to shoulder the blame. She had been taught to believe only in what she could see. Paranormal manifestations were fine in books and movies, but they did not exist in the real world. Nor did curses. Accidents and disease had claimed many people in earlier centuries. Losing entire families was not unusual. But the credulous could easily terrify themselves into believing some supernatural phenomena was at work.

She turned to the summary of the Marquesses of Broadbanks that had accompanied one of the stories. The family was patriotic, but unlucky. Four lords had died childless only because their sons had earlier perished at Waterloo. A later marquess lost both sons in the Crimea. Other heirs had died in China, South Africa, India, Ireland, both world wars, the Falklands, and the Persian Gulf. In fact, the only military man in two hundred years who had returned alive was the sixth marquess, who shot himself a week later.

She removed the military from her list of potential employers, then chided herself for foolishness.

There was no pattern to the accidents, though she suspected that many of them proved fatal only because of the deplorable state of medicine in earlier times. She had nearly convinced herself that the curse was no more than media hysteria when she noticed the dates.

Seventy-one dead marquesses and death by accident or in war of twenty-nine heirs. Every fatality took place on March 15, June 15, September 15, or December 28.

Cherlynn slipped through a staff entrance, escaping into the early dawn. She had spent the rest of the day and a largely sleepless night formulating plans. Somehow she had to neutralize the curse. Given the current publicity, selling the title was out of the question, and she suspected that giving it away would do no good unless the recipient was willing to take it on. Fat chance! CNN had carried the story, so virtually everyone on the planet would have heard the details by now. She had no idea how to proceed, but learning about the family seemed an obvious first step. Thus she purchased a railroad ticket to Dover where she joined an afternoon bus tour to Broadbanks Hall, former seat of the Marquesses of Broadbanks.

An enterprising reporter had managed to catch her on videotape as she exited Buckingham Palace, but the image had featured her ratty flyaway hair. Today she had pulled it into a neat coil. Sunglasses, baggy jeans, and her assumed name of Heddy Anderson allowed her to pass unrecognized.

Little remained of the estate that had once stretched along several miles of the English Channel and included some of the richest grazing and agricultural land in the county. Even the park had shrunk until the four follies that used to offer grand vistas of lake, wood, and shore, now marked the corners of the property. All were in ruins. All were surrounded by overgrown thickets. The National Trust only maintained the house and formal gardens. But the Regency wing and grounds were renowned, which had placed Broadbanks high on her itinerary when she had planned this trip. Little had changed since the sixth marquess commissioned Repton to redesign the park in 1812. That marquess had also redecorated the house, scandalizing the neighbors, according to Lady Travis, by refusing to allow his wife any say in the results—which suggested good judgment on his part; another letter had condemned the marchioness for her utter lack of style. Cherlynn would soon decide for herself. The only redecorating since the sixth marquess had been the addition of plumbing and electricity.

She stayed at the back of the tour group when they entered Broadbanks Hall, so she could absorb as much as possible without drawing attention to herself. Yet room after room offered no insight into the people who had lived there. Not that Broadbanks was dull. It had grown from an Elizabethan core, one wall of which had belonged to an earlier fortified manor. By the time the last addition was built in the late eighteenth century, the Hall sprawled across twenty acres, boasting two hundred rooms in a dozen wings. Courtyards, sheltered gardens, and terraces filled odd corners.

Only the Regency wing and the Elizabethan core—which held the great hall and state apartments—were open for the tour.

At first, Broadbanks Hall seemed much like other English great houses. The carving on the main staircase took her breath away, as did the ornate *stuccatori* ceilings and intricate marble fireplace surrounds. Faded fabrics graced furniture and windows. Elaborate paneling glowed in the study and library. Threadbare carpets and patched wallcoverings tried to remain unobtrusive.

But the gallery triggered uneasiness. Forty-eight portraits lined its walls. The last had been completed barely a month before the forty-ninth marquess relinquished the estate to the National Trust in 1916. The marquesses represented every manner of man—thin to stocky, short to tall, light to dark, homely to handsome—but they had two things in common. Every picture had been commissioned the day its subject acquired the title. And beginning with the seventh marquess, who acceded in 1815, every subject observed the gallery through haunted eyes. The first four marquesses looked stern. Number five was arrogant. The suicidal sixth was missing.

"Your first visit, dearie?" asked an elderly lady.

Cherlynn jumped. "Yes. And you?"

"Oh, no. I come here often. Broadbanks is fascinating. You should try one of the October tours. Those talk about the ghosts instead of babbling about the curse like Mrs. Tibbins is doing today," she said, naming the guide. "Inevitable, of course, with poor Lord Broadbanks selling the title and all."

"Don't you believe in the curse?"

"Go on with ye!" cackled the woman. "It's real enough. An' powerful strong. My great-grandmama had the tale from her grandmama who married one of the Broadbanks grooms. He heard the gypsy utter the fateful words himself. But no one knows if it truly attaches to the title or to the head of the Villiers family."

"You mean selling the title may make no difference?"

"Maybe. Maybe not. But curses are dull things. Ghosts are more interesting. Broadbanks is the most haunted manor in England—all those horrible deaths, you know. The best-known ghost is the sixth marquess, who haunts the library where he shot himself. Any number of people have seen him. He first appeared the day his wife died in Scotland, leading many to conclude he had previously been haunting her. A more enigmatic ghost occasionally appears on the cliff path, but he has never been positively identified. At least nine family members perished out there and we can't see him clearly enough to identify his clothing. The most elusive one lives in the great hall. It is probably female, but even that is uncertain. All anyone's ever seen is a flash of blue. Theories range from a servant to the fifth marchioness, who was said to fancy blue. Of course the most frightening ghost is the gypsy, but only the marquesses see her. She is not confined to the estate, and her appearance always presages a death. None has survived the sight by more than forty-eight hours. At least one—the sixtieth, I believe—died on the spot."

"Mabel Hardesty, if you're cackling on about ghosts again, why don't you come up here so everyone can hear you," chided the guide, but it was clear she had a soft spot for the old lady. Mabel happily complied.

Mrs. Tibbins paused in the doorway to the great hall, waiting patiently while the last of her charges trickled through. Mabel was expanding her tale of ghostly wonders. "I hope she wasn't annoying you, my lady," she whispered. "It's been eighty years since a Broadbanks last set foot in this house. I want the occasion to be a positive one."

"You know?" She cringed.

"How not? Stay after the others leave and I'll show you the rest of the place. Don't worry about reporters. I doubt those outside recognized you. They are hoping to see the stars."

Cherlynn raised a brow.

"We're turning the Hall over to a film crew at five o'clock, so they can shoot Jane Austen's *Mansfield Park*. This will be your last chance to see the place until autumn."

"Thank you." The words lent a different twist to the urgency that had propelled her to Broadbanks this day. What had she hoped to find? It had not been used by the family since World War I. Had she thought the sixth marquess might materialize to explain how to break the curse? If any clues existed, surely one of the many previous marquesses would have found them. Her incentive was no stronger than theirs. They had all faced early death.

Unless it was the gypsy herself who had impelled this visit. Perhaps she had needed Broadbanks Hall to connect with someone outside the Villiers bloodlines.

"Oh, my God!" she muttered under her breath. It was June 15.

Perspiration instantly soaked her shirt, bringing on clammy chills from the cool air. She fought down her fear. This was a perfectly ordinary English great house full of perfectly ordinary tourists. No one was going to leap out and strike her down. Besides, she had seen nothing resembling a gypsy—which showed how superstitious she had suddenly become.

Biting her lip to control incipient hysteria, she concentrated on Mrs. Tibbins's lecture, turning obediently to examine the portrait above the mantel.

It was the missing sixth marquess. His expression was grim, his eyes revealing fathomless grief and stoic determination. Neither was suited to his face. The drawing room had held a painting of five children, commissioned when this man was fourteen. In the group he had been happy, radiating life and laughter with a face designed for smiling. What had happened in the intervening years to turn him into this dour shell? It couldn't have been the curse, for this portrait had been completed before it was cast, if Lady Travis's letters were accurate.

She drifted closer until she stood directly below him, mesmerized by his haunted countenance. Even through pain and desolation, his mouth remained sensuous. With melting warmth added to the chocolate brown eyes and a light breeze ruffling his short brown curls, he would be a lady killer. Those muscular shoulders bespoke athleticism. She could see him laughing as he effortlessly controlled a team of fractious horses.

Stiffening, she tried to back away, but her feet were rooted in place. Where had that image come from? New shivers attacked. A writer needed a healthy imagination, but nothing in this portrait pegged him as a sensuous Corinthian. Deep furrows plowed his forehead above eyes nearly black with despair. Lines dragged his mouth into bitterness. The weight of the world bore down on his shoulders, bending his back into a permanent stoop. She wanted to pull him into her arms and comfort him, to remove his burdens and free him from care. Her hand stretched upward, straining to reach those sagging shoulders. Empathy flowed from her fingertips. His countenance matched her own reflection during those last weeks of her marriage, reviving her pain, her helplessness, and that overwhelming certainty that she had no future. He had been right about his own prospects, and unless she could do something, hers were no better.

Mrs. Tibbins was gathering her flock to lead them into the gift shop. Ruthlessly suppressing her thoughts, Cherlynn turned to follow.

Unseen hands grabbed her shoulders and pushed. Hard. As she fell, she caught a glimpse of blue out of the corner of her eye. Then her head hit the stone hearth, and blackness engulfed her.

Chapter Two

June 15, 1812

Drew Villiers, by courtesy Earl of Thurston, made an unnecessary adjustment to his cravat and sighed. Procrastination served no purpose. Even contracting some dreadful disease that would keep him away from the great hall would change nothing. His fate had been irrevocably sealed three months ago. The contracts were long since signed. This was merely the public acknowledgment of a *fait accompli*.

He indulged in one last grimace before forcing his countenance into *ennui*, which was as close to pleasant as he could manage. How discouraging to discover at six-and-twenty that his range of emotions had permanently shrunk. Fury now stood in for passion, grief for joy, hatred for love, and bitterness overlay everything. But somehow he would survive.

Emily.

His cowardice was yet another cross he had to bear. He had committed solecism upon solecism in the past two days, refusing to greet her when she arrived, pointedly ignoring her in the drawing room, and abruptly reversing course when she had approached along the hallway that afternoon. Charles had noticed, of course, but assumed that he was avoiding a potential scene. Charles had often joked about his sister's virulent case of calf love. Drew had never contradicted him, though he knew that Emily's feelings went far beyond infatuation. As did his own. The pain on her face at his pointed cut had matched the agony stabbing his own heart. She deserved an explanation, but cowardice had won in the end. If he got close enough to gaze into her eyes, to feel the heat of her touch, to smell the delicate lilac that always enveloped her, he would be incapable of carrying out his sworn duty. If Charles had not been his closest friend, he would not have invited them to his betrothal ball—or would at least have arranged for them to stay elsewhere. But again fate had conspired against him.

Emily. My love.

No! He could not allow her to remain in his thoughts. After this evening had destroyed the last vestige of hope, then perhaps he could explain. They had made no vows—

His conscience rose in protest. While he had put nothing into words, he had implied plenty—with hints, with mutual plans, with kisses that would destroy her reputation if they became known. And he had meant every one, not that it mattered now. Dishonor faced him regardless of his course, so he could only choose the path that harmed the fewest people. Emily was better off without him, a fact she would realize soon enough. If she was lucky, his caddish behavior would teach her to hate him. If not, his explanation would make her despise him for all eternity. He would make sure of that. Either way, the break would be clean. She would return to Yorkshire with Charles. Next Season she would go to London to choose a husband who was worthy of her. He himself would not be there. He would rusticate here in Kent, dutifully attending to business. In time, he would put the memories aside and find contentment.

"Hah!" His snort was lost in the banging of his bedroom door, which he slammed with far more force than was necessary. These mental perturbations were naught but smoke. He was not ignoring Emily so she would learn hatred or prudence or even cynicism. He was a coward. If he got close enough to speak with her, nothing could keep him from sweeping her into his arms and carrying her off—which was what he should have done three months ago. If only he had married her out of hand . . .

Instead, cowardice had trapped him. He should have stood up to Fay. He should have immediately confessed to his father. But pride and cowardice had held his tongue. Pride, cowardice, and the knowledge that Emily would repudiate him anyway once she learned the truth. He could bear being a cad in her eyes, but he could not bear her condemnation once she learned he was a—

He turned down another hallway. If only he had contacted

his father by post. Or chosen another day. Or another time. If only he had stopped for dinner instead of pressing on into the evening. If only Fay had been home where she belonged...

He deliberately emptied his mind. The past was over. His future was set. He could survive only by concentrating on the present. *Set one foot in front of the other. Descend this last flight of steps smoothly. Don't picture the first marquess distracting Charles II's attention so he would not witness the dishonor his descendant would bring to the title bestowed by that monarch.*

Nodding coolly toward his father, he took his place in the receiving line. Broadbanks had suffered spasms for the past week, but he seemed healthy at the moment. Drew held himself rigidly erect and set about doing his duty. Everyone who knew him noted his grim expression, but no one dared comment. And fate offered one small reprieve. Charles and Emily delayed their entrance until after he led Fay into the opening waltz. But his eyes locked onto Emily's bent head the moment she arrived, her obvious anguish stabbing his soul. It took all his resolve to tear his gaze away.

Lady Emily Fairfield followed Drew with her eyes. He waltzed as if his partner had the plague, holding her so far away that her hand had no chance to reach his shoulder and their fingertips barely touched. Describing his expression as grim implied more warmth than was evident. But she took no comfort in the sight.

"Smile!" hissed Charles.

How could she smile when ice encased her heart? She could feel the blood drain from her face to pool around the shattered remnants of her soul.

Betrayal.

So this was what it felt like. Her governess had warned her against men who teased and cajoled, promising the moon when they had no intention of delivering. But she had never suspected that Drew was such a man. He was her brother's best friend! A man to be admired, liked—and eventually loved. He had been her life for four years, since the day he had moved to Thurston Park, the estate adjoining her brother's seat at Clifford Abbey. She saw him whenever he visited Charles. For the past year, she had also encountered him in the woods common to the two estates.

She had lived for those meetings, her love too powerful to allow other interests. Body. Mind. Soul. She was his and would do anything for him.

He had hinted that he returned her love, though he had never spoken the words. When he left for Broadbanks in March, she had thought he was informing his father of their betrothal, though again, they had never uttered a formal vow. Propriety demanded that he seek agreement from his family and hers before speaking of marriage.

Fool! she cursed herself. Why had she thought him devoted to propriety? Memories of his kisses still flooded her with heat. How could he? Or she?

When he had remained in Kent, she had been saddened, but not alarmed. His brother had recently died. Drew would have much to do, and proposing marriage during deep mourning was inappropriate. When the invitation to this house party had arrived, she'd sighed in relief. The marquess must wish to meet her before approving the connection.

But nothing had gone as expected. Lord Broadbanks had been confined to bed, and she had exchanged not a single word with Drew. But the death knell for her hopes was her maid's report that Drew would announce his betrothal to Fay Raeburn at the ball.

She knew who Fay was, though she had not heard the name before. Fay was the neighbor Lord Broadbanks had chosen as Drew's bride. Fay was the reason Drew lived at Thurston. He despised her, distrusted her, and swore his father could not force him into marriage. He had vowed to wed when he chose and whom he chose. Now he had chosen Fay. His face proclaimed that he had not chosen willingly, but that was small consolation for a broken heart. So many dreams shattered. So many hopes in ashes.

She wanted to flee the ball, but that would only draw attention to herself. Pride demanded that she hide her pain. And so she donned the facade of gaiety. This was her first society ball—and her last. She would never see London

THE SECOND LADY EMILY 33

now. Drew was all she had ever wanted. Wedding another would make her pain worse. And so she would return home. Charles had already agreed to leave at first light. For a time she would remain at Clifford Abbey. Once Charles married, she would retire to a quiet cottage and concentrate on gardening.

Only once did she falter during the interminable hours before supper. Her eyes accidentally met Drew's from across the room, and she could not drag them away. This might be the last time she saw him. She wanted to show him how badly she hurt, but she couldn't. His own anguish was too obvious. And so she looked upon him with love one last time. He responded in kind, then paled alarmingly and wrenched his gaze away, stumbling as he slipped from the room.

How long she stared at the empty door she did not know. Her trance broke only when someone grabbed her shoulders and shoved. She hardly had time to gasp before her head struck the stone fireplace. Then nothing.

Drew's eyes burned. He had not cried since boyhood, so it took a moment to recognize the need. Why had he looked into her eyes? Anguish already tortured him. He didn't need confirmation of her pain. To regain his composure, he slipped across the hall, ostensibly to check the preparations for the supper that was to be served in barely half an hour.

Twenty minutes later, he was returning to the great hall when the music ceased in the middle of a country dance. A crowd clustered around the fireplace, parting almost reluctantly when he appeared.

He nearly fainted.

Emily lay crumpled on the hearth, blood already pooling under her head.

"What happened?"

Twenty people spoke up at once, but even after sorting out their words, he knew little. No one had seen her trip, but the consensus was that she had misstepped and fallen.

"Summon Dr. Harvey from the card room," he ordered a footman, gingerly scooping Emily into his arms. She was still breathing, but very shallowly. "And find Lord Clifford," he added to Lady Clifford, who had always been worthless in a crisis and was already on the verge of hysterics.

Cherlynn's eyes flickered open as someone shifted her body. Where—? Dozens of people clustered around, at least three times the number on the tour.

She winced as pain exploded through her head.

Regency clothes. The man lifting her wore an intricately tied cravat and smelled exotically of sandalwood. The movie cast, of course. How long had she been unconscious?

The light hurt, so she closed her eyes. Powerful arms clasped her against a muscular chest and drew her head against a broad shoulder. Who—? She tensed, relaxing only when a soothing whisper tickled her ear, vowing eternal love. She was safe. Protected. Blackness descended.

Drew fought down his panic. Emily was badly injured, though he refused to put the severity of her wound into words. Blood still welled from a deep cut on her head. Even without touching it, he knew that the skull was depressed. He had seen a man die from a similar blow after falling during a hunt.

He carried her upstairs, trying not to jostle her. Fear, rage, love—even confessions of his crimes—poured into her ear as he pleaded with her to fight for life. An eternity later, he laid her gently on her bed, pressing kisses to her mouth, her eyes, her cheeks. His own tears blinded him, but he suppressed them and forced control on his body.

Already, footsteps approached. He could not afford weakness. The ball must resume. Tragedy changed nothing.

He found a towel and pressed it against the cut, trying to stop the bleeding. Once the doctor took over that chore, he returned to the great hall, uncaring that blood streaked his clothing. How better to announce the end of his life?

Chapter Three

Drew prayed harder than ever before, but it didn't help. Emily was still unconscious.

Most of the guests had departed the morning after the ball. Some had murmured about the impropriety of announcing his betrothal while adorned with the blood of one of his guests, though no one had mentioned it to his face. By now, only Charles, Emily, and their mother remained.

Lady Clifford rarely visited Emily's bedside, which was just as well. The few times she had come sent everyone's temper soaring. She started each visit with a litany of complaints and furious admonitions. When Emily failed to respond, she invariably fell into mild hysterics, bewailing the change of plans the accident had precipitated. But her biggest concern seemed to be that Emily would die, thus keeping her from London during the Little Season. Drew was relieved when she quit coming altogether.

Charles was genuinely concerned for his sister, but he had no idea of how to help her. Fortunately, his fear and frustration kept him too preoccupied to notice how much time Drew spent at her bedside. Such devotion was beyond the duty of even the best host. Not that Drew was useful in a sickroom. He could only trust Dr. Harvey to save her.

But as hours turned to days, he feared that Harvey's efforts would fail. The restless movement that had characterized her first two days had ceased. She now lay motionless, her face like wax. And it was all his fault. He hadn't needed Charles's morning tirade to confirm it. His cowardice had hurt her. Displaying his own love, pain, and longing was a self-indulgence that could only have increased her agony, making her clumsy. And the shock of learning that he had turned his back on her despite his feelings could have killed her will to live. He could not be more responsible for her fall if he had pushed her.

As the hours of his vigil dragged by, he plumbed the depths of his soul, shaking with shame at what he found. Cowardice. Fear. Weakness. His inability to deal honestly with the world had destroyed the one decent thing in his life. He had courted Emily in secret, fearful that announcing his intentions would lead to a battle, though in retrospect, he couldn't name the presumed opponent. The match was a good one, undeserving of secrecy. He'd made even bigger mistakes after traveling to Broadbanks to announce his intention to wed. His father's ill health had made him unwilling to do anything that might bring on another attack. Thus he had bowed to pressure and accepted a betrothal to Fay. *Coward!* Now the woman he loved lay dying and he faced a living hell. Why hadn't he put love first and consigned the rest to the devil?

An hour earlier, Charles's infernal pacing had finally shattered his control. "Get some sleep," he'd ordered sharply. "You're doing no one any good by making yourself ill."

Charles had protested, of course, but he'd given in once Drew promised to summon him if there was any change.

Now he rested his head on the fragile hand clasped in his own and prayed. Three days had passed. Her skin was transparent, her face stark white, her breathing shallow and fast. By the second night, she'd been feverish. Dr. Harvey had mumbled what sounded like incantations as he poked and prodded. But his only treatment was bleeding her twice a day to release the evil humors consuming her body.

Each time, protest had choked Drew's throat, for she had bled copiously after her fall, but he knew of no alternative, so he remained silent. Besides, Charles was her brother and guardian. And Charles had agreed. All Drew could do was send to London for Dr. McClarren, a friend trained in the latest Scottish techniques, who could provide a second opinion—assuming Emily was still alive when he arrived.

She was so pale. Normally creamy, her cheeks now resembled the white marble effigy of Queen Elizabeth that rested in a Westminster Abbey chapel. But she looked better than she had all day. He stared again, needing to affirm that hope was not tricking his eyes. The moment Charles had left, he had removed the mound of pillows Dr. Harvey insisted they use to prop her into a half-sitting position, claiming that excess blood in the head would prevent the wound from healing. Drew disagreed. He had seen a few genuine faints in his six-and-twenty years. Each victim's face had turned stark white, returning to normal only after lying down. Thus consciousness must require blood in the head. Since he had lowered her—being careful to prop towels around the wound to remove any pressure—a hint of color had returned. She remained unconscious, but her breathing seemed easier and her pulse was steadier.

A commotion announced the return of the doctor.

"Any change?" Harvey asked as he entered the room. His face snapped into a frown as he noted Emily's new position. "Are you mad? Allowing blood to rush to the head will kill her!"

"She is resting more comfortably," he swore. Normally he deferred to experts, but he was suddenly seized by the certainty that Emily's life was in his hands. "The change in position has not caused any bleeding."

Dr. Harvey rested his palm on Emily's forehead. "But it is making her fever worse. I will blood her once more to drain the humors, but if she does not respond, I must try a blister."

Drew froze in horror. Blistering was a last resort that sought to wake a comatose patient by inflicting excruciating pain to the chest or shoulder.

"My God!" The thready whisper was hardly a sound, but it exploded through the silence like a bomb.

"She's awake." Drew's legs weakened in relief.

"That's encouraging, certainly," said Harvey. "But I must still blood her to drain the fever."

"*No!*" Emily moved restlessly, though her frenzy would have gone unnoticed if he had not been watching so closely. "Can't . . . believe . . . England . . . barbaric," she managed between gasps for air. "Not . . . third . . . world."

"No," Drew echoed. "She has lost enough blood already."

Emily's eyes cracked open, then widened in obvious horror at the sight of the doctor, who was already grasping her arm in preparation for his work.

"Quack!" she gasped. "Filthy. I'll sue. Remove those dirty hands this instant."

"She is delirious." Harvey pulled the box containing his lancet from a pocket.

Drew took in Harvey's appearance for the first time. Blood spattered his jacket sleeve. Dirt clung to his fingernails. A malevolent odor of food, sweat, and disease permeated his clothing. Closing his fingers over Harvey's arm, he pulled him away from the bed. "Leave her alone," he ordered coldly. "Your services are no longer required."

"You wish her to die of fever? She is clearly out of her head."

He couldn't explain his instincts, for Emily's delirium was obvious. On the other hand, changing her position had revived her despite Harvey's claims to the contrary. Praying that he was not making a mistake, he hardened his expression.

"I am not the one who is killing her. She is closer to death now than when you commenced treatment. Good day, sir."

Snorting in fury, Harvey slammed out of the room.

"Water."

He poured a glass of barley water and gently raised her shoulders so she could drink. The motion drained every vestige of color from her face. He quickly lowered her. Using a spoon, he managed to dribble nearly a pint of water into her mouth before she was satisfied.

"No bleeding," she begged thinly. Her fingers scratched against the sheet in agitation.

"No bleeding, my dear," he promised, stilling her hand with his own.

"How much"—she stopped to catch her breath—"blood lost?"

"Six cups," he admitted. "But you also bled freely when you fell."

"Need . . . transfusion," she whispered. "I'm . . . AB positive. Any blood . . . will do."

He shook his head. Her delirium was clearly worse. "Rest

now, my dear. You are feverish. Pray God it will not grow worse."

"Aspirin . . ." Energy exhausted, her voice trailed away as she slipped back into unconsciousness.

Pain finally nagged Cherlynn awake. Something was wrong. She sifted her memory. London. Christie's. Queen Elizabeth. Broadbanks. Hands on her shoulders. A blue flash, yet no one had been near her. Or was she recalling a nightmare? The subconscious could be very strange. Hers had connected the actors in their Regency costumes with a doctor from her current book, producing a nightmare in which she had been victimized by just such a hidebound charlatan. Ridiculous, of course. It was nearly the twenty-first century.

Where was she? The effort to crack one eye open left her panting. Even the auto accident hadn't made her this weak. Her head seemed to float tenuously above her body, each heartbeat reverberating inside. Sharper pains identified the spot that had hit the stone hearth. She scanned the room as best she could without moving her head. The partially open curtains of her canopied bed revealed a small table and a chair occupied by a woman wearing a blue uniform jumper. The room was not part of a hospital, though the woman might be a nurse. Where was she?

Exhaustion closed her eye. But the view nagged at her mind. The woman was wearing a skirt so long it would reach her ankles when she stood. Impractical. But the answer was obvious, she realized in relief. It was a Regency maid's costume. One of the actresses must know enough first aid to look after her until the ambulance arrived. In the meantime, they had moved her into a bedroom.

"Water," she begged, recognizing an urgent need. Her voice came out in a seductive whisper instead of her usual growl. Her mouth was dryer than she had thought.

"Oh, my lady, thank heaven you are finally awake," said her companion. "Everyone will be so relieved." She turned as if to leave.

"Water," she repeated, reminding herself that she was now a marchioness and entitled to be addressed as a lady.

The guide must have revealed her identity. Inevitable, of course, now that she needed medical care. What would the tabloids make of this accident? *But it wasn't an accident.* Goose bumps tickled her arms.

"At once, my lady." The woman grabbed a glass and spooned the foulest-tasting water imaginable into her mouth.

"No straws?" she grumbled between sips. "How long until the ambulance arrives?"

Confusion gave way to motherly solicitude. "Now don't you worry about a thing, my lady. Dr. McClarren warned us you might be unsettled when you finally woke," she said soothingly. "Four days unconscious will do that to a body."

"Four days?" she croaked. Good God, why was she not in a hospital? But waves of weakness dragged at her mind. Her mouth refused to work.

"You were right, my lady. Whatever happened to tear his lordship away, he cares for you. He's hardly left your side in all that time."

Water dribbled down her chin, the weakness so pronounced she could no longer swallow.

Footsteps approached the bed.

"She's awake, Lady Clifford," reported the woman.

"So I see. And about time, too. Thank you, Grace."

"Who—?" choked Cherlynn, opening her eye again. A middle-aged woman was shooing the maid away. She also wore a long gown, but hers was made of muslin. A lace cap adorned black hair shot through with silver.

"I told Charles you would be right as rain after a good sleep," she said in satisfaction. "I can't wait to leave. Now that everyone is gone, I have no one to converse with. Lady Ledbetter has invited us to Brighton for the summer. You must convince Charles to go. You can claim weakness. The journey to Yorkshire will be too arduous, so you need the healthy air of Brighton. Yes, that will do quite nicely. Rupert Ledbetter is staying with his mother. Despite being a younger son, he is a comely lad who will inherit a considerable fortune from his grandmother. He can squire us about until Thurston's wedding. He won't do as a husband, of course, but his credit is good enough to restore yours."

Cherlynn tried to interrupt the flow of words, but no sound emerged.

"I am quite disappointed in Charles. Including you in this party has done you no good at all! He should have left you at Clifford. You haven't entered society yet and hardly know your brother's friends. But even youth won't excuse your gauche behavior. One would think you eight rather than eighteen. What happened to your manners? No lady would fall so inelegantly. I nearly swooned from mortification. Lady Colburn succumbed to vapors on the spot, and Miss Raeburn couldn't get away from you fast enough. Poor Lady Redtree burst into tears and had to be helped from the room. To think that a daughter of mine could cause such a scandal! That is why we must go to Brighton to repair the damage. If people think you are afraid to appear in public, you will never find a husband. Now enough of your megrims. Four days abed for a mere bump is beyond frivolous. You must speak to Charles immediately." The woman reached out as if to jerk her to her feet.

"Wh-who are you?" she managed, shrinking away.

Lady Clifford jumped back, emitting screeches that reverberated through Cherlynn's pounding head. "Ungrateful wretch! You have been listening to that so-called doctor's nonsense. He must think that keeping you abed will increase his fee. Don't ever address your mother so foolishly again."

Mother. The petulant voice continued, but she ceased trying to make sense of the words, welcoming the return of blackness.

The next time she woke, a man occupied the chair. Or was she still dreaming? She recognized him—the sixth Marquess of Broadbanks, whose portrait hung above the great hall fireplace.

Identifying him brought relief. This was either a nightmare or a fever-induced hallucination, which explained the woman who claimed to be her mother. Would Broadbanks think he was her father?

He met her eyes. "So you are awake again." His voice sent shivers down her spine. It was deep but soothing, the voice that had banished the doctor.

"I doubt it. You're dead."

His brows disappeared into the brown curls draped negligently over his forehead. "When did that happen?"

"A long time ago."

"Dr. McClarren feared you might be muddled, but your head will clear as your strength returns. You have me confused with one of my ancestors. I am Lord Thurston."

"You are the sixth marquess," she insisted in irritation.

Something that might have been pain flashed in his eyes. "Not yet, though my father, the fifth marquess, is in failing health. Try not to think too much, Em."

"God, what a nightmare," she murmured. But she could not seem to wake up, so she might as well go along with it. Both his words and his dress placed him in the Regency. She and her subconscious needed to have a good, long talk. "Was it Dr. McClarren who bled me to death?"

He smiled. "No, that was Dr. Harvey. You complained, so I dismissed him. It won't happen again."

"Filthy quack. Did Dr. McClarren give me a transfusion?" She doubted it, given her continued weakness.

"What?" His brown eyes held confusion.

"Never mind." It had been a stupid question. Her subconscious was aware that Regency doctors knew nothing about transfusions. "Where am I?"

"Broadbanks Hall, Kent."

That fit well enough, but she abruptly shivered. He had addressed her as Em. "Who am I?" she quavered.

He frowned. "Do you not recall?"

"Who am I?" she demanded louder.

His hand soothingly stroked hers. "Confusion. It was to be expected. You are Lady Emily Fairfield, sister of my closest friend Charles, Earl of Clifford. Your own home is in Yorkshire, but you were attending a house party at Broadbanks when you fell. Your mother is resting just now, having succumbed to megrims when you fainted during her visit. That was two hours ago."

"Lady Emily Fairfield?" she asked, still in shock, though the dream at least made macabre sense now. Lady Emily's accident had disrupted the betrothal ball of the sixth marquess. The girl had died four days later, according to one of

Lady Travis's letters. Her mind was spinning historical facts into a story. "What is the date?"

"June nineteenth."

"I mean the year," she insisted.

"1812."

"Thank God! This really is a dream. I'll wake up in the hospital any minute."

"Are you all right?" he asked anxiously. "Should I summon the doctor?"

He looked so frightened that she needed to comfort him. "I will be fine as long as I get proper care." Another wave of weakness sent her thoughts in a new direction. Perhaps improving the lot of this dream girl would awaken her faster. It was worth a try anyway. "That quack nearly killed me. I must build up my blood if I am to survive." She concentrated, diverted for a moment by thoughts of Willard. She had never expected to be grateful for his obsession with health food and natural supplements. What would be available in 1812? "I need iron," she murmured. "From infusions of stinging nettles. And liver—at least half a pound a day, cooked gently in milk without grease. It won't equal a transfusion, but it's the best I can do."

"The doctor won't allow it," he said with a grimace. "You can have nothing but gruel and barley water for at least a week."

"Do you want me to die?" she demanded. "I must rebuild my blood before my brain withers. I need iron. And protein. I hate liver, but it is the most concentrated source of both in this accursed world. And I need fruit. Fresh fruit. Especially apricots. They are high in iron. So is parsley, watercress, and spinach—but don't cook those. What I wouldn't give for a bottle of multivitamins."

"Emily?" The fear was back on his face.

She sighed. "You listened once and prevented that quack from bleeding me to death. Follow your instincts, my lord. I may not remember my name or my history, but I know how to restore my health."

Drew tried to ignore her words, but her eyes pleaded too eloquently. She was terrified, yet she honestly believed that this strange diet would help. Did he dare agitate her further by refusing?

He couldn't. He was responsible for her condition. The cruelty of his treatment had cut his conscience to ribbons in the days since her fall. He would do anything to save her, even if that meant flying in the face of convention, wisdom, and medical advice.

"Very well, Em. I'll find whatever you need."

"Thank God!" She relaxed, her pallor again frightening him.

"Let me get this straight." He fetched a sheet of paper from the escritoire. "Infusion of stinging nettles. Fresh watercress and parsley. Apricots. Liver"—he grimaced, but forced himself to continue—"cooked without grease. Is that right?"

"Thank God you're rational, my lord," she murmured. "That will take care of the blood loss. For pain and fever, I need infusions of yarrow and black willow bark. And to fight infection, six fresh garlic cloves a day. Powdered purple coneflower root would be even better, but it's an American plant that may not be available in a country apothecary shop."

He wrote down the names, shaking his head in perplexity, but she was too weak for further questioning. Protests raged through his head, but he thrust them down. If satisfying Emily's demands was the only way he could serve her, then he would willingly do so.

"I will see to it," he vowed, stroking the hair from her forehead. "Trust me."

She nodded.

"One more question, Em. Do you remember your accident?"

"Somebody pushed me." Her eyes drifted shut.

Shaking his head, he departed.

Chapter Four

Drew stared at the library fire through the glass of brandy held loosely in one hand. Charles was similarly occupied.

"Am I to have any say at all in the care of my own sister?" demanded Charles suddenly.

"Surely you don't approve of Harvey bleeding her to death!"

"Of course not! I should have fired the man myself, but I was too worried about Emily to think clearly. And I agree that McClarren is her best hope for recovery. So why are you ignoring his advice?" Anger underlay his voice, only precariously controlled.

He sighed. "Do not make too much of this. She is clearly delirious from fever, but she wishes something solid to eat—and who can blame her? McClarren also warned against agitating her. Talk to her yourself if you think refusing her demands is the best course."

"I already have," Charles grumbled.

"Did she recognize you?"

"No. I was prepared for that, for both you and McClarren had warned me. What I hadn't expected was her determination. She doesn't sound like herself. She doesn't act like herself. Have you ever known Emily to put herself forward?"

Drew shook his head. Charles had put his own impressions into words. Emily was sweet, kind, and beautiful. But she was also the most biddable girl he knew. It was one of her attractions, for she was the antithesis of Fay. He would never have faced a wife who would intrude on his time, make irritating demands, or try to control his behavior. Emily would have served him faithfully, responding to his every whim, but without substantially changing his life.

"It is most unlike her," he agreed. "But that is all the more reason to tread softly. She is confused, and she must be terrified. Agitating her can only worsen the effects."

"But liver? Cooked without fat?" Charles emptied his glass and poured another. "It's not healthy."

"Of course not, but she is obsessed by the blood Harvey took. You must admit that liver is very bloody. At least she did not request a glass of the stuff."

"True, but nettles are almost as bad." Charles shuddered in disgust. "That is precisely my point. Emily faints at the mere mention of blood, let alone the sight of it. Why would she discuss the subject?"

"I've been wondering that very thing. And not just the part about diet. You've seen the list of remedies she demanded. Some of them I've never heard of. Do you suppose that her meekness has been an act all these years? You must admit that her demeanor has always conformed to what she was taught. But her am-amnesia"—he stumbled over the word he had heard for the first time from McClarren—"made her forget those teachings, allowing her true character to surface."

"Fustian," snorted Charles. "Even as a rebellious child she was never like this. I was talking to McClarren before dinner. Though he has no personal experience with lost memory, he knows several doctors who do. Not one has ever encountered profound personality changes. Bewilderment, fear, anxiety, and even anger, but never new traits."

"What did she say that bothers you so much?" Charles was more upset than he had ever seen him. They had been friends since Eton, though they often disagreed with each other. Charles was traditional, disdaining the newfangled notions Drew often espoused, but even their most heated debates had never upset him the way Emily's accident was doing.

"Besides not recognizing me?" Bitterness filled Charles's words.

"She doesn't know anybody," Drew said in excuse, but that wasn't strictly true. Her first words to him had been *You're dead.* The idea may well have come from a dream, but she had recognized him and connected him with Broadbanks. "How odd," he murmured.

"What? That she knows none of us? You are the one who reported that she remembered nothing."

"No, not that. When she first awoke, she thought I was the marquess. Why would she know that my father is Broadbanks?"

"But amnesiacs' brains are not completely blank," said McClarren from the doorway. "They recall many things. Take Lady Emily, for example. She has no trouble speaking, recognizes most common objects, and seems to have a firm understanding of medicine and the human body. What she cannot produce are memories of her childhood or of the people she knows."

"But the condition is temporary," said Drew hopefully.

"Usually." The doctor pulled a chair closer to the fire and sat down. "In most cases, the problem corrects itself within a short time, though I know of at least one victim who did not return to normal until six months after his accident."

"Six months!" exclaimed Charles.

"And there have been a few who never remembered. We know little of how the brain works. A man in Edinburgh suffered a blow to the head some years ago that wiped out all memory of who he was. He recovered from the injuries and was building a new life when he was again struck in the same place. When he recovered consciousness, he had regained his memory, but recalled nothing of the two months that separated his accidents."

"So Lady Emily might forget these days?" asked Drew sharply.

"I think it unlikely. In most cases, restoration of memory does not erase what happened during the amnesia episode."

McClarren left to check his patient. Charles accompanied him.

Drew stared into the fire. Emily's amnesia was almost a blessing. Since she had no memory of their relationship, he was able to sit with her and talk to her without constraint, though he had to admit that her nearness was taxing his control. But that was a small price to pay for a few days of contentment. It was all he would have in his lifetime.

Yet he could not forget her words when she first awoke. Even delirium could not explain some of them. How could she have undergone such a total change? The Emily he loved would never have defied a doctor, even such an unprepossessing one as Dr. Harvey. The Emily he loved would never have made demands that ran counter to what others advised. And it was not just the liver. She had been specific about fruits, vegetables, cooking methods, and quantities. When he had delivered the first infusions to her an hour before, she had elaborated on the health benefits of each item, claiming attributes that he had never considered, using words with which he was unfamiliar. But she had sounded so sure of herself that he had acceded to every request—even to the demand that her windows be opened and the draperies drawn back to allow excessive light into the room.

He had asked McClarren about the herbs she specified. While the man had not personally used a couple of them, he had agreed that none should cause any damage.

Had she received divine knowledge in answer to his fervent prayers? He doubted it. God would hardly grant favors to a sinner such as himself. And when her memory returned, she must reconcile herself to his betrothal. She had loved him for years. One of her few deviations from strict propriety had been to tell him how much she cared. He had long suspected that her feelings were more powerful than his own, a fact that prompted a nagging sense of guilt. Had he taken advantage of her? After Fay's determined possessiveness, Emily's selfless devotion had seemed a blessing. She would be a perfect wife, catering to his every need without intruding on his privacy or objecting to his activities. His own love was strong enough to keep him faithful. . . .

At least it was now. Had losing her deepened his feelings? Life with Fay would be anything but congenial. And Emily's pain would make it worse. Poor Em would actually be better off dead. So why would a loving God bring her back to a life that promised misery? She had been on the verge of death only a day ago.

And that was another puzzle. How could someone who had hardly been able to breathe, and who had not had enough energy to move so much as a finger, be ranting and making demands on him with such vigor?

He headed for the kitchen. From the moment that he had yielded to those demands, he had taken the full responsibility. The servants were so horrified at his unconventional orders that he could not demand obedience. If this odd regimen killed her, he wanted no one else to feel guilty. He was already damned. One more death would make no difference.

Cherlynn awoke in a pool of sweat. For the first time since falling, her mind was coolly logical. She could think. She could remember. Her fever had broken.

She glanced around the room, but someone had shut heavy curtains, blocking any trace of light or air. Only a couple of deep shadows marked the location of furniture. She hated being shut in. But as she tried to sit up, her body protested.

Her head still throbbed. Whatever analgesics they had given her must have worn off, which was probably what had awakened her. But she felt weak, weaker even than the morning after Willard had driven them into a tree, triggering a miscarriage that destroyed their unborn son. Her subsequent hemorrhage and infection guaranteed that she would bear no more. But she thrust that tragedy away, focusing instead on her current weakness. Surely she had not been ill long enough for her muscles to atrophy! Her mind was hazy, but she shouldn't have been in bed longer than two or three days.

Or had she? Snatches of hallucinations and voices lingered in her mind. Her fever must have reached at least 105 degrees to have produced delirium. If she had been that ill, then she could easily have lost a week of her life. Or more.

Fighting dizziness, she carefully rolled toward the edge of the bed and sat up, stretching her feet toward the floor. Once she switched on the lamp, she could take stock of her situation. But the floor was not where it should have been. By the time she realized that, it was too late to prevent a fall.

New waves of pain rolled through her head. She must be in a hospital for the bed to be so high. But she could not recall ever seeing a hospital so dark—nurses were always popping in and out and left the doors to the lighted halls open so they could keep an eye on the patients. But English hospitals might be different, she surmised, recalling that she was no longer in Massachusetts.

She lay on the floor for several minutes until she felt strong enough to stand. Why had no one noticed that one of the patients had fallen out of bed? But a new puzzle deflected the question. When she put out her hand to grasp the bed, she encountered a set of steps. Using them to pull herself up, she next discovered that the bed was a four-poster with a complete set of bed curtains. Even English hospitals would hardly include something so unsanitary.

Those fragments of hallucinations returned. Had they been real images? Perhaps she had not been taken to a hospital after all. It was possible that she was being housed at Broadbanks.

No lamp rested on the bedside table. She lurched to the window and fumbled her way through the curtains, sinking thankfully onto a window seat. Moonlight faintly illuminated a grand vista of formal gardens. Catching a glimpse of the thin crescent that floated above a tree, she grimaced. She had last noticed the moon the night before leaving for England. Some rapid math confirmed that a full week had passed since her fall.

The cool air chilled her soaked nightgown, raising goose bumps. Looking down, she cringed at the sight of heavy cotton clinging to her body instead of her preferred nylon. Hopefully whatever second gown had been loaned to her was more comfortable. If not, she would have to sleep nude and pray that the other side of the bed was dry.

She was moving slowly toward the door, where she expected to find a light switch, when it opened.

"What are you doing out of bed?" demanded a male voice. One hand held an oil lamp that pushed the darkness into the corners.

But Cherlynn did not see him. She had been facing a dressing table when the door opened, and now froze in shock. The girl in the mirror was a stranger. Long jet-black hair raged wildly about a face so white she might have been a ghost. An elegant neck disappeared into the ruffled nightgown, whose damp fabric clung like skin, revealing tall slenderness and shapely curves.

She fainted.

Drew shoved the lamp onto the table as he sprang forward to catch Emily. What was she doing out of bed? And where was the maid who was supposed to be watching her?

At least she hadn't hit her head again. And she seemed to be stronger. Perhaps the weeks of forcing all manner of strange foods and potions down her throat had helped. Or perhaps she was possessed by the devil as the servants whispered. He grimaced at the tightly shut windows. Some beliefs were too strong for even direct orders to overcome. A fear of the night air was one of them.

But at least she was stronger. With relief came awareness. She was soft and feminine. Holding her was spiraling intense need into his loins. He tore his mind from the woman in his arms and carried her to the bed. But the moment he set her down, he realized that both her gown and the sheets were soaked. That must be what had driven her to her feet.

Pulling the coverlet loose, he wrapped her warmly and deposited her on the couch. The fire was nearly dead, but the scuttle was full, so he set about warming the room. The maid would be dismissed.

"Emily," he called urgently, chaffing her wrists to awaken her. He needed smelling salts, but didn't know where she kept hers, and he could not leave her. "Are you all right?"

She blinked. "What happened?"

"You unwisely got out of bed," he murmured. "Why did you not ring for help?"

"The mirror," she murmured. "It wasn't me."

"Mirror?"

"When the light came on. The reflection wasn't me."

"I know you dislike looking rumpled," he said with a sigh. "But we could not brush your hair properly while you have been so ill. We feared the tugging would harm you. Your injury is only beginning to heal."

"Who are you?"

He fought renewed pain, reciting the litany with which he

was all too familiar by now. "Lord Thurston. You fell during the ball and struck your head. You have been recuperating at Broadbanks Hall ever since. We feared that you would succumb to your fever, but it appears that it has finally broken. Your brother and mother are also here, but both are resting at the moment. I can fetch them if you like."

"No!" She seemed to be making a mental struggle, but her question when it came was unexpected. "How long have I been ill?"

"Nearly three weeks."

A shudder wracked her body. He tucked the coverlet closer. "It can't be." Her voice was pleading. "The moon is a waning crescent. It can only have been a week."

"Relax, Emily. You are still disoriented by the fall." He brushed the hair from her brow, feeling her puckered forehead, a sign that she was deep in thought.

"The date. What is the date?"

"July 4, 1812." He had answered this question so often that he added the year almost automatically, though he had never considered it a vital part of the date.

"The Fourth of July," she murmured to herself. "I'll miss the fireworks."

"Emily?"

She shook her head, then winced. "Nothing, my lord. You call me Emily?"

"I shouldn't, of course."

"Because it is not my name?"

"You still don't remember, do you?" He sighed, his thumb idly stroking her palm. She didn't seem to mind the impropriety. "You are Lady Emily Fairfield, sister of Charles Fairfield, seventh Earl of Clifford. I am his closest friend. But that does not give me the privilege of addressing you by your given name. Forgive me."

"Of course. I am sorry to be such a bother." She frowned. "Do I recall a doctor bleeding me?"

"Yes, but I put a stop to that at your request. The new doctor agrees that routine bleeding does more harm than good."

"So I was not hallucinating." She sounded disappointed. "And you are seeing that I get the food I need to recover."

So harping on food had not been a product of delirium.

THE SECOND LADY EMILY

"You needn't fear for your recovery, Lady Emily. But if it is to continue, you must return to your bed."

"No. Being bedridden for three weeks explains why I am so weak. I need exercise."

"In the morning, if you remain free of fever. Now let me summon a maid to change the bedlinen, and we will get you tucked back up."

"What time is it?"

"About two."

She glared. "You can't awaken some poor girl in the middle of the night! Get me a couple of sheets and I'll do it myself."

"What?"

They argued for several minutes before he finally gave in and collected the sheets. Not that he would allow her to make up the bed. She would swoon the moment she stood up. He did it himself. Poorly, but after subjecting him to such stubborn insistence, she could sleep on wrinkles. She had to change her own nightgown, of course. But aside from grumbling over the style—at least he thought that was what she found wrong with the garment—she managed. The effort tired her so much that she fell asleep the moment her head hit the pillow.

Succumbing to temptation, he placed a lingering kiss on her forehead before he left to track down the maid who was supposed to keep watch in her room.

Chapter Five

She paced slowly from window to door and back. Each time she passed the mirror, her eyes searched the glass, hoping to see her familiar image restored. Who would have thought she could long to be short and fat with frizzy brown hair, gray eyes, and a plain face? But she had never anticipated finding herself in this predicament.

Each pass brought new disappointment. Cherlynn Cardington never lurked in the mirror. Instead, long black hair rippled to her waist, and China-blue eyes stared hesitantly from a pale oval face, their depths reflecting shock, fear, and lingering disbelief. Hands repeatedly skimmed her figure, trembling at the change from chunky to slender.

Acceptance gradually subdued the shock. This was no dream. The flesh and blood her fingers touched matched the image in the mirror.

Lord Thurston had left her with much to ponder, not least of which was his parting kiss. Their argument had wearied her, so she'd taken the coward's way out by pretending sleep, raising new questions. When his lips had pressed against her brow so gently, it had taken all her willpower to remain motionless. Before she spoke with anyone else, she needed to figure out what was going on.

His claims validated the scraps of memory from her illness. If they were all true, then she was no longer Cherlynn Cardington, failed wife, unsuccessful author, and unwilling marchioness.

Again her eyes locked onto the vision of beauty in the mirror. Lady Emily Fairfield. Lady Travis's first letter had described the accident during Thurston's betrothal ball. If this was the fourth of July, then the girl had died of her injuries sixteen days ago. Thus she must now occupy Emily's body. Her own fall on the same date in the same room must have wafted her into the past. But why?

She moved to the open window. The maid had implied that Emily loved Lord Thurston. His concern and tenderness suggested that he returned her regard. He had been at her bedside nearly every time she'd surfaced from her delirium, feeding her, supplying the remedies she demanded, bathing her face with cool water—not typical Regency behavior. Even Emily's brother had visited only rarely, and her mother even less.

She returned to the mirror, forcing her thoughts past her renewed headache as she recalled everything she had read about Emily. There wasn't much. The press had concentrated on the curse. Since Emily had had nothing to do with the Broadbanks fortunes, even the tabloids had ignored her. Her only knowledge had been gleaned from that single letter and the maid's comments.

Mabel's voice echoed in her ears, prattling about ghosts. Cherlynn replayed her tour of the great hall from her sight of the sixth marquess's portrait to the weight of hands on her shoulders. Throwing open the clothespress, she gasped. A ball gown hung inside. A silk gown dyed a very familiar shade of blue.

Emily had not died until four days after the ball, yet she had seen the great hall full of people dressed in Regency gowns. Thus Emily must have voluntarily vacated her body early so that Cherlynn could save her life. Once that was accomplished, the girl would return, sending Cherlynn back to a time when transfusions and life support were undoubtedly keeping her own body alive.

Nerves again set her pacing. Nerves and her determination to build some stamina into Emily's flaccid muscles. No wonder Regency ladies seemed delicate and never did anything. Even this mild exercise made her gasp for breath.

Forget Regency ladies. Think about your own problems. Emily's body was well on the road to recovery. Thurston knew the regimen well enough to assure that it stayed that way. He would dismiss any words uttered during her delirium, but now that she was rational, talking risked exposing her identity, something Emily wouldn't want. Yet the girl hadn't reclaimed her rightful place.

It didn't require a rocket scientist to figure out why. The man Emily loved was betrothed to another in an era when betrothals were nearly as binding as marriage. And that wasn't all. The sixth Lady Broadbanks would call down the curse that would destroy his family and prompt his suicide in only three years. Emily must expect her to break his betrothal. Only when that was accomplished, would she return to her own life, allowing Emily and Thurston to live happily ever after.

Worded like that, it sounded like she must selflessly serve a stranger. But Emily wasn't the only one who had a stake in ending Thurston's engagement. The outcome would affect every Broadbanks in the future, including her. She had visited the family seat to learn more about the curse. Now she had a unique opportunity to prevent it. Instead of railing at Emily for putting her through this agony, her time would be better spent figuring out how to proceed.

Or *if* she should proceed.

She took another turn about the room.

Time travel had fascinated her ever since she'd seen *Back to the Future* in her youth. Her library contained many books with time-travel plots. A theme common to many of them was the havoc that could result from even tiny changes in history. Again she stared at Emily's face. The girl was not asking for a small change. Removing the curse would allow hundreds of people to live full, productive lives and would result in hundreds more being born. The fifth marquess was a powerful man. His relatives held positions of influence in government, the military, and society. What would happen if all those men and women continued their lives unfettered? How could she, an insignificant American, come to be in the right place to be wafted back if there was no curse? At first glance, Emily's actions could create a really nasty paradox.

On the other hand, she doubted that Emily could have acted alone. If that were possible, millions of people would have changed their lives—innocent victims of random violence, repentant sinners, persons disabled by accidents, and so many more. Thus there must be a higher authority who processed requests for intervention. If that were the case, then she could trust that power to maintain the balance of the universe by preventing such a paradox. Whatever steps she took now would not destroy the integrity of time or prevent her from touring Broadbanks on June 15, 1998.

It was a comforting thought, and she could only pray it was true. Her track record for clear thinking wasn't very impressive.

Again she contrasted the laughing, fourteen-year-old Thurston with the grim sixth Marquess of Broadbanks. And with the haunted man who had lingered at her bedside. Andrew Villiers, Earl of Thurston. Charles called him Drew. Emily would also have done so, at least in private. Drew. She liked the name. He deserved better than death by suicide at age twenty-nine. She would save him from Fay, and save herself as well.

The first step must be investigation. She couldn't free Drew unless she understood why he and Fay were betrothed. His personal feelings were obvious. Spending hours at Emily's bedside—often with no one else in the room—bespoke his love. Unless her understanding of Regency propriety was completely off, his behavior was scandalously compromising and could ruin Emily's reputation if word of it leaked out. He had also wrested control of Emily's convalescence from her own brother. Both actions must stem from his fear of losing her. So why was he betrothed to Fay?

His father might have arranged it, of course—Lady Travis had hinted that was so when she mentioned the long friendship between Lords Broadbanks and Raeburn—but why would a marquess force an alliance with a baron's daughter when an earl's sister was available? No matter what criteria one judged by—breeding, wealth, character, personal preference—Emily was clearly the better match.

So she would start by learning how the betrothal arose. Halting before the mirror, she met Emily's unexpectedly blue eyes. "I'll try to help you," she whispered. "But I can't guarantee success. I've bungled every task in my life. There's little hope this will be any different."

Half an hour of pacing had expended her scant energy. She climbed back into the high bed, arranging the mountain of pillows behind her so that she was half sitting. Her eyes noted the bell pull, but she resisted the urge to summon her maid. Before she spoke to anyone else, she must decide what to say.

As she drifted in semi-slumber, she recalled the tour guide's words. Drew's will had ordered that his portrait hang in the great hall as long as the house stood. And now she knew why. Emily was the ghost in blue who had haunted the site. He had wanted to spend eternity gazing at her. Had he felt guilty for loving her when he was bound to another? Had he been responsible for her fall? She would have to work the answers out for herself. They were scarcely questions she could ask him.

And they weren't the only puzzles. Why had Emily chosen *her*? She was hardly the sort one turned to in an emergency. But reviewing her life showed why she might be suited to this particular task. Her two years of working for the committee had taught her to gather and assimilate data, piecing facts together to make a picture. If she was to solve a mystery, such a skill would be useful. She had no family or close friends who would miss her if anything went wrong. Plus, she knew much about the Regency era—knowledge essential to anyone who wrote about the period. Then there was the information on herbal medicine she had learned from Willard. How ironic that he had actually saved her life.

But Emily could have found a helper long ago if those were the only requirements. Many people fit that description. Cherlynn Cardington was so ordinary, she was negligible. Thus it must be the title. In buying the Broadbanks title, she had purchased everything that went with it, including the curse. So she had a personal stake in the outcome. Or the title may have been the conduit that allowed Emily to bring her back. She might be the first available marchioness who knew how to survive the injury that had originally killed the girl. No family member had visited the house since it had been turned over to the National Trust during World War I. Ghosts were usually tied to a specific location. If the title was the conduit, then Emily would have had no opportunities in over eighty years—which didn't do much for her confidence. Had the girl grabbed her because she was the only choice instead of the best?

"Enough." Rehashing how she got here accomplished nothing. She needed to consider the stakes instead of wallowing in her own inadequacies. Seventy-one dead marquesses, including Drew, who had blown his brains out on September 15, 1815. His kiss again tickled her forehead. She could no longer see him as a historical entity, or even as the grim-visaged portrait of a man long dead. He had fought hard to save her life, willing to try anything, no matter how odd, if she claimed it would help her survive.

"He does not deserve to die."

Her expression firmed. If she was to carry this out, she must start thinking of herself as Emily and must try to act like Emily. She could help no one if they locked her away for insanity.

"You rang, my lady?" Dawn had broken over an hour earlier, allowing sunlight to stream into the room. The maid's face suddenly changed to horror. "The window is open again! You'll catch your death, and no mistake."

"Stop!" Her voice halted the maid in her tracks. "Leave it. Fresh air will speed my recovery."

"Still delirious," muttered the maid.

Cherlynn bit her lip. She had no idea what Emily had been like, but suspected the girl had been a wimp—biddable and conformable, as she would have said in one of her books. Though she would try to emulate that in public, there was no hope of fooling the maid. Everything she recalled from her illness confirmed that Emily had confided freely in this servant. Amnesia wouldn't account for all her differences, so she needed an explanation for the change.

"I am not delirious," she said gently, "though this illness has left me weak. I need your help—and your silence."

The maid's eyes blazed with suspicion.

"My head has healed and my fever is gone, yet my memory has not returned," she announced slowly. "You must teach me about myself and the people I should know. Announcing my condition to the world will harm my family, but I cannot wait patiently for the affliction to right itself. I must live as though it is permanent."

"Very wise, my lady."

"What is your name?"

"Grace."

"Very pretty. It fits you." Grace was about thirty, with a willowy figure and ease of movement that did not match the literary description of the servant class. "Have you served me long?"

"Since your birth. I started as a nursery maid, but was assigned and trained as your lady's maid at your request."

"I trust I have good judgment. Let's start with my family. I have spoken with Charles and my mother, but I know little about them."

She listened for nearly an hour as Grace described Charles, Lady Clifford, and a younger sister, Mary, who had remained at Clifford Abbey. The more she learned, the more daunting her assigned role seemed. Emily was a typical Regency miss, barely educated and dependent on others for everything. She never raised her voice, never put herself forward, never disputed a gentleman. All in all, she sounded like a boring doormat. Impersonating her would be impossible. But that explained why the girl had dumped the job of preventing the curse onto her shoulders. The real Emily wouldn't have known where to start.

And the task was potentially more dangerous than she had first suspected. If she acted like Emily, she would have little chance of learning enough to break Drew's betrothal. But asking the necessary questions meant that Emily must undergo a character transplant. Damn! How was she to keep the damage to a minimum so that Emily's return wouldn't cause worse trouble? There was a limit to how much she could blame on amnesia.

She snapped her attention back to Grace's words, which had moved on while she was lost in thought.

"If only that man hadn't intruded," Grace was saying stoutly. But her face suddenly flushed.

"What man?"

"Nothing, my lady. I've tired you with all this talk."

"What man, Grace? Lord Thurston?" At the maid's

THE SECOND LADY EMILY 61

flinch, she continued. "I already know that he and I had an understanding that has since been abandoned. What was it?"

"Not now, my lady," begged Grace. "If you don't remember, it's all for the good."

"Hardly. I need to know how to behave. Since I remember nothing, learning the facts can hardly bother me. It would merely be a story about strangers."

"Very well," agreed Grace, though she was obviously uncertain what she should do. "You have known each other most of your life. He has occupied the next estate for four years and is Lord Clifford's closest friend, so he was often in the house. Some years ago you formed a *tendre* for him that blossomed into love. Last fall he began courting you."

"Why has Charles not mentioned it?"

"His lordship didn't know," admitted Grace. "Lord Thurston wished to gain his father's approval before openly pursuing a connection. When he left for Broadbanks in March, you believed that he would announce his intention to wed you and would return within a fortnight. But he did not. You clung to your certainty long after everyone else had learned the truth. His betrothal to Miss Raeburn was announced at the ball three weeks ago, but the arrangement had been made when he was a child."

"So it was contracted by the families," she murmured, frowning. Either Emily had been a complete widgeon—a distinct possibility, though not one she could broach to the loyal maid—or Thurston was no gentleman. He had not behaved as a dishonorable cad during her illness, but that meant nothing. She'd been in no shape for dalliance. And her impressions of him might all be wrong. She had a long history of poor judgment. Perhaps his hovering had had a more prosaic purpose—making sure that delirium did not reveal their relationship.

He must have had dishonorable motives for pursuing Emily. No gentleman during the Regency could get away with terminating a betrothal. Never mind that his bride was unworthy. Yet if Drew had pursued Emily solely for seduction, why had the girl brought Cherlynn back through time? Emily had been certain of his love. Had he gone home to terminate the understanding, but found himself outmaneuvered? It was a comforting theory, but she didn't know him well enough to judge.

"My lady?"

"I'm sorry. I was thinking of something else. Help me dress now. I need to sit up if I am to regain my strength."

"It's far too soon," protested the maid.

"Nonsense. Remaining in bed weakens you more than illness does."

"You don't sound at all like yourself," admonished the maid.

Of course she didn't, but she must convince Grace that all would be well. She would need the woman as an ally if she was too succeed. "I am not myself," she said slowly. "Perhaps if I tell you why, you will understand. But the tale is to go no further." She stared at the maid until the woman nodded, then dropped her voice into the cadence of storytelling. "My earliest memory is of falling. I awoke in a brightly lit meadow full of wondrously strange flowers in colors for which we have no name and shapes that cannot be described. One moment I was alone; the next a man stood at my side. He radiated peace and harmony, but his words denied them to me. 'It is not your time,' he began quietly. 'You must complete a great task before the garden will be open to you.' I protested, for I wished to stay, but he insisted. Before he sent me back, he laid a hand on my head and promised me success. I can only guess that he bestowed gifts to aid me, but I do not wish the world to view me as odd. Thus you can speak of this to no one. And you must teach me all that I have forgotten so that others do not guess the truth."

"You saw God. . . ." The awe on her face was too much.

"He did not introduce himself, but I do not believe so. At most, I met a messenger. And he did not define my task. All I can do is live my life as best I can—with your help."

Grace nodded.

"But I now have urges I cannot deny, even if they counter convention. Compulsions this powerful can only have come from him. One of these is to revel in fresh air, even at night, though I will ask for an additional comforter to keep me warm. Another is to rise from this bed and regain my strength. I will expect you to accede to my wishes, but we will not speak of this again."

"Are you finally recovering?" asked Charles as he approached her couch that afternoon.

"Physically, though I still remember nothing before my fall," she replied calmly. "But I wish to minimize that fact in public. Have you any idea why I tripped so clumsily? People are bound to ask."

Charles sighed. "I did not actually see you fall, so I can only guess. You were quite blue-deviled that evening."

"Because Lord Thurston was to wed another?" she asked bluntly.

His eyes widened, but her matter-of-fact tone calmed him. "No. Because he had spoken not a single word to you since our arrival two days earlier. Despite our many discussions of your air dreams, I doubt you accepted his betrothal until the ball itself. A group of ladies were discussing it just before you fell. Confirmation may have shocked you into staggering back and tripping on the hearth."

"Gauche of me." Her mind was working furiously. "So we never had an understanding."

His face registered shock, but he apparently recalled her condition, for he reined in his fury and sighed. "We've had this discussion too many times, Em. You were obsessed with the man, but Drew would never behave so dishonorably. He paid no more attention to you than to Mary, knowing that his father expected him to wed Miss Raeburn. You knew that, but you were ever one to ignore facts. I hope you have learned your lesson."

"Perhaps this illness has steadied me."

"I am glad to hear it. We will remain here until Drew's wedding—which should be plenty of time to assure your recovery—then go to London for the Little Season. I let you talk me out of a Season last year, but it is time to seriously look for a husband."

She made no protest, allowing him to direct their conversation into impersonal channels while her mind tried to make sense of these new facts. Grace claimed that Thurston was serious but secretive. Charles didn't think he had singled her out. So whose head was in the clouds? If Drew had courted Emily secretly, it didn't speak well for either his intentions or his honor. But perhaps Emily had magnified simple courtesy to fit her own fantasies. Grace had only Emily's word for Drew's behavior.

She had no way of knowing. And despite the fanciful tale she had spun, she had received no special powers to solve this mystery.

Chapter Six

Another fortnight passed before Cherlynn was strong enough to leave her room, and even then she wasn't up to the lengthy dinners typical of the Regency period. She spent her days trying to improve her stamina. Her own mother had once tried to turn her into a dancer. She had hated every minute of those classes, but now she blessed them. The stretching routines dancers used warmed her up for her daily regimen of calisthenics, aerobics, and the kicks and dodges learned in a self-defense course. Her physical exertions probably delayed her recovery for a few days, but the conditioning might prove vital. The few facts she'd gleaned about Fay made the girl sound dangerous when crossed. Terminating Drew's betrothal would hardly sit well.

Few callers intruded. Drew had ceased visiting once her fever broke, though he continued to supply whatever foods she requested. Charles likewise avoided her company, which relieved some of her stress. His visits always included animadversions against her dietary regimen despite its obvious success. If he learned about her exercise program, he might very well commit her to Bedlam. Dr. McClarren returned to London, promising to return when he judged she would be completely restored to health. Thus her only regular visitors were Lady Clifford—whose diatribes were a trial she found hard to endure—and Lady Anne, Drew's shy young sister, who stopped briefly each afternoon to inquire about her condition.

A fortnight of exercise energized her until she could no longer remain in her room. She had come to England to research the Regency period. What better source would she find than actually living in it? But being here was of little use if she stayed cooped up in a bedroom. On that thought, she set out to explore the house, or at least the Regency wing. She was familiar with the layout from her tour, but the decor was very different than she recalled—which was only to be expected. The faded Regency furniture occupying the National Trust property had been installed by Drew after he acceded to the title. Most of the rooms now contained heavy seventeenth-century pieces that she found oppressive. Whatever Drew's morals, she had to admire his taste.

The fifth marchioness had decorated the morning room in a lighter French motif that had survived into her own time, but she again noted differences. Accustomed to the faded splendor of 1998, she found the original furnishings almost garish. Yet a moment's thought explained the bright colors. German chemists would not discover the artist's palette hidden in petrochemicals until the mid-1800s. Many natural dyes were expensive. Thus using a broad range of bright colors indicated wealth. That was even more true because the Regency also lacked good color fixatives, so every cleaning dulled the fabric.

Moving on from the morning room, she entered the library—which contained only half the volumes she had last seen on its shelves—and avidly perused the titles. No one had thought to supply Emily with books during her convalescence, and she hadn't wanted to make an issue of her differences, but she was bored out of her mind. A section in the corner contained a collection of gothic novels, each inscribed *Elizabeth Villiers,* Anne's older sister, who was now Lady Lindleigh, mother of two children. Apparently Anne had purchased no novels of her own. Even Jane Austen's first published work, *Sense and Sensibility,* was absent, though it had come out more than a year before.

But no matter. Grabbing the first volume of *Otranto,* she settled contentedly into a chair and was devouring its pages when the door opened to admit Thurston.

"You like novels?" he asked in surprise, identifying the book in her hand.

"I love them," she answered truthfully before recalling that she was supposed to be Emily. Lady Clifford was both empty-headed and dictatorial, so the girl probably disapproved of them. But since these books belonged to his sister, he could hardly revile her for reading them.

"Are you sure you should be up and about so soon?" The frown this time was merely worry.

"Of course. It is two weeks since my fever broke and five since my fall. Prolonged bed rest weakens the body, delaying recovery."

He collected a newspaper from the desk and sank into a nearby chair with a sigh. "I don't know where you get these odd notions, Lady Emily. You never showed any sign of medical pretense before."

"Since I have no recollection of that, I will have to take your word for it. But what is the news today?" She nodded at the paper, hoping to distract him to a less personal topic.

"Would you like to read the society page?" More surprise laced his words.

"Perhaps later. I was wondering how Wellington is doing in Spain. He would have taken Badajoz last spring, but I forget where he went from there."

Thurston's shock abruptly shut her mouth. Again she had forgotten her role, speaking aloud without thinking, annoyed because she couldn't recall the sequence of battles and hadn't thought to check the newspaper for herself. Was Wellington in Madrid yet? It didn't matter. If she was to carry off this masquerade, she must hide her research, suppress her knowledge of current events, and concentrate on pursuing Emily's goals. That would require thinking every comment through before uttering it. Especially around Drew, whose image of Emily must remain unchanged if the girl was to return. Unfortunately, after weeks of receiving his personal attention, she felt far too relaxed with him, which made it hard to remain aloof. She should not have stayed in the library to read. Books always made her lose track of time and place.

He swallowed a couple of times, then apparently decided to humor her. "I do not know what Wellington is doing right now. He does not announce his plans in advance, and the papers are still printing arguments over the sack at Badajoz." He glanced at the *Times*. "Parliament is debating Wellington's latest request for supplies. They will doubtless refuse to increase the amounts."

She tried to ignore him and remain silent as Emily would have, but he wouldn't let her.

"Come on," he urged, meeting her eyes. "You're dying to say something. Out with it."

He was right. "How shortsighted to keep the army on poor rations," she scoffed. "How can anyone expect him to win if they deny him the men and material he needs?"

"True. But many people believe that victory is hopeless and we should forget the whole thing."

"Nonsense. Napoleon is not invincible, as his asinine move into Russia proves."

"He is winning there," he said softly.

"For the moment. It is only July."

"What does that mean?" He was clearly puzzled.

"Have you ever been to Russia?"

"Of course not!"

She tried to drop the subject, but the expectant look on his face prompted one last comment. "It get very, very cold there. No one unaccustomed to the weather can stand the winters."

"Napoleon is not stupid," he countered sharply.

"But he expects his troops to live off the land. They will never find food and clothing for six hundred thousand men."

Thurston surged to his feet. "Where did you hear that?" he demanded. "No one knows how many troops the Emperor sent to Russia!"

She swayed, feeling the blood drain from her face. "I-I don't know," she said finally, falling back on her supposed amnesia. Fleeing to the window, she gazed at the gardens. *Damn you, Emily! I'm going to screw this up. You can't expect me to ignore a topic so dear to my heart. Couldn't you at least give me an idea of how to go on in this plagued world? Look at me! Five minutes with Drew and I've already blown my cover. At this rate, he'll despise you by morning!*

Emily remained silent.

"Damnation," he muttered so softly she barely heard the epithet. He slipped up behind her. Placing his hands on her shoulders, he gently turned her to face him. "Forgive me, Em," he said soothingly. "You did nothing wrong. I shouldn't have ripped you up. But you've never evinced an interest in world affairs before. I was surprised."

"Is knowing about the world in which I live so terrible?" she asked in return, shivering at his touch. "This void in my mind is frustrating. I have to learn the rules all over again. And they make no sense! How can anyone stand to live in ignorance?"

"Don't think about it now," he urged. "The memories will return. And you needn't hide your interests completely. Ladies like your mother disparage learning—which explains why you've hidden it so well—but I know several bluestockings who get along quite nicely in town."

She shuddered. She should not have attached that label to Emily. But it was too late. Hopefully Drew would not bandy his knowledge about and would be relieved when Emily returned to her uneducated self. This masquerade was going to be harder than she had imagined. Breaking from his grasp, she fled.

Drew watched Emily leave the library, then returned to his seat. He was still in a state of shock, for she had never given the slightest hint that she read anything beyond *La Belle Assemblée*. Despite loving her, he suddenly felt that he did not know her at all. Did amnesia induce alien traits? Or had it merely stripped away a facade of pretense, allowing the real woman to shine through?

It was a frightening thought. If he could know someone so well, yet be so wrong about her core, how could he judge anyone? And why had she hidden her interests from him? Didn't she trust him? Pain stabbed his heart at her betrayal. Despite her protestations of love—which had surpassed all bounds of proper behavior—she had shared none of herself with him. It hurt.

Charles arrived, pouring himself a glass of wine before taking the chair Emily had just vacated.

"Anything noteworthy in the *Times*?" he asked.

"Emily just asked the same question. She had some startling—but astute—observations on Napoleon's campaign into Russia."

Charles's glass landed on the floor, spattering wine in all directions.

"So you didn't know, either." He felt better knowing that even Charles was ignorant of her interests.

"Impossible," Charles snapped. "The girl hasn't a thought in her head beyond clothes, gossip, and music."

"So I thought. But not only is she *au courante* on the war, her understanding of tactics surpasses that of many gentlemen."

"Fine praise, indeed. I know how much you chafe at being the heir. Wellington could use you."

Drew stared at the fire to hide the pain that twisted his face. "My last hope of a commission died with Randolph. I must secure the succession and stand ready to assume the title. Father is not well. McClarren believes he will be gone within the year."

Charles raised a questioning brow.

Bitterness filled Drew's voice. "He has suffered numerous spells since the one at William's funeral, though no one bothered to inform me." And that was intolerable. Anger flared. It was time to assert his rights. He had been in a fog since Randolph's death, too morose to question even glaring insolence from the servants or the secrecy that had left him in the dark for so long. "Something is amiss with his heart. Since each attack is worse than its predecessor, it is only a matter of time before one proves fatal."

"My condolences. Did Emily mention how she learned so much about the war?" he asked, moving the conversation away from the emotional pit over which it hovered.

Drew was glad to set aside his problems. Not even Charles would stand by him if the full truth emerged. His deceit weighed more heavily every day. If not for the succession, he might have ended his life by now. "She recalls nothing," he reminded his friend. "I can only assume that her memory loss is why she is exposing her foibles. She no long realizes that such interests are unladylike."

"Then she must be a better actress than I had suspected. She has always been a model young lady with never a hint of anything more. Perhaps she has been slipping into my study to read the papers while I was otherwise occupied. But it is odd that even the servants have never caught her at it. Humphreys would have heard if anyone had seen her there," he added, naming his valet. "But I cannot understand why she would bother. Or, if she is truly interested, why she would hide it from me. I have never disapproved of anything she has done."

Only because she's never done anything unconventional, at least nothing you know about. "Your mother would," he said aloud with sudden understanding. "How often have I heard her condemn others for something as innocuous as mentioning a well-known poet. She even criticized Lady Peabody one afternoon for allowing her daughter to read Maria Edgeworth's *Improving Tales for Young People,* claiming that reading and writing should be restricted to invitations and letters between close friends."

Charles sighed. "I had best talk to Emily. She will have forgotten Mama's intolerance. McClarren fears that any upset could worsen her condition, but Mama will ignore that if she thinks Emily's behavior is unacceptable." He hurried after his sister.

Drew summoned a servant to clean up the wine, then frowned, again pondering Emily's secrecy. He had thought them even closer than siblings. She had loved him with an intensity that sometimes stifled him. Yet despite meeting him scores of times without a chaperon, she had never said a word about reading for pleasure—an activity far less damning. It hurt.

His hands tingled where they had grasped her shoulders. His love burned as hot as ever, now accompanied by an unexpected lust. Did that arise because she was now forbidden fruit? He tried to accept the explanation, but her accident had allowed more than her intelligence to surface. Her eyes revealed a spark of passion he had never noticed before. It animated her, adding seductive grace to every movement. Touching her had been a mistake, sending heat into his loins that awakened powerful desires. They had no future, a fact his body had better accept.

Swearing, he headed for the stables.

* * *

Cherlynn looked over her shoulder. No one was in sight, so she ducked into a seldom-used sitting room and exhaled in relief. One of the unexpected aspects of Regency life was the plethora of servants. It wasn't their existence that bothered her as much as their constant presence. Those who had grown up in the aristocracy didn't even think about them, but she was aware of every one. No matter where she went, she was surrounded by people who watched her every move so they could serve her properly. But they provided no companionship, instead raising persistent worry about blowing her cover.

Drew's shock yesterday had been bad enough. Charles's had been worse. He had followed her back to her room, where he read her a lengthy lecture about Lady Clifford's intolerance, then pressed her for details of where she had learned her information. Her claims of amnesia merely increased his irritation until she finally feigned a headache and all but passed out in order to get rid of him. Since the men of this era considered women to be weak, then weakness was her most powerful weapon. It put another twist on Regency relationships, but she preferred honesty to guile.

And it raised yet another question about Drew. How could he and Charles be close friends? Unless he was also horrified at the idea of female intelligence. It might explain his love for Emily.

She must be more careful. Remaining silent on the grounds that her amnesia left her uncertain of the proprieties might work. And acting demure. If she kept her eyes on her lap, she would avoid meeting Drew's gaze. There was something about him that challenged her, making her forget Emily, forget the curse, and forget the years that would soon separate them.

In the meantime, she had to assuage her boredom. She had purloined a copy of *Tom Jones* from the library and sought out this unused room so she could relax for a while. Sighing in relief, she sprawled onto a couch and was soon engrossed in the lascivious tale.

She was chuckling softly when a knock sounded on the

door. It opened as she dropped the book and bolted to her feet.

"My lord!"

As Drew sauntered into the room, she sat down atop *Tom Jones* and tried to compose her shattered nerves. The adrenaline rush from fright drove her heart into high gear and left her muscles quivering.

"What are you doing in here, Em?" he asked curiously. "Your mother is hysterical because you are missing."

Damn! Lady Clifford hadn't called on her in two days. Why now? Drew waited expectantly for her answer. "I was looking around and stopped to rest for a moment."

Skepticism flared in his eyes. Recalling her plan, she dropped her gaze to her hands, realizing too late that in this context, the action made her appear guilty. Stronger invective raced through her mind. She had always been a rotten actress, even with a script. How was she to manage without one?

"You needn't pretend with me," he said softly, joining her on the couch. "You slipped away to read, I suppose. But despite your mother's admonitions, there is nothing wrong with gothic novels like *Otranto*. Most of the girls who come out each Season enjoy such tales."

"But Charles and Mama do not." Thank God he hadn't seen the title. She had collected *Otranto* from the library while the family was at dinner the night before, and finished it after dismissing Grace. Only then did she realize how starved she had been for mental stimulation. It was impossible to go back to staring at the walls, but there was little else to do. Lacking a Regency lady's accomplishments, reading was her only time filler.

"I won't tell."

"But you already did," she reminded him, making the mistake of meeting his gaze. He was staring at her with such longing that she nearly reached out to touch his cheek. But guilt rapidly filled his eyes.

"I'm sorry, Em. It wouldn't have happened if you both hadn't caught me by surprise. I'll handle it better in the future. Trust me."

"Can I?" She had meant the question as an innocuous

comment, realizing only as he blanched that he would believe she referred to the entire Fay-Drew-Emily imbroglio. Heat washed over her face, making this second *faux pas* even worse. Emily had chosen her unwisely. She was going to fail, condemning Emily to bitter unhappiness, Drew to an early suicide, and herself to the Broadbanks curse.

He visibly pulled himself together. "Of course you can. But for now, you must return before your mother disrupts the entire household with her frenzy."

Without warning, he grasped her hand and pulled her to her feet, then picked up her book. "I'll slip this into your ro—" His voice died as he saw the title. "My God! You're reading Fielding!"

"So?" The fat was in the fire anyway. She would *not* apologize.

"Emily, ladies never read Fielding."

"Why? He's quite humorous."

He was pacing the floor, one hand tangled in his curls as he tried to form a coherent response. "Agreed, but his stories are bawdy."

"Which contributes to the humor. And they are excellent studies of human nature. Being human, ladies should learn about personal relationships. Ignorance puts us at the mercy of liars, seducers, and unscrupulous men who wish to prey upon us."

"But protecting you is the duty of your family."

"Who aren't always available," she countered. "And Charles is hardly the most competent protector. He is so blinkered, he sees only what he wishes to see." Why else had he missed the myriad liaisons between Drew and Emily?

"Astute of you," he conceded, then sighed. "We haven't time to debate the question now, Em. I will deliver the book to your room and slip it under your pillow. But you'd best be careful. If it is discovered, Charles will likely incarcerate you for life. I dare not consider what Lady Clifford would do. She makes a formidable opponent when riled."

Chapter Seven

A week later, Cherlynn and Lord Broadbanks paced slowly through the formal gardens. Though his arrogant expression matched the portrait hanging in the gallery, his pale face, swollen fingers, and irregular breathing hinted at heart problems. Her father had suffered similar symptoms before he died of congestive heart failure, but the absence of twentieth-century drugs made the marquess's situation worse. He was caught in a vicious cycle of angina attacks which forced him into bed rest, reducing his stamina so his heart had to work harder when he arose, bringing on more angina.

Recognizing his illness changed her plans. She had considered probing his friendship with Lord Raeburn and the betrothal he had arranged for Drew, but she now abandoned the idea. He did not have long to live in any case—a heart attack would kill him on September seventeenth—but emotional shock might hasten that end, complicating an already messy situation. The very fact that he was walking with her was a change from history that could affect his health.

If only he had not insisted on joining her. She didn't want him to collapse while in her company. Had she known that he was on the terrace, she would have left through the front door—she had slipped outside to be alone. But by the time she'd spotted him, it had been too late to escape.

He had not yet joined the family for dinner, but she'd recognized him from his portrait, even though Reynolds had painted it thirty years before. Without that, she would never have pegged him as Thurston's father. Aside from brown eyes, they looked nothing alike. Broadbanks was tall and wiry with the most aristocratic face she had ever seen. Hauteur suited him. As did disapproval. Within moments he revealed himself as a belligerently opinionated man who despised new ideas. His notion of right and proper had been carved in stone in his youth, mellowing not one iota in the intervening years. Too bad she hadn't anticipated how passionately he would defend even unimportant ideas.

"The park is lovely, though personally I prefer a vista closer to Repton's naturalism," she replied to a question. Hiring Repton to redesign the estate had been Drew's first move after gaining the title. She had seen the results in her own time and found it more relaxing than the rigid Italianate garden of 1812.

He snorted, his face purpling alarmingly. "The man lacks discipline. How are we to maintain order if we surround ourselves with chaos?"

She bit off a caustic reply. Irritating him would do his heart no good. Nor would it help Emily's reputation. So she did not point out that Repton was every bit as controlled as his predecessors. The result might look natural, but every plant was carefully placed and shaped to achieve that effect. Nothing was allowed to spring up on its own.

And his basic premise had merit. A person's surroundings *did* influence his character. Children growing up in violent neighborhoods accepted violence as normal, making them more apt to use it as a problem-solving tool. In like manner, youngsters surrounded by books and whose parents appreciated learning were more likely to become readers.

She forced her mind back to the marquess, who had forgiven the untutored statement of a mere girl, but was now set on educating her. "My great-grandfather inherited both the estate and the title from his uncle, the first marquess, in 1697. The estate was on the decline at that time—the first marquess having been a better warrior than a manager—but the second marquess dedicated his life to restoring it. It is a legacy I intend to leave to my heirs." His voice caught, reminding her that he had lost both of his younger sons—William in battle early in 1811, and Randolph only a few months past.

"And a beautiful legacy it is," she agreed, letting her eyes wander over the view. The rigidly formal style assured that man's hand was obvious in every planting. Each tree or

THE SECOND LADY EMILY

shrub was trimmed to a precise shape. Every hint of imperfection was instantly removed, whether dead leaf or faded flower. It reminded her too much of a Renaissance painting. But she kept her mouth shut. Not knowing what Emily would have admired, she chose to be the shy maiden.

The path turned a corner, which she cut too sharply, impaling the skirt of her muslin morning gown on a rosebush.

"Phooey!" A thorn scratched her hand as she wiggled the fabric free. Again she was jeopardizing her cover. Emily would not have been so careless.

Long skirts were the pits. Actually, she hated skirts of any length, preferring jeans and T-shirts. Her casual garb was another trait Willard had criticized. But now she had no choice. Emily's dresses constricted her, making it impossible to move freely.

And the gowns weren't all that constricted her. She had often included clothing descriptions in her writing, but had never fully understood how those garments affected the wearer. The reality had led to an argument with Grace the first time she had dressed to go downstairs. Emily had a less formal relationship with her maid than was usual between lady and servant—probably because they had been together for eighteen years. As a result, Grace felt free to protest when Cherlynn ripped off the corset and refused to put it back on.

" 'Tain't proper," the maid insisted. "You'll destroy the fit of the gown."

Cherlynn nearly countered with "Bullshit," but caught herself in time to change it to "Fustian! The gown is so loose it would fit a woman six months with child. I can't breathe in that thing. Do you want me to faint from lack of oxygen?"

Grace's frown reminded her that oxygen might not have been discovered yet.

She sighed. No wonder Regency ladies were always swooning. "Grace, I can't explain. But I know that squeezing my body into unnatural shapes is harmful." After years of battling fat, Emily's lithe figure was heavenly. She had no desire to change it.

"Did your messenger tell you that?"

It took her a moment to recall the tale she had spun. "He must have. Where else would I get such an idea?"

"But why would he want you to ruin your reputation?" Grace asked, her satisfied smirk making this lethal blow to the argument even more irritating.

Further discussion had led to a compromise. She would wear the corset, but only if it was laced so loosely that it nearly slid off. Deliberately flouting the rules of proper dress would attract attention she did not need. It was bad enough that she had none of Emily's accomplishments. Lady Clifford had asked her to perform on the pianoforte in the drawing room the previous evening. She couldn't. Two years of piano lessons back in grade school did not constitute talent. She couldn't even read the notes. Lady Clifford had decided that Emily was being obstreperous and had read her a blistering lecture when they were alone, but Cherlynn couldn't rectify the situation, vowing instead to draw as little attention to herself as possible. And so she walked with Lord Broadbanks and encouraged him to talk. If she kept her own mouth shut, she wouldn't give herself away.

"Fortunately, Drew is finally taking his duty seriously," he said as they turned back toward the house. "Randolph's death demonstrated how vulnerable we are to fate. He needs to secure the succession, a fact he could no longer ignore, offering for Miss Raeburn the next day."

"I thought that the marriage had been arranged years ago," she said in surprise, then modified her tone. "At least that's the impression my brother had."

"Lord Raeburn and I had often discussed the possibility, but Drew was free to make his own decision. He spent five Seasons in town, so has had ample opportunity to meet other candidates."

They had reached the steps to the house. Lord Broadbanks's valet waited to assist him inside, so she bade him farewell. But the hair on her arms was standing on end.

Needing time to think, she slipped back into the gardens and headed for the nearest folly.

Contradictions piled atop contradictions. No wonder Emily was staying away. The poor girl must have been too confused to think straight. Charles swore that Drew's betrothal had been contracted in childhood. Either the arrangement was common knowledge, or Drew had mentioned it. Yet Emily had told Grace that Drew waited only for parental consent before proposing to her. What game was he playing? Lord Broadbanks claimed that Fay was merely a suggestion and that Drew was free to marry where he would—thus validating Emily's words. But that left Drew looking like a cad, for after leading Emily to expect marriage, he had offered for Fay anyway. She didn't want to believe he was dishonorable. And surely Emily would have learned the truth after her death if not before. The fact that Emily had brought her back should be proof that there was more to learn than she had yet discovered.

She stepped on a rock, turning her ankle. "Damn!" she muttered under her breath. She had been striding along with her usual gait, forgetting yet again that she was no longer Cherlynn Cardington. Footwear was another penance. Emily was apparently one of those widgeons who tried to appear dainty by cramming her feet into slippers that were too small. Even the half boots that were presumably made for walking pinched her toes. But that wasn't the worst of it. Shoemakers hadn't yet discovered that feet had shape. Every slipper was identical, with no distinction between left and right. Nothing supported her arches. She would give anything for her Reeboks.

The path entered a stand of trees. If memory served, it would emerge behind the Grecian folly that marked the northeast corner of the 1998 grounds.

A cat slunk behind a rhododendron, obviously hunting. It didn't know how easy its life was. It had only to sneak up on a bird or rodent, pounce, and it had all it needed. If only her goals could be achieved so simply. But she must question people if she was to succeed. And those questions couldn't reveal her purpose. Damn!

Why was Drew betrothed to Fay? She had to understand that before she had any hope of preventing the marriage. But no one had given her a definitive answer. She could hardly ask Drew. Amnesia could forgive a multitude of sins, but she doubted it would excuse that one.

A new thought struck, and she gasped. She was merely a

guest at Broadbanks. Now that she was recovered, would Charles decide to leave? He had mentioned staying until the wedding, but Lady Clifford was pressing harder each day to move to Brighton, citing the benefits of sea air for convalescents. Yet Broadbanks was also near the sea. Had Emily recalled that her movements were at the mercy of her mother and brother? Somehow she must deflect Lady Clifford without involving Drew.

She frowned. Her conditioning program was essential, but perhaps she should claim continuing weakness. And she must work harder to conform to proper conduct lest Charles decide to remove her from the public eye to protect her reputation.

Rounding a corner, she spotted the folly just ahead. It was more charming than she had expected, and not just because it was in good repair. Trees had not yet taken over the hillside, thus the view was stunning. A picturesque lake nestled in the valley, a herd of deer sheltering in the trees at one end.

But the folly was occupied. The last thing she wanted was people. Lady Clifford's insistence that she be constantly accompanied was stifling. In fact, this was the first time she had escaped the house without Grace. She was slipping back into the woods when voices halted her in her tracks.

Drew sank onto a bench in the Grecian folly and tried to relax, but the view over lake and valley refused to work its usual magic. His life was a disaster whose proportions grew larger by the hour. In less than two months he faced marriage to a woman he despised, but even that wasn't his worst problem. He could no longer trust his own judgment.

Every time he spoke to Emily, she revealed new interests. He had stopped visiting the sickroom the day she first left her bed. The decision had wrenched him, for he enjoyed talking with her, but he had already pushed propriety too far. So he waited until she was strong enough to leave her room.

Now he didn't know what to think. If the exchange in the library had shocked him, discovering her engrossed in *Tom Jones* had left him dumbfounded. In the week since, he had deliberately tested her knowledge, casually mentioning a number of subjects young ladies were not expected to understand. She had followed his lead every time, engaging him in stimulating discussion.

But as enjoyable as the exchanges had been, he found them uncomfortable. And not just because she always caught herself and retreated into a shell. Her knowledge was breathtaking. She knew everything Shakespeare had written, and had argued interpretation with him. She showed a surprising familiarity with Wordsworth, Scott, and Pope, loved Fielding and Mary Wollstonecraft—which would send Lady Clifford into strong hysterics if she learned of it—and admired a poet named Blake whom he had not heard of. After that last conversation, he had combed the library and actually turned up a book by the fellow. But Emily couldn't have read it. The pages remained uncut.

How had he missed her intelligence and education all this time? He'd known her for years. It was true that he had paid her little attention when she was younger, but could even a consummate actress hide such interests during childhood? And why maintain the charade with him? She'd had ample opportunity to trust him with her secret, for they had often met in the woods that separated Thurston Park from Clifford Abbey. The day they had talked of marriage, he had mentioned Odysseus—hoping that his trip to speak to his father would not resemble that man's journey home—but her eyes had held only the blank stare of incomprehension.

And you were disappointed. A wife with whom he could hold a rational conversation would be a real treasure. Emily now proved to be just such a person.

"Devil take it!" he muttered. Emily was off limits. Why had she divulged her interests now? It was bad enough to rue the loss of her beauty and sweetness. Must he also regret losing a keen mind?

Footsteps climbing the hillside interrupted his reverie. Fay. She stormed across the folly to loom over him.

"I won't have that girl at Broadbanks any longer," she hissed, her face twisted in fury. "It's all over the village that you tended her sickbed and practically live in her pocket now that she is recovered. How dare you insult me so! If she is well enough to leave her bed, then she is well enough to return to Yorkshire."

Damnation! The servants must be spreading exaggerated tales. Why did they hate him so much? But Fay needed to learn that he had limits beyond which nothing could push him. "We may be betrothed, but that does not give you the right to rule my life," he replied calmly. "Your father allowed you to act the hoyden, but I expect decorum from my wife. And obedience."

Her expression changed to contrition. One hand touched his sleeve in supplication, making his skin crawl. "You are making me a laughingstock, Drew," she protested. "It is your duty to protect me."

"Duty?" he snorted with a mirthless laugh. "You've had all the duty you'll ever get from me. Don't push your luck."

She stomped her foot. "Is this how you treat the woman who has loved you for so many years? You'll both regret insulting me. I won't have your doxy here another day."

"Insulted? Impossible. Your lack of breeding shines, as usual," he taunted, injecting coldness into his words. "Lady Emily is the sister of my closest friend and the daughter of a highly respected earl. She was more a lady in her cradle than you can ever be."

Fay laughed. "So masterful, my love. But you forget with whom you speak. I know that you fancy yourself in love with the chit. She has to go. Either she leaves tomorrow, or I will visit your father. He doted on Randolph, you know. The poor boy could do no wrong. The shock of learning that you murdered him would have a detrimental affect on the dear marquess's health."

"So precipitous," he drawled, hiding his fear and loathing. But part of him wished she would divulge everything. It would remove the responsibility for hurting Broadbanks from his shoulders and destroy his credit enough that jilting Fay would seem a mild transgression in comparison. "You would cut off your nose to spite your face. Lady Emily will remain here until the wedding. Despite taking an occasional turn about the gardens, her health is still precarious. A lengthy journey can only harm her. And she would hardly arrive home before she would have to return for our nuptials."

"She needn't go all the way to Yorkshire if her health is

that bad," sneered Fay. "Clifford could just as easily house her in London. She would be closer to her doctor there anyway."

He rose, his expression forcing Fay back a step. Ice dripped from every word. "This discussion is pointless. Lady Emily stays. Run to my father if you must, but you are correct that he doted on Randolph. Learning that I killed my brother would infuriate him. Do you know what he would do?"

"Die. Leaving you with more blood on your hands."

"You underestimate his strength. He would cut me off without a shilling. The inheritance I received from my grandmother would support us in a cottage, but no more. And that is not all. He has the connections to force a bill through Parliament removing me from the succession. The only reason he hasn't already done so is because I begged him to. I would rather join Wellington than take over his honors."

"You lie. He has too much pride in family to ever do such a thing." But her voice revealed uncertainty.

"Exactly. So much pride that he would do anything to prevent the marquessate from falling into the hands of a Cain. But just so we understand each other, if you do anything to damage my reputation, I will terminate this accursed betrothal in an instant. The only reason I agreed was to spare my father distress. Once that is no longer necessary, I care nothing for my own credit."

"Very well, my lord." Fay's fury was barely controlled. "Your mistress stays—for now. But you will rue this day."

He watched as Fay swept down the steps and disappeared. Not until her horse cantered across the valley did he relax. Then a wave of desolation left him shaking. He should have followed Randolph over that cliff when he'd had the chance. There had been a moment when the urge to jump had nearly overwhelmed him. But cowardice had frozen him in place, accepting even dishonor in lieu of taking his own life.

And cowardice was still directing his actions. Fay was right. He already rued the exchange. He should have let her expose him, but he didn't want Emily to know he was a murderer. Perhaps he deserved Fay after all.

It was all he could do to walk back to the house.

The moment Cherlynn identified the speakers, she slipped between the shrubbery and the rear wall of the folly where she could hear without being seen. Within moments she realized that Fay was Emily's deadly enemy. But even that knowledge receded under the weight of Fay's other revelations. Drew had killed his brother. And despite his claims, he was terrified that Broadbanks would die if he learned the truth. Had Fay also heard that note of panic in his voice?

That explained his betrothal. He had fully intended to wed Emily, but when he came home to discuss the match with his father, something had happened that left Randolph dead. Fay knew what it was and had used that knowledge to blackmail him into marriage. Emily's expectations were clear. The girl had not only lost the man she loved to Fay's manipulation, the man himself had lived every day of his life in fear of exposure.

She shifted when Fay left, catching a brief glimpse of her. Even livid with fury, Fay was beautiful. Blonde hair clustered in natural ringlets. The slender body emitted an aura of fragility that would raise protective urges in most gentlemen. But that was as false as her protestations of love. She untied a massive gelding and leaped into the saddle. The athleticism needed to control her fractious mount belied any hint of weakness, just as grasping greed belied her pretended jealousy.

Drew remained in the folly. Cherlynn considered slipping away, for he would probably stay until his temper was under control. But he suddenly strode out and headed for the house. Her one glimpse of his face made her recoil in shock. After Fay's threats, she had expected fury or possibly resignation. Instead, his face was twisted in an agony so intense it took her breath way.

She gave him time to get well away, then slipped into the folly and sat down on the curved bench that hugged the rear wall. What must Drew be suffering? Fay's blackmail had forced him to jilt the woman he loved. No wonder he hadn't spoken to her before the ball. Shame would have tied his tongue. And what could he have said? It was better that Emily believe him a cad than a criminal.

But now she had a bevy of new questions. How had Randolph died? Drew must have been involved, but she could not believe that he had deliberately killed his brother. Such an action was out of character. He had often accosted her since she had left her room, their discussions revealing a sensitive, caring nature that complemented his intelligence. Drew was not a man who used violence to solve his problems. Nor was he a man who could kill a brother in cold blood. Even her own history of poor judgment couldn't make her this wrong.

Appalled at her vehemence, she ran through her impressions again. Her feelings were growing too strong. His allure was obvious, for he was a man like none she had ever known—physically powerful, blatantly masculine, devastatingly sexy. Yet it was the contrasts that made him truly memorable: his gentleness, his concern, his aura of carrying a burden too heavy for even Atlas to bear. The desolate face in his portrait had mesmerized her. The reality was even more striking. But falling in love would be a grievous mistake. Emily loved him, and Emily would ultimately have him—by his own choice. She wouldn't even be around to wish them well.

She deliberately focused on business. This new information made her task even harder. She must save Drew from Fay without revealing his part in Randolph's death. She must prevent Fay from spreading tales. And she must convince Drew that Emily would forgive that death, no matter what he had done. That last might be the toughest. He had alluded to his misdeeds shortly after Emily's fall, claiming that she would hate him if she learned the truth—at least she thought that's what he'd said; she'd been out of her mind with fever at the time.

Perhaps learning about Randolph would help. If his death was an accident, Fay would lose most of her bargaining power. If he had deserved death, Drew's actions were excusable. Either way, he could break the betrothal with minimal social censure.

Who was her best source of information? Broadbanks had

apparently idolized his second son, so he would hardly be reliable. Besides, she had no desire to hasten his death by agitating him. She shook her head. Drew's sacrifice had been in vain, for his father had died just after the wedding. What a pity.

She suppressed all extraneous thoughts. At this point Drew was also a poor source. Once she discovered what kind of man Randolph had been, she could decide how to approach Drew.

That left Anne. The girl was eighteen, but horridly shy. It had taken several visits to the sickroom before she relaxed enough to exchange more than ritual greetings with Emily. Not until they had met in the morning room just yesterday had they become friends.

"Pardon me," Cherlynn had said, turning to go when she realized that Anne was curled in the window seat with a sketch pad and pencil. "I did not mean to intrude."

"You needn't leave," she protested. "I am relieved that you are feeling better. Has your headache gone?"

"Long since. My real problem was that first doctor, who nearly bled me to death." She paused, deliberately taking a deep breath and vowing to control her tongue. "You sketch?" she asked politely.

Anne flinched, but hesitantly held out the pad. "My governess does not consider it proper sketching," she reported shyly.

Recalling Miss Anders, who had accompanied Anne on her calls, Cherlynn grimaced. The woman would probably condemn eating and sleeping if she thought Anne found the activities enjoyable.

She flipped pages, awe growing with each new picture. The pad was filled with detailed drawings of trees and flowers, showing the stages of development from young shoot to leafy plant and from flower to fruit. The trees included silhouettes of their characteristic shapes and intricate renderings of their bark patterns. "But these are marvelous! You must be a naturalist."

"I only sketch to occupy my time," Anne protested.

"Perhaps, yet these are the best I've seen," said Cherlynn. "They should be published."

"Oh, no." Horror filled Anne's eyes. "I could never! And I know little about the plants themselves. Pictures are never enough."

She reined in her enthusiasm. *Regency! This is the Regency. Ladies would never stoop to trade, and a female who turned to commercial art would be considered fast.* "It is your decision, of course. But don't lose these." She paused for a moment. "May I ask a favor of you, Lady Anne?"

The girl nodded, though she was clearly surprised. The question must have broken another rule. Despite reading hundreds of books set in this era, she knew only the importance of proper behavior, not the details of what propriety entailed.

"My memory shows no signs of returning any time soon, and it is terribly frustrating not to know how to go on. Now that I am on my feet again, I will undoubtedly meet many people—you can't always dine *en famille*—but the thought of committing a *faux pas* frankly terrifies me. Would you instruct me in etiquette? I would ask my brother, but he is too frustrated over my problem to make a comfortable teacher."

"Of course." She was clearly pleased to be consulted. "I cannot imagine suddenly forgetting everything one has been taught." And without further ado, she had set in.

The afternoon had been the most enjoyable that she had spent in years. Their budding friendship filled a void that she usually ignored. She had made no new friends since leaving Willard. Nor had she ever acquired the kind of lasting friends that others took for granted. School; college; work; marriage. People had moved through her life who seemed to like her when they were together but who quickly forgot her when she moved on. Once she returned home, she must work on finding some real friends. Loneliness took too great a toll on her emotional resources.

Anne was again in the morning room. It seemed to be her favorite place. The girl craved solitude almost as much as Cherlynn did herself.

"Your father mentioned Randolph when we were walking in the garden, but he seemed so saddened that I hesitated to ask for details. How did he die?"

Anne jumped, but controlled herself immediately. "He

fell from the cliffs just outside the estate boundaries." She sighed. "It seemed too fantastic. I had just finished reading *Julius Caesar*—'Beware the Ides of March'—and then Randolph died on that day."

"How tragic," she murmured, but her skin crawled and her mind was whirling. The cliffs. Nine members of the family would die there, all on March 15. What did Randolph have to do with the curse? It had not yet been uttered. Fay was Marchioness of Broadbanks when she triggered it. Or so the story went. But it couldn't be that far wrong. Mabel Hardesty was a direct descendant of an eyewitness.

"Yes. Papa had his worst spell just afterward. He hasn't been the same since."

"From the shock, I suppose."

Anne nodded. "Randolph was always Papa's favorite. It was never a secret, not that Randolph deserved such favor," she added under her breath.

But the words carried. And this was exactly the information Cherlynn needed. "Why?" she asked softly.

"I—" She stopped in confusion. "Please forget I said that."

"Of course I will, but I suspect you need to talk. I know one is not supposed to speak ill of the dead, but I am more concerned with the living. If you keep irritation locked in your heart, it will make you bitter. Whatever you say will go no further."

Anne appeared undecided, but she soon sighed and turned to stare out the window. "Randolph had a mean streak," she confessed. "He lashed out at anyone who annoyed him—not in anger but in revenge. He delighted in hurting people. And terrorizing them. When I was five, he shut me in the priest's hole, knowing that I was afraid of the dark and that the release was too high for me to reach. He didn't free me for three hours, and I doubt he would have done so then if Papa had not been showing visitors through the Elizabethan wing where they would have heard my cries."

"How awful! Why didn't you tell someone?"

"Who would believe a child? Randolph had the sort of charm that could sell sin to heaven. Besides, he would have done worse if I had even hinted at his actions. I learned to stay out of his way when he was home from school. And to ignore anything I saw."

"That is an unconscionable burden to place on a child," she said softly, then remembered that she was supposedly the same age as Anne, with no experience of the world.

But Anne saw nothing wrong with her statement. "It is over. I wish I could mourn his death, but I can't. It saved untold multitudes from his fury, and it saved Papa from having to admit that Randolph had sold his soul to the devil."

"It must have been difficult for Lord Thurston to return home to a death."

"Drew arrived the night before Randolph's body was found, though Randolph must have been dead by then. He was last seen in the Blue Parrot's taproom. If he indulged to his usual extent, it is no wonder he fell from the cliffs. Many is the night I heard him return home in his cups. Again Papa did not know because he always retired early. The servants learned long ago never to say anything against Randolph if they valued their jobs."

Poor Anne. Cherlynn extracted a sampling of Randolph's deeds. The man was a sadistic monster who had terrorized the girl, belittling her interests, destroying her enjoyment of any gathering, and harming any people or things she liked. No wonder she was painfully shy and had no confidence in herself or her abilities. Having a dragonish governess who forbade everything fun had finished the job. And Randolph had used even her shyness against her, convincing Broadbanks that Anne was too delicate to attend school. Thus she had no close friends.

"What about your other brother?"

"William? He had been in Portugal barely a month when he fell. And not even in a pitched battle. It was some nameless roadside skirmish in which he was the only English casualty."

"But he is just as dead," she said with a sigh. "So Lord Thurston is all you have left."

Anne nodded. "But he is so morose these days. I don't know if it is Randolph's death or if something happened earlier. Except for William's funeral, I'd not seen him in years." She glanced hopefully at Cherlynn.

"I cannot help you there, at least until my memory returns. You say he is not usually so glum?"

"He has always been full of life—which is one reason he and Papa never got along. Papa demands proper decorum, which he interprets as solemnity and complete control of one's emotions. Drew loves to laugh—or he did—an attitude more suited to the lower classes. And they argued often about the estate—planting, investments, and other things I don't understand. Drew finally got tired of it all and moved to Thurston Park."

A knock on the door cut off any reply. Drew stuck his head into the morning room, his eyes lighting at the sight of Emily.

"I was going to ask Anne to ride with me. Are you up to joining us?" he asked.

She stifled her panic. She had been on a horse only once in her life—astride, using a western saddle atop a lethargic trail horse who did nothing but plod in the wake of his peers. "Do I ride?" she asked hesitantly, hoping the answer was no, though he wouldn't have asked in that case.

Drew's expression softened. "You ride quite well, but if you wish, we can test your memory with a refresher lesson before we go into the park."

"Very well."

"I will pass for now," said Anne softly. "Perhaps another day."

The animal Drew chose for Emily's first ride was small, as horses went, but appeared enormous to Cherlynn. The sidesaddle included a leaping horn—the second horn that would supposedly keep her in her seat when jumping fences.

Drew noticed the direction of her eyes. "We won't do any jumping today," he assured her. "In fact, you've never been much for cross-country riding, but the extra horn will improve your security."

"Thank you." A comment found in most historical romances was the instability women endured on sidesaddles, so she wasn't looking forward to this. All she could hope was that Emily's muscles remembered what to do. Unfortunately, only a few primitive reptiles had helper brains in their extremities that might make that possible.

She had read many stories in which the heroine was tossed onto her horse—and had written that very line more than once—but she had never appreciated just what it meant.

"Easy," murmured Drew as he grasped her waist with both hands. His touch burned clear to her toes. Lifting her effortlessly, he set her gently onto the saddle, twisting her so she faced forward. A glare had already sent the grooms back to their jobs so only he would witness her skill or lack thereof. It allowed her to relax.

"Keep your back straight and your hips square," he suggested, adjusting the single stirrup. Her right leg curled around the horn, while her left rested loosely against the horse. She nearly asked why it did not fit against the leaping horn, but remembered reading that a lady only tightened her grip on the horns when actually jumping. The position was surprisingly comfortable.

"Are we ready?" he asked, swinging onto his own mount. The restive bay sidled under the sudden weight, but he controlled it easily. Her horse paid no attention. Lovely placid animal.

Riding was an exciting new experience. Drew kept her in the meadow behind the stables until he was satisfied that her lost memory had not impaired her abilities. She found that the sidesaddle was actually easier to sit than a cross-saddle. Or perhaps the horse was unusually smooth gaited. They did nothing strenuous in deference to her recent injuries. But an hour of riding through the park gave her a sense of freedom that she had hitherto lacked.

She might have known that Drew had an ulterior motive for his attention. "Did riding trigger any memories?" he asked as he helped her dismount near the Roman folly that overlooked the Channel. On clear days like today, one could glimpse France on the horizon.

"Nothing. It might have been my first time on a horse except that my muscles seemed to be familiar with the motion," she admitted truthfully.

He sighed, but his eyes contained both disappointment

and elation. She suddenly realized his problem. He loved Emily and wanted to spend as much time with her as possible—especially since Fay had made it clear that Emily would not be welcome in her home. But if Emily recalled their past, he would no longer be able to treat her as a friend. She might even turn on him. And so he was trapped between desire for her recovery and the need to keep his perfidy a secret.

But that last was impossible. One of her tasks was to prove that Emily would forgive him. And now was the perfect time. No gentleman could abandon her here. Settling onto the stone bench, she invited him to join her, then turned her eyes to his.

"Tell me about the day Randolph died."

Chapter Eight

Drew jerked back in shock, but Cherlynn's hand on his arm kept him from rising. "I need to know why you feel responsible for his death," she continued relentlessly.

"Why?"

"I can't explain." She shrugged. "But it's vitally important. Trust me. Please?"

"Who told you I killed him?" Resignation sagged into his shoulders even as fear threaded his voice.

"No one else knows," she assured him. "I was walking in the gardens this morning and thought to visit the Grecian folly. But it was already occupied. I did not intend to eavesdrop, but I couldn't force my feet away. I am asking for the details because I don't believe you are capable of murder, and it's not worth sacrificing your life over an accident."

His face was stark white. "I never wanted you to find that out, Emily." Suspicious moisture glinted in his eyes.

"I don't need protecting from the truth, Drew," she vowed, tightening her grip on his arm. "Nothing you can tell me could be worse than imagination."

"Are you sure? What happens when your memory returns, reviving the rules you are now ignoring?"

"Whatever rules limit my life, I will still judge you on the merits. But I cannot judge at all if I don't have the facts. Please, Drew? Tell me how Randolph died."

He restlessly paced the folly. "You won't recall, but for the last four years I've split my time between Thurston Park and London. My father and I disagree about many things, so it was easier for both of us. Randolph remained here, taking over the estate's management when Father's health began to fail."

He paused to look out over the Channel. "The arrangement was acceptable to all parties and allowed me to leave immediately after William's funeral despite Father's recent attack."

She nodded, ignoring the break in his voice.

He pulled himself together and continued. "I didn't return until March. Some business arose that required consultation with Father." He glanced at her, but she kept her face expressionless. This wasn't the time to discuss his relationship with Emily. But it might help if she clarified his feelings for Fay.

"Was your father the only reason you stayed at the Park, or did Fay have something to do with it?"

"My dealings with my betrothed are private," he said haughtily, suddenly becoming the quintessential aristocrat.

"Please, Drew. I have to know everything." Her pleading softened his eyes, but not his stance.

"I am to bare my soul, though you refuse?"

"I didn't refuse to explain. I said I can't. Perhaps that will change once I'm fully recovered. All I know now is that I must understand everything." It was close enough to the truth that she felt no guilt over her lie.

He walked away, and for a moment she feared he would leave her there. But he moved into a breeze and ran his fingers through his hair in frustration. Several minutes passed in silence before he returned to the folly. After taking another turn about the floor, he propped his shoulder against a column and again stared at the Channel.

"Fay is the only child of my father's closest friend," he said on a long sigh. "Raeburn House is unentailed and will be her dowry. Father and Lord Raeburn often discussed the desirability of a match between Fay and myself, but left the ultimate decision to us. Yet she acted as though the betrothal were carved in stone, assuming that I would succumb to pressure. So she was less than pleased when I informed her five years ago that I wasn't interested. She tried many wiles to change my mind. When her tantrums and possessiveness grew wearisome, I moved to Thurston Park."

"So your absence was a way to avoid Fay?"

"That was the impetus for the move, but the advantages

of being apart from my father kept me away. And living near Charles, of course."

She could easily see why he'd left. Fay was spoiled and selfish. Even at fifteen, she had probably been unscrupulous. At twenty, she was deadly. "What is the problem with your father?"

"We've spoken of that many times," he protested.

"None of which I recall."

He sighed. "We have several. I both love and respect him, but we disagree on nearly everything."

The love was obvious. Why else would he sacrifice his life to spare his father pain? He wasn't the type to cower in fear. "Everything?" she asked in surprise.

"I wanted to buy colors, but he refused. Although Randolph would make an unexceptionable marquess should I die, he would not allow the heir near danger."

She nearly contradicted him, but caught herself. Either he was unfamiliar with Randolph's true character, or he was skirting the subject out of guilt or respect for the dead.

Again he sighed. "But mostly we disagree about the estate. He refuses to try anything new, despite my successes at the Park. Even Coke's stunning results won't sway him. Unfortunately, Coke is a Whig."

"As are you, I suppose," she guessed, then noted his nod. "Politics have ruined even more relationships than religion." That earned her a puzzled stare. Biting her tongue, Cherlynn returned to business. "So you were on your way home to speak with your father. What happened?"

He turned back to the view. "The weather was unusually warm for March. I was so eager to conclude my business that I pressed on rather than stopping for the night. I had outpaced my baggage carriage and was nearing Broadbanks when I caught up with Randolph. Naturally, I dismounted to talk to him."

"Of course."

"Not until we exchanged greetings did I realize how foxed he was—nearly three sheets to the wind. Normally, drink only intensified his tendency to sneer at others' foibles and ridicule pretensions. But something must have already irritated him that evening, for he was argumentative and suspicious from the moment he saw me."

"Did he start a fight?"

He shook his head. "He was surprised at my arrival, for I hadn't bothered writing ahead. Thus he immediately assumed that I was sneaking home to check on his stewardship."

"Why would he care? You already said he was doing a good job."

"Of course he was!" He glared at her. "Father was satisfied..." But his voice trailed away, his expression changing to horror as thoughts raced past his eyes. "Why would he care?" he echoed in a whisper. "He'd been helping for three years before assuming the entire job. Father often praised his efforts. Yet this year, Father was too weak to check on him."

"Surely, if there was a problem, it would have surfaced by now," she reminded him, mostly because she did not want to accuse a man she had never met.

"Not necessarily. I've been in too much shock to review the books." Both hands threaded his hair as frustration and horror increased. If Anne's tales were accurate, Cherlynn had no doubt that Randolph was not the paragon Lord Broadbanks assumed, but Drew could investigate that on his own now that his suspicions were raised.

"Later. Continue the story," she urged.

He took another restless turn about the folly. "Randolph demanded to know what I was doing here. I explained my business, seeking to reassure him that it didn't concern him. He disagreed."

"Why?" She knew she was putting him on the spot, but the truth was too important.

He scowled. "I was considering marriage, but wished to have Father's blessing before speaking with the girl's guardian."

"The proper approach, but hardly Randolph's affair. You have a duty to secure the succession."

"It wasn't his affair, but he exploded in fury, catching me off guard with a blow to the stomach. I knocked him down—as he should have expected, for I was always the better fighter—then demanded an explanation."

His mind retreated back to that cliff top as he continued his tale. He'd forgotten her presence, so she remained silent.

Randolph had been both drunk and furious—a lethal combination. "You were promised to Fay from the time she was two," he shouted, staggering to his feet to renew his attack. "She counted on you, doted on you, loved you every day of her life. She wouldn't even look at the rest of us because of you. And now you plan to jilt her?"

"There was no promise," Drew countered sharply, panting a little as he sidestepped Randolph's onslaught. "It was only a dream fostered by our fathers. Fay has known for years that I wouldn't wed her, for we discussed it more than once. I won't let the dreams of two old men trap me into a marriage that would be hateful for both of us. And she can't seriously claim to love me. She is a manipulative witch who loves only herself."

"I won't let you hurt her," screamed Randolph, kicking out at Drew's groin.

Drew sidestepped, but couldn't avoid the blow completely. "The only dream she harbors is getting her hands on the Broadbanks wealth. No matter what lies Fay tells, I know what a woman in love looks like, and Fay doesn't even come close. If you are so concerned for her future, marry her yourself."

"She won't have me," he gasped, reeling from a blow to the stomach. "Not without Broadbanks."

"Which proves how little she cares for either of us. Emily will make a better Broadbanks chatelaine than Fay ever could. Fay destroys everything she touches, as this encounter proves. Why else are we fighting over her?"

But Randolph didn't listen. Like so many men who were the worse for wine, he couldn't let an idea go once he latched on to it. So he fought on. Before it was over, Drew shoved him over the cliff, falling back to smash his own head on a rock. He did not regain consciousness until Fay arrived.

* * *

Cherlynn let out a ragged sigh. "How can you call that murder?" she asked softly, ignoring his mention of Emily. He hadn't even been aware of doing so. "It was an accident. Or at worst, self-defense. He was obviously trying to push you over the side. By killing you, he could have both Broadbanks and Fay."

His eyes widened.

"Think, Drew," she demanded. "By his own words, he wanted Fay, but she wouldn't take him without the title and estate. He let her follow her heart, but when you declined to wed her, he saw only one way to make her happy—by killing you. If he had been sober, the thought wouldn't have occurred, and certainly would not have taken root." She uttered the lie with a straight face. Randolph sounded jealous of everything Drew had. For twenty-four years he had been the second son, expected to make his own way while his older brother needn't lift a finger to acquire untold power and wealth. Many men would scheme to rid themselves of the impediment, but Randolph was dead. There was no point in defaming him now. "If you had lost that fight, you wouldn't be here today."

"Thank you for the vote of confidence, but I could have won without pushing him over the edge. I will forever bear the burden of having deliberately killed him."

"Why would you do that?"

"I—" He frowned. "How can anyone remember their thoughts when in the heat of an argument?"

"Do you remember pushing him?"

His shoulders sagged. "Not exactly, but Fay saw the end of the fight."

"That's why you accepted my amnesia so easily," she said triumphantly. "You've forgotten, haven't you? Do you remember hitting your head?"

He frowned before hesitantly replying. "Yes. It all happened in slow motion. I was swearing. I had meant to roll as I hit, but I came down on a rock. There was a blinding pain and a lot of stars. The next thing I knew Fay was bent over me. She had seen the whole thing and agreed that Randolph had clearly been in a belligerent mood. She chided me for shoving him over the side when he paused for breath, but swore she would never tell a soul. She didn't want her husband to be suspected of killing his brother."

"And the implication was clear," she finished. "Either you married her or she would tell everyone that you had deliberately killed Randolph."

"Exactly. I couldn't do that to my father. He has always doted on Randolph. The shock of finding me a murderer would have killed him."

"But you aren't a murderer," she swore stoutly. "And I'll prove it. Show me where this fight took place."

He started to protest, but shrugged and tossed her back onto her mount.

The cliffs where Randolph had died were barely half a mile from the folly. The road turned inland to avoid rough terrain and skirt Broadbanks Hall, but an ancient footpath followed the cliff tops, offering a shortcut to men and horses. Woods crowded the hill, thinning at the edge into a clearing a hundred yards long by twenty yards wide. Gulls soared on the wind while others picked through the rocky detritus piled at the foot of the cliffs, looking for edibles washed ashore.

Drew remained silent as he searched for the exact spot.

"Here," he finally said. "This is the rock I landed on. Randolph's body was found just below."

The rock was a dozen feet from the edge.

"How exactly did you land?" she asked.

He pantomimed his actions, stepped back a pace, then gingerly laid down with his head on the rock.

"You are sure that you landed precisely like that?"

"Positive."

"Then you are no more guilty of killing your brother than I am."

"What?"

"How did you fall here, if you were close enough to the edge to push Randolph over?" she asked.

He looked from the rock to the cliff several times. His feet had been angled inland when he awakened.

"Do you see what I meant?" she demanded. "Do it again. I am Randolph. We are struggling." She stood between him and the cliff. "Fay claimed that Randolph stopped to catch his breath." She let her hands drop to her sides. "Now shove me over."

"I see. If I push, you might possibly go over, but I'm not likely to catch you far enough off guard to make you stagger that far. And when I stumble back, I land in the wrong place."

"Precisely. To land where you did, you must have started here." She moved to a spot nearly twenty feet from the edge. "I don't care how drunk he was, a push at this point would not get him anywhere near danger."

"But he did go over."

"Of course he did. But the only way *you* could have killed him was to pick him up bodily and toss him there. Not only would you remember doing so, I doubt he would have cooperated enough to make it possible."

"So it was an accident after all." He sounded relieved.

"True, but not in the sense you mean. Since you remember falling, you can't have been conscious when he went over the side. You would have had to stumble around for quite some time before going down if the fight had been responsible. I think he fell over later."

"What are you saying?"

"It was an accident, all right. But you were in no way involved. Randolph knocked you into that rock. Perhaps he stumbled afterward, or perhaps his exertions on top of too much wine disoriented him so he turned in the wrong direction. Whatever the cause, he fell on his own."

"You're saying that he simply stumbled over the edge after he had knocked me out?" he asked.

"Exactly. You had nothing to do with it."

"But why—"

"—would Fay swear otherwise?" she finished. "Since she claimed to have seen the fight, she must have heard everything you told Randolph. There was only one way to prevent her dreams from going up in smoke. Once you got home and talked to your father, it would be too late."

"So she convinced me that I had murdered my brother." His voice had turned deadly.

"Don't do anything rash," she said as he surged to his

feet. "You can't break your betrothal without cause. The scandal would kill your father. And if he has only her word versus yours, whom will he believe?"

She could see the admission in his eyes. Broadbanks would believe Fay over his own son. It hurt, and she longed to comfort him, but she couldn't. Pulling him into her arms was much too improper for Emily and would only push her own feelings closer to the brink of disaster.

"So what do you propose?" he asked at last, weariness now etched on his face.

"You can't let her get away with blackmail. But we need to find evidence to either support your claims or call her veracity into question. Jilting her will cause enough gossip without adding suspicion of murder."

"I will gladly live with ostracism if it rids me of that witch," he swore.

"I know, but you should try to avoid it. What would it do to your wife and children?"

He gave her a sharp look, but she hid her knowledge of who that wife would be. "Fay was the only witness. What evidence might there be after four months?" he asked.

"If she lied about this, she must have lied about other things. All you need to do is expose one deliberate falsehood."

"True." He nodded. "Thank you, Em. You may have just saved my life."

That was truer than he knew. And perhaps he could uncover some useful evidence. But this didn't let her off the hook, she admitted when she reached her room. If Drew could handle everything from here, why hadn't Emily returned?

Stupid question. Evidence must exist that only she could find. *Am I reading this right, Emily?* Impossible though it seemed, there was something that would prove Drew's innocence.

She shook her head. This seemed an ideal task for the *Mission: Impossible* team. Too bad she didn't know enough psychology to set up the kind of mind games that might trick Fay into confessing.

Stopping in front of the dressing table, she again stared at

Emily's beautiful face. The day had been a surprising success. She had looked for and found evidence that Randolph was not the paragon Lord Broadbanks assumed. She had discovered why Drew was betrothed to Fay and had proved him innocent of any crime, demonstrating that Emily would stand beside him through thick and thin. Never in her life had she accomplished so much in so little time.

Emily's blue eyes widened as the realization hit. She was approaching this problem differently from any other—with confidence. Emily believed that Cherlynn Cardington could help her. Accepting that faith had saved her from most of the dithery *can-I, should-I* soul searching she usually indulged in. Not to mention the paralyzing fear of failure. Had her own insecurities prevented her from succeeding all these years?

She paced the room. Yes, they had. She had often refused to try things, so sure of failure that the effort seemed wasted. Even when she made a push, her attempts were often hesitant or tentative, retreating at the least hint of resistance. Her persistence in writing was more a reaction to Willard's taunting than confidence in her abilities. And the excuses came easily. Her limited dates in high school and college got blamed on her plain looks and pudgy body—as did the lack of respect she received from fellow House aides, the Cardingtons' hatred, and much of Willard's disdain. Yet today's successes had nothing to do with Emily's appearance. They were a combination of her own intelligence, a sympathetic ear, and logic.

Now that she thought about it, she had often blamed her body for her failures. Had she been hiding behind fat so that she needn't put her real self on the line? She had first started gaining weight during childhood—about the time her mother forced her into dance classes.

Damn! Once she returned home, she must see about improving her outlook. Expectations were very powerful. If she expected to fail, she would.

Drew locked himself in the study before dinner. He had meant to examine the estate records, but he couldn't forget Emily's astonishing performance. She had pushed, prodded, and cajoled him into admitting facts he had suppressed. Such manipulative behavior was the antithesis of what he wanted in a wife. Yet he couldn't condemn her for it. None of her pressure promoted selfish goals. It had opened his mind to possibilities he had never considered and left him kicking himself in disgust. Why hadn't he asked those questions before?

Randolph was suddenly an enigma. Had he had a guilty conscience? That would throw suspicion on his stewardship. And it didn't do much for Drew's own pride. He knew Randolph had died in debt. He knew his brother was a gamester. Yet he had never audited the books. Was Randolph in love with Fay? His words certainly implied such feelings.

More importantly, how had Emily recognized the possibility? He was beyond being irritated by her secrecy. The workings of her mind fascinated him. Her logical deductions astounded him. How had she come to be so astute?

His fingers tingled, recalling the feel of her waist as he helped her mount. He should have merely formed a step with his hands, but the temptation had been irresistible. And her amnesia might have demanded an explanation of what she should do. But touching her recalled their embraces and kisses, reviving the memory of her firm breasts and sweet lips. Was it possible that he might yet have her?

It was a dangerous dream. First he had to find evidence that Fay was a liar. Then he had to rid himself of her unwelcome presence without upsetting his father. Only when that was accomplished could he consider the future. In the meantime, he must treat Emily with the respect due the sister of a close friend. He could afford no hint of dishonor if he hoped to win a my-word-versus-your-word contest with Fay.

Chapter Nine

Cherlynn talked quietly with Anne, but her nerves were stretched to the breaking point. Though she had been dining with the family for a fortnight, tonight was the first time that guests were expected. Lord Raeburn and Fay would be among them.

Ever since she had overheard Fay's tirade in the folly, she had dreaded meeting her. Originally Emily had been dead by now, which increased her nervousness. She was breaking new ground simply by being here. Thus she had no inkling of the outcome. Fay's animosity could easily create problems that would make Drew's situation even worse.

Remember Anne's lessons in proper conduct! The rules were extensive and very precise. Committing them to memory was no challenge. It was forcing herself to think every action through before performing it that was driving her crazy. She had to behave conventionally. These people would meet Emily repeatedly once she married Drew. She must not be handicapped by Cherlynn's mistakes. It was bad enough that Drew was puzzling over Emily's changed demeanor.

She sighed. After their frank discussion on the cliffs, she had avoided him. The confrontation had been necessary, and would have been impossible to carry out using Emily's persona. But he had been shocked at her forthright manner. And curious once he had cast aside his guilt—which was why meeting him was dangerous. Assuming Emily's meekness around Drew was nearly impossible. He sparked her own personality too easily. But neither of them would benefit by exploring it. Drew loved Emily, a situation that must remain intact. He could not become disillusioned over Emily's apparent deceit, nor could he become attached to her new character. Thus she must ignore her own traitorous feelings. He had kissed her more than once during her convalescence when he thought her asleep, and she'd been trying to forget the touch of his hands at her waist ever since they'd returned from the cliff. She could not afford to form a *tendre* for him. *Please, let me free him from Fay before I do something stupid!*

She forced her mind back to the dinner guests. There were worse problems than revealing her growing infatuation. Fay was already furious over Emily's residence, accusing Drew of conducting an affair. After his refusal to send Emily away, Fay might try to accomplish it herself.

She shivered. There was no *might* about it. Fay would definitely seek to drive Emily away. Would she settle for unobtrusive insults, deliver a direct cut to a guest in her fiancé's home, or set up a compromising situation that would destroy Emily's reputation? Drew's threats might keep Fay in line while in company, but they wouldn't restrain her in private. How far would she go?

Lady Travis's letters depicted Fay as a woman who cared little for convention when it stood in the way of her goals. Cherlynn had learned nothing that would counter that image. Historically, once Fay had actually married Drew, she had abandoned all self-control—as the letter describing Drew's will made clear.

> *His wife should have expected such Judgment, for despite his three-year Absence, Broadbanks remained in touch with his steward. Banishment to Scotland is a small price to pay for her Scandalous Conduct. Even had he not caught her en flagrante with a groom the day he returned from the Army, he must have known about her activities. Her name has long been Notorious. She has No Shame and less Discretion. It is a Wonder her Nursery is not brimming.*

Another letter had noted that Lady Broadbanks routinely abused servants and tenants. Any failure to instantly obey her orders met with punishment. Since arrogance and scorn for the servant class were common in the aristocracy, Fay must have been bad indeed to have elicited such censure.

Would her behavior have been better if she had not schemed for Drew's title and wealth? Knowing that he despised her must taint her pleasure, which could make her lash out in frustration.

Cherlynn grimaced, nodding at another of Anne's admonitions about Regency etiquette. It was a waste of time to delve into Fay's motives. Good or bad, evil or deluded, the girl must be stopped before she destroyed Drew's family.

Hardwick announced the Raeburns.

Fay was stunningly beautiful. The glimpse at the folly hadn't done her justice. She was almost fairylike, with spun gold hair and golden eyes. The delicate, heart-shaped face would turn the heads of even jaded gentlemen. In contrast, her bosom was decidedly voluptuous, but not a gentleman in the room seemed to mind. It was shown to advantage by an embroidered green silk gown similar to one Cherlynn had seen at the Victoria and Albert, but it looked far better than she had imagined. She hadn't been able to picture what the faded color and lifeless fabric had looked like when new.

Broadbanks would not join them until dinner, so Drew was acting as host in the drawing room. And doing it with an ease Cherlynn could only envy. She had always been tongue-tied when Willard expected her to entertain guests—*because you worried about the impression you were making instead of trying to make them feel comfortable. You let him convince you that you could never belong to his world.* What an idiot she had been. She'd had just as much right to be there as his friends.

Her eyes followed Drew as he moved about the drawing room. He was mouth-wateringly handsome tonight, dressed more formally than usual in a burgundy jacket trimmed in black velvet. He was a far better man than Willard, treating everyone with equal respect, his warmth the same with the vicar as it was with Charles. But his expression turned remote as he welcomed the Raeburns. She could see the banked hatred in his eyes as he brought them over for introductions.

"Lady Emily . . . my betrothed, Miss Fay Raeburn. You may have met at the ball."

His voice stumbled over the words, but it was the malevolence blazing in Fay's eyes that sent chills tumbling down her spine. Murmuring something innocuous, Cherlynn wrenched her eyes away.

"Lord Raeburn," continued Drew.

"My lord." She offered her hand, remembering to turn it palm down so he could pay homage to it. He was a distinguished gentleman, running slightly to fat as he progressed through middle age. But the worry lines on his face hinted at a difficult life. With a daughter like Fay, that was hardly surprising.

Drew next presented Miss Testmark, Fay's companion, a fiftyish cousin so colorless that Cherlynn had not even noticed her until that moment. The woman had an uncanny ability to fade into the background. And she was precisely the sort who would stay there, seeing, hearing, and saying nothing. Such a one would make an abominable chaperon for a girl like Fay. Little better than no companion at all, in fact.

But the biggest surprise was the last member of the Raeburn group.

"And this is Fay's cousin, Mr. Frederick Raeburn," said Drew. "He arrived only yesterday from America."

"Mr. Raeburn." She again offered her hand.

"Lady Emily."

Drew kept Fay on his arm when he left to welcome more arrivals, his motives clear. He was keeping Fay close so she could not annoy Emily. Thus he must also expect trouble.

"What part of America are you from, Mr. Raeburn?" she asked, turning her attention to the newcomer. He looked nothing like his cousin. At least four inches taller than Drew, Frederick's wiry frame was topped by blazing red hair and the bluest eyes she had ever seen. And his face was deeply tanned—unlike the other gentlemen, who affected very pale skin—with none of the freckles she would have expected to accompany such coloring.

"Virginia, ma'am."

"Really? What part?" She nearly mentioned that she had been born in Virginia, but forced herself to slow down and think before talking.

"We had a farm in the hills west of the capital."

"Richmond?" she murmured, but that made no sense. The mountains were nearly two hundred miles west of there.

"Washington."

"Ah, out by the Shenandoah River. Beautiful country. Or so I've been told," she added hastily.

Drew rejoined them and addressed Frederick. "You use the past tense. Have you sold the farm?"

"Yes." He shrugged. "My family was killed by Indians in March—I was away in Baltimore at the time. Farming wasn't for me, so I returned to England, hoping the connection with Uncle Toby would help me start a shipping business here."

"You poor man," murmured Anne compassionately. "Your entire family?"

"Yes. Parents, three brothers, and two sisters." His lips moved as he struggled to control his voice. *So much blood.* Cherlynn saw the words rather than heard them. Something fretted at her mind, but she could not bring it into focus. Perhaps later.

"Quite a tragedy," agreed Lord Raeburn. "But we are glad you turned to us in your hour of need. I can put you in touch with some people in London." He frowned. "Not quite the thing for a baron's heir to be dabbling in trade, but as you're American, most folk will make allowances."

Drew went to greet a new arrival, taking Fay and her father with him.

"Virginia must be beautiful," said Anne shyly.

"Very." Frederick smiled almost protectively at the girl. "I will miss the mountains, but I was planning to leave home anyway."

"To set up your shipping business in Baltimore?" murmured Cherlynn.

"It is the nearest good port," he agreed. "But I couldn't stay there now. I needed to come home."

"You were born here, then?" she asked.

"My mother and Lady Raeburn were sisters. Pa was Raeburn's heir when they married, so they lived at Raeburn House for a time. But it wasn't a comfortable arrangement. Pa never expected to come into the title—who would have predicted that Aunt Faith would produce but one girl—so he was determined to make a place for himself. We left for America just after Fay's birth, but I was only two, so I recall nothing of England. Even after Aunt Faith died five years ago, Pa did not seriously expect to get the title. Uncle Toby was still a young man who would probably marry again. And may yet. He is only fifty."

"So that is another reason to build your own business," Cherlynn said with a nod. "Wise man."

"Tell me about your farm," asked Anne. "Unless talking of it is too painful," she added uncertainly.

"The land is too beautiful to bring pain," he said softly. "The Shenandoah runs along one of the valleys enfolded in great ridges that extend for hundreds of miles. But they are cozy mountains for all that, covered with forests and sheltering an abundance of game."

"The mists that cling to the slopes often change their color from green to blue," murmured Cherlynn, recalling the hills of her childhood. "But it is autumn that truly marks their splendor."

"Exactly." He was so caught up in memory that he did not notice her slip.

"There are more rugged mountains to the west," she added, then chided herself for forgetting her role. "I have heard that the Lewis and Clark expedition encountered massive rocky mountains."

"That is true. President Jefferson sent them to explore the land he purchased from France. They returned with tales of broad grasslands covered with beasts larger than cattle, of rock pinnacles so tall they scrape the sky, and of narrow gorges through which rivers tumble in wild fury. They are not men prone to exaggeration, so we must believe them. But I prefer the tranquil beauty of the Shenandoah."

As do I, but she kept the thought to herself this time, then prudently moved away to converse with Lady Clifford, leaving Anne and Frederick in a discussion of American wildflowers.

Dinner was enjoyable. Drew had seated Emily next to Lord Broadbanks, placing Fay on his own right at the foot of the table. Cherlynn alternated between lighthearted exchanges with the marquess and Frederick's spirited descriptions of an America she knew only from books. But two things marred the meal. Fay glared daggers at her whenever Broadbanks chuckled. And her feeling that Frederick was hiding something important grew stronger. He must realize that this was an inauspicious time to start a British–American shipping company. He had sailed from Baltimore barely a week before war broke out. Americans would soon be burning York. Had he fled for some reason?

It really wasn't her business. She had enough mysteries on her hands. It was better to relax, enjoy an evening like so many she had described in books, and revel in being accepted as an equal.

An unfortunate thought, for it recalled that mortifying gathering that her in-laws had hosted during her one visit to their home. The guests had looked down their noses as if she were some form of vermin. Her clothes had been hopelessly casual, though even if Willard had warned her, she couldn't have afforded anything suitable. At least she no longer had that problem. Emily's wardrobe contained gowns for every possible occasion. And Anne's tutoring had given her confidence that her manners would pass scrutiny. All she had to do was watch her tongue, and she appeared the perfect Regency miss.

Far too soon for Cherlynn's peace of mind, Anne rose to escort the ladies to the drawing room. She managed to stay near Lady Clifford and the vicar's wife for nearly half an hour while Anne played quietly on the pianoforte, but Fay eventually cut them out.

"You certainly don't look too ill to travel," she said as soon as they had moved out of earshot.

"But looks are so often deceiving, don't you find?" She stared pointedly at Fay's own appearance. This was no time to project Emily's sensibilities.

"I want you out of this house."

"Sorry to disoblige you, but you are not my hostess, Miss Raeburn," she said implacably. "My brother and my doctor will determine when I leave. The last time I checked, you were neither." Her shoulders tensed as Fay's hands tightened into claws.

"I will soon be the mistress of Broadbanks Hall," Fay

hissed. "And I will tolerate no interference. If you have some idea of comforting my husband, forget it."

Cherlynn drew herself up to Emily's full height—which topped Fay's by a good six inches—adopting the same haughty expression Drew had used in the folly. "Your manners are sadly lacking, *Miss* Raeburn. You are not Lady Thurston yet. Nor will a title cover your many flaws. If you hope to be accepted as a lady, you must watch your tongue. Not even Lord Thurston's credit will excuse such insolence in London—assuming he would even take you there. He is a stickler for propriety, as you must know."

An evil smile crinkled the corners of Fay's mouth. "I know everything necessary about dear Drew. And I know how to handle anyone who tries to interfere with my life. Either leave or you will find your reputation in shreds."

She must have heard the gentlemen's approach, for she glided away without waiting for a response. When the drawing room door opened moments later, she presented the picture of a demure angel who had been waiting patiently for them to arrive.

Fay's outburst hardened Cherlynn's resolve to free Drew from her clutches, but she must tread warily. Emily's reputation must remain untarnished. And Fay was not her only problem. Frederick had drawn Anne aside for another lively discussion, reviving her uneasiness. His dinner conversation had fascinated her, evoking mental comparisons between the Virginia of 1812 and that same valley in her youth. If she understood his descriptions, she had grown up barely two miles from his family farm. But she had difficulty imagining the wild grandeur he knew. Perhaps that was why she had so much trouble selling her books. Too much of the modern world had crept onto their pages.

Her uneasiness suddenly burst into rampant suspicion. Thoughts of her childhood recalled her fourth grade teacher and an interminable class on Virginia history—her own interest in the past had not materialized until high school. Miss Martinelli had lectured on relations between the settlers and the local Indian tribes, closing with the comment that the area had had no further Indian problems. But the events she had described occurred in the eighteenth century.

An Indian massacre that had wiped out an entire family of peaceful settlers less than a hundred miles from Washington would hardly have been ignored. Had Frederick done it himself? *So much blood.* Like Lady Macbeth, he sounded as though he had been there.

Another mystery. One she needed to solve soon. Not only was he lying about his past, he was related to Fay and could be in league with her. And he was paying particular attention to Anne. Were the Raeburns trying to destroy Drew's family? Yet Lord Raeburn was supposed to be Broadbanks's closest friend.

Anne was apparently infatuated with the American, and Cherlynn could understand why. His charm was palpable, reminding her of Willard, whose charm had been legendary. Thus she must discover his motives very soon. It was even more urgent than ending Drew's betrothal. Anne was too naïve to suspect secrets, and too kind-hearted to bounce back from emotional pain. After enduring Randolph's deliberate cruelty, deception by someone she trusted would destroy her.

But the drawing room was not the place to question him closely. Exposing his lies would reveal more knowledge of America than she could account for to anyone who knew Emily. And that was especially true of Drew. He was confused enough already. It would be best if he knew nothing of this investigation.

Thus she moved on to speak with Vicar Rumfrey, keeping only a casual eye turned to Anne. She paid little attention to his words until he started enumerating the year's tragedies.

"So many deaths," he murmured, half to himself. "It's uncanny for so small a parish."

"Have there been so many then?" she asked idly.

"Five so far, and it's only August. Mrs. Boggs was hardly a surprise, of course. She had been ailing for months. And the same could be said for Bobby Duggan. 'Tis the others that are so tragic. Poor Jack Gardner died back in March, as did Ben Lockyard. Jack had been fighting and was still unconscious when he was found. He died two days later without ever waking enough to tell us what happened."

"He said nothing?" asked Cherlynn, curious at his odd wording. She shivered.

"He was fevered and mumbling deliriously at first, but it made no sense. He kept urging someone to run—possibly Ben, though they were found two miles apart. Most folks figure it had something to do with smuggling, but whether he was running goods himself or had stumbled onto a landing, no one will say. And most folks don't care. Lord Randolph's death claimed their attention."

"He died at the same time?"

"Possibly. Miss Raeburn and I discovered his body the next morning. What a shocking sight for a girl who had accepted Lord Thurston's offer barely an hour before. I am amazed that she did not fall into hysterics. Lord Randolph had fallen over the cliff just west of Broadbanks. Plenty of men had seen him drinking at the Blue Parrot, so there was little question how it came about, but his death sat heavily on Lord Broadbanks's shoulders. It was a lucky thing that Thurston had returned home, for his brother had run the estate ever since his lordship's health worsened. Now that duty rests with the heir."

She refrained from comment. Fay had lost no time in turning up the body once Drew had succumbed to her blackmail. The vicar would have made a perfect witness. He was dull enough to be easily led. If Fay ever decided to expose Drew for his supposed crime, she would convince Rumfrey that he had seen the irrefutable clue that proved Drew's guilt. She might even have planted such evidence before she dragged him out there.

The vicar moved on, allowing an elderly spinster to commandeer her attention. Miss Langley lived in the village.

"Mrs. Rumfrey just told me the most shocking story!" she said without preamble. "Jaime Potts lost more in a card game last night than he can possibly pay. He'll be in debtor's prison by week's end."

"I'm afraid I don't know the man. Is he accustomed to deep gaming?"

"Oh my, yes!" said Miss Langley, glad to have a new audience. "He's a terrible card player. And not much better at other things." She launched a lengthy monologue that described Jaime Potts as a farmer whose finances usually flirted with ruination because he spent most of his meager income on drinking and gaming. His bad luck and lack of skill were legendary. Many avoided playing with him either from compassion or because winning was too easy to be fun.

After disposing of Jaime's current ill fortune, Miss Langley moved on to caustic comments about Maude Gardner, who had run off some months earlier; the innkeeper's daughter, who was looking unusually pleased with herself; and a host of other local girls and boys, who she implied were unchaste.

Cherlynn listened with half an ear, making appropriate noises whenever the lady paused, but her attention remained on Anne and Frederick. They were still together. Anne must have lost all sense of time. If she didn't circulate among the guests, she would draw undue notice and speculation, particularly from people like Miss Langley.

Finally excusing herself, she moved off to pry Anne loose. How ironic that the student must rescue the teacher from a social *faux pas*.

Chapter Ten

"You are mad, Potts!" sputtered Lord Raeburn, his face purple with indignation.

"I know what I saw, my lord," insisted the farmer implacably.

"My daughter would never behave so dishonorably." But his voice lacked conviction.

"Ask her to explain why she didn't discover Lord Randolph's body until the next day."

Jaime Potts watched complacently as Lord Raeburn's face darkened even further. He hadn't meant to put the touch on Raeburn. Everyone knew better than to annoy the man's daughter. But his luck had turned sour, threatening him with debtor's prison if he didn't come up with some cash. He'd considered selling his information to Lord Thurston, but the man would hardly complain about an action that had saved his life. Miss Raeburn would never do, of course. She'd see him in debtor's prison before lifting a finger to help him, even if that meant exposing his tale to public scrutiny. But Lord Raeburn was different. Since the man hadn't been there, the careful wording that condemned Fay's actions without actually lying would go unnoticed. Raeburn wouldn't want his own name tarnished by his daughter's misdeeds. And a swell would never miss thirty pounds. Or so he'd thought.

"I won't pay you a farthing," snapped the baron. "If Fay has erred, she will make a public confession and restitution. But she won't be cowed by your drunken fantasies. Wait here while I fetch her. Let's see if you dare accuse her to her face."

Potts frowned once Lord Raeburn left the room. This was not going as planned. He had expected Raeburn to give up the paltry sum to save his family name from disgrace. Miss Raeburn needn't have known anything about it. Would Raeburn arrest him for blackmail? It didn't matter. The choice had come down to transportation or debtor's prison. He'd chance the first to escape the second. And it was too late to turn back.

What would she do? Rumors had long hinted that she was a witch. She might ill-wish his farm. Even worse, he was one of the Broadbanks tenants, so she could make trouble for him once she became lady of the manor. Ignoring the voice that berated him for joining that card game at the Blue Parrot, he pondered how to approach this confrontation. Would Raeburn really expose his own daughter, or was he bluffing? Should he change tactics and approach Lord Thurston or Lord Broadbanks instead? But that alternative was no more viable than before. Broadbanks had caught him lying in the past, so he would never believe this tale. And though Thurston and Fay were betrothed, it was an arranged match, so he might not care for her enough to cover any misdeeds.

It was too late to change course anyway. Raeburn had already heard his accusations. Recanting would leave him in even worse trouble. Damn his luck of late! What was taking the man so long?

The door opened, admitting Fay. "So you believe you saw something odd?" she asked, her sultry voice raising the temperature of the room several degrees. "Why did you wait so long to mention it?"

" 'Tweren't my business."

"But now it is?" She moved closer, her eyes moving slowly from the top of his head to the tips of his toes.

"I've hit on hard times, ma'am. I've nothing else to sell."

"Not necessarily," she murmured. "You've any number of options. Have you considered accepting a job?" One hand slid up to caress his cheek.

He looked frantically at the door, stepping back to keep the witch at a distance.

"Papa left the negotiations to me," Fay said, her feral smile raising both heat and panic. She slid fifty pounds into his hand. "You're a fine figure of a man, Jaime Potts." One finger trailed lightly down his chest. "You're working for me now, and I'll expect more than sealed lips for my money."

God help him, he couldn't refuse.

Cherlynn sat in the drawing room, idly leafing through Anne's copy of *La Belle Assemblée*. She had declined to accompany Anne and Lady Clifford on their visit to the vicarage, citing continued weakness, but the lie was wearing thin. It wouldn't hold up much longer.

Since the dinner party, Lady Clifford had stepped up her campaign to spend the remainder of the summer in Brighton. And her thinking had clearly shifted. While she had originally claimed that public appearances would rescue Emily's reputation after her fall, now she seemed determined to marry Emily to Lady Ledbetter's son Rupert. The lad sounded liked a typical Regency wastrel who had not a brain in his head. Emily would be miserable with such a husband. But why was Lady Clifford so anxious for the match? Granted, Lady Ledbetter had been her bosom bow at school, but that was no excuse. As a baronet's younger son, Rupert was hardly a desirable mate for an earl's daughter.

She froze. Damn! It was her fault. Emily had hidden her relationship with Drew from her family. But his hovering in the sickroom and their *tête-à-têtes* since must have started rumors. Fay might even have contributed to them. She'd threatened to destroy her reputation. Fearing Emily had been irredeemably compromised, Lady Clifford wanted her married off before the tale spread beyond Broadbanks.

Thus she faced yet another danger. So far, Charles had resisted Lady Clifford's pleas. But that could easily change, especially if her behavior made him suspicious. He would not tolerate her hanging out after any man, let alone one who was betrothed. And if he discovered Drew's feelings, he would not only leave post haste, but would likely terminate his friendship. Thus the pressure was increasing, the available time was rapidly running out, and she was caught in a trap of her own devising. If she was to discredit Fay, she needed to talk to people, yet the weakness that held Lady Clifford at bay tied her to the house.

Anne's return jerked her thoughts away from this conundrum.

"We just heard the saddest news," she said, but her voice held ambivalence.

"Terrible," concurred Lady Clifford, not at all sincerely. Her expression was smug. Plotting already animated her eyes. For all her uneducated stupidity, the woman could be deviously shrewd when she wanted something—a fact both Grace and Drew had mentioned.

Anne shook her head. "Lord Raeburn suffered an apoplexy last night and is said to be at death's door."

"How awful!" Her mind raced. This could change many plans, mostly for the worse. "Will that mean postponing Lord Thurston's wedding?"

"He must!" exclaimed Lady Clifford. "It would be scandalous for Miss Raeburn to wed during mourning." The words made her thinking obvious. Without the excuse of an imminent wedding, Charles would have to take them to Brighton.

"Lord Raeburn is not yet dead," protested Anne softly. The abashed countess flushed at losing her composure.

"And he could recover," added Cherlynn. Apoplexy was a euphemism for stroke. Even without the clot busters and other wonder drugs of her own time, stroke was an unpredictable ailment. But she could safely foretell Raeburn's immediate future. Since Emily had done nothing to bring on the attack, history remained unchanged, so the wedding would proceed as scheduled. "It would be gauche to don black prematurely."

"Of course," admitted Lady Clifford, heaving a disappointed sigh.

"Did you hear other news at the vicarage?" asked Cherlynn.

"Billy Turner will be calling the banns soon," said Anne, naming the son of one of the tenants. "He has offered for the innkeeper's daughter and will help run the inn. His father will miss his assistance, though."

"Has he no brothers?"

"Three, but only one is old enough to do a full day's work. Perhaps one of the Fallon boys can help."

"I'm sure your father and his steward are more capable than either of you at solving estate problems," said Lady Clifford blightingly.

Anne flushed.

"Anything else of interest?" asked Cherlynn, biting her tongue to keep from lashing out at Lady Clifford. If even women had considered themselves inferior, it was no wonder they had been subjugated for so many centuries.

"Jaime Potts seems to have turned his gaming luck," reported Anne. "Last week, he was half a step from debtor's prison, yet this week he not only paid all creditors, but has money to spare. But most of the talk was about Lord Raeburn and speculation of what his attack will mean for Drew."

Lady Clifford excused herself to speak with Charles, leaving Cherlynn to wonder how long it would be before she would have to leave Broadbanks. But this might be the best time to question Anne about Fay. From the gleam in her eye when it sounded like the wedding might be delayed, she suspected that Anne did not relish the thought of having Fay as a sister-in-law.

"What will you do after your brother marries?" She hadn't come across Anne's name in the historical records, though she had not looked closely at the Villiers family before her accident.

Anne jumped. "I will be making my bows next spring."

Not if her father died in September. "I don't like to think about you sharing a house with Fay," she said instead. "She doesn't seem overly pleasant."

"We will manage."

"I doubt it. You grow tense just thinking about it. I owe you a great debt for helping me overcome my missing memory, and can promise that your words will go no further."

Anne hesitated, but the temptation proved too great. "The prospect does trouble me. So far Fay ignores me, but rumors abound about her vindictiveness."

"She hurts others?"

"So people claim. The servants are nervous. Turnover at Raeburn House is high, and it's not unusual for departing workers to leave the area without a word—even when their families are local. But that is not all. Whispers call her a witch, citing the man whose family died hideously when he refused some request; the widow who lost her home, her jointure, and her friends after crossing Fay; the shopkeeper whose business collapsed; the doctor whose patients turned against him. . . ."

"But how many of the rumors are true?" she interrupted to ask as the shadows deepened in Anne's eyes.

"Who can tell? These are not stories bandied about in respectable drawing rooms. You hear them whispered in corners and servants' halls."

"How specific are they? Do any name the victims?"

Anne shook her head. "Which shows they have little basis," she added firmly. "I am a ninny to listen to them."

"Not necessarily. Such ubiquitous stories must arise from something other than irritation at an arrogant, overbearing manner."

Anne giggled.

"Lord Thurston hasn't been here in years, so why have you paid attention to Fay?"

"I always knew she would insinuate herself into our family," said Anne with a sigh. "Father wished it even if Drew did not. For many years I hoped she would settle for Randolph. They were two of a kind and good friends besides."

"Friends?" She could not picture Fay as anyone's friend.

"Well—" Her face reddened. "I did see them in the Roman folly one day, though they were otherwise occupied and did not notice me."

"Lovers, then." She kept her voice so matter-of-fact that Anne's blush receded. Could this information help her? Ending a betrothal on the grounds of an affair between Fay and Randolph would hurt Lord Broadbanks nearly as much as suspecting Drew of killing his brother, especially since Anne's tale was her only evidence. And what would the vindictive Fay do to Anne?

But this validated Randolph's own words during the fight. He had fallen in love with a kindred spirit, yet she refused to give up Broadbanks and a title for him. Thus Randolph must have tried to kill Drew.

Which did not explain why Fay hadn't intervened to help

him. Together they could have tossed Drew over the cliff and taken Broadbanks for themselves. Randolph would have married her willingly, giving her a husband who cared instead of one who despised her.

Stupid! Randolph had fallen to his death. Once her lover was gone, Fay would have had no choice but to coerce Drew into marriage.

Assuming she loved Randolph, of course. She may have been using him in her feud with Drew. Fay was vindictive. Drew had repudiated her and now loved another. She couldn't allow him to get away with it. Would she taunt him with her liaison once they were wed? Even worse, would she start rumors that he had killed Randolph? The wedding would release all restraints on her tongue.

She listened with half an ear to Anne's descriptions of how Fay had played on her insecurities to make her miserable. Not because Fay had any particular grudge against the girl, but to exercise her sadistic powers. And again, to hurt Drew.

The rest of Cherlynn's mind tried to plot her next move. There was little point in sharing this with Drew just yet. It would hurt and enrage him, but he could do nothing about it without harming his family. That impotence would make life even harder for him. But if Fay had been coupling with Randolph, she probably took other lovers as well. Lady Travis had noted overt affairs soon after the wedding. They had probably started long before, if the one with Randolph was any guide. Finding proof of such a liaison would fulfill her mission, for an unchaste, licentious bride was anathema to powerful lords.

The moment Anne went upstairs to change, Cherlynn escaped the house. She needed a plan. How was she to find hard evidence of Fay's affairs? It wasn't something one advertised even in her own era. In the Regency, such goings-on would be cloaked in so much secrecy that she had virtually no chance. Fay's reputation for vindictiveness would seal even the loosest lips. *Come on, brain, think!*

Moving past the formal gardens, she turned along a path that followed the stream uphill into a forest, enjoying its pleasant gurgle and the way sunlight filtered through the trees to highlight random plants. Anne knew nothing beyond Fay's fling with Randolph and a few vague rumors. This was not drawing room talk, so the area gossips would be of minimal help. Drew might know of possible paramours, but he was a last resort, and his four-year absence wouldn't make things any easier. Fay had been barely sixteen when he had left. Perhaps Grace could question servants and villagers.

She was turning over the pros and cons of that idea when the path opened into a charming clearing. Thick grass covered the hillside. Butterflies probed a handful of late summer flowers. The stream chattered over a short fall. But the clearing was already occupied.

Frederick jumped, yelping as he nearly landed in the water. "Goodness, you startled me, Lady Emily!" he exclaimed.

Having done nothing to hide her unstealthy approach, she refused to apologize. "What were you watching so intently that you didn't hear me coming? I've been humming since I entered the wood."

He flushed, then nodded toward the trailing bough of a willow that was perched on the stream bank. A butterfly finished easing out of its cocoon, its wings still damp and wrinkled.

"How beautiful," she whispered, watching in awe as the creature stretched, pumping fluid into almost invisible veins. Its wings straightened, their color growing more brilliant by the moment. "Anne would love to sketch it."

"She is calling at the vicarage this afternoon," he replied absently.

"And how do you know that?" she demanded, abandoning her vigil over the butterfly. Anne had originally intended to go shopping, changing her mind at breakfast when Lady Clifford expressed a wish to call on Mrs. Rumfrey.

Embarrassment stained his cheeks. "I sometimes run into her when I am out walking," he admitted.

That he would bump into Anne while walking fully three miles from Raeburn House was odd enough, but using the plural within days of arriving meant that the meetings were planned. Anne was slipping off to assignations, a fact that would ruin her if it became public.

Yet this was precisely the opportunity she needed. She drew herself upright. Once she discovered what he was hiding, she could decide what to do about this latest development. "You are in England now, sir," she reminded him sharply. "You may not arrange assignations with well-born young ladies. Even accidental meetings will not do. Do you wish to destroy her reputation?"

"Of course not," he countered.

"Have you requested permission to court her?"

"I am not courting her."

"Then what do you call it?" she demanded, rounding on him. "Seduction?"

"God, no!" he exploded with such force that she believed him.

"Why not call upon her in the usual way? As Lord Raeburn's heir, you would be welcome. Or do you fear to face Lord Thurston because you've lied about your background?"

"What?" He honestly looked perplexed. "I was born at Raeburn House. What's to explain?"

"I was referring to the tale of America you spun so eloquently. Surely you know that the last Indian attack in the Shenandoah Valley occurred during the French and Indian War. I don't recall the exact date, but it was at least fifty years ago. What happened to your family?"

He blanched. "I thought Englishmen considered America to be a wasteland populated only by hostile Indians," he confessed.

"But I am not an Englishman."

He looked her over. "Obviously. Female to the bone. And educated, as well." He sighed. "Despite crossing the ocean, my luck is as wretched as ever."

"The jig is up," she said softly. "Are you really Frederick Raeburn?"

"Oh, that part is perfectly true," he assured her. "In fact, everything I said was true—except for the details of my family's end."

"You really did lose your family?"

He paced the bank for several minutes. She sat on a nearby boulder, studying his face and the hands clenched behind his back. He did not fit the image of the Regency buck she had formed after reading so many novels. And not just because his clothes were looser and more casual than those worn by Drew and Charles. His movements were freer and more purposeful, even in this moment of aimless motion. His complexion was different as well, his face tanned and his hands calloused from hard labor. She recognized an animal magnetism that boded ill for Anne if he turned out to be a fraud.

"We emigrated to the United States when I was two years old," he began at last. "I remember little of the early years beyond cramped rooms and empty bellies. My mother was in a family way most of the time. Two brothers died in infancy, leaving me with three brothers and two sisters by the time I was ten."

"I'm surprised she survived such excess."

"So am I, and I wish she had not." The last comment was an aside to himself, but his tone was so harsh she could not help but overhear. "Pa finally gave up trying to support a growing family in New York, so we moved west, settling in the hills overlooking the Shenandoah. It is pretty country, rich in game, but most of the land he bought was too steep to plant. We barely managed to coax enough from the ground to put on our own table, let alone sell. Pa was always a dreamer, accepting claims that the property was five hundred acres of good farmland. He bought without ever looking at it."

"He wouldn't be the first to fall victim to land fraud," she concurred. Even in the twentieth century, misrepresentation was a common complaint in the courts.

"Nor the last. I helped in the early years, clearing small fields and planting crops. Pa's mother was Scots, so he brought in a cousin who helped him build a small whiskey distillery. Malcolm stayed for a year before moving on to find his own land farther west. We later heard he'd been killed by Indians in the western wilderness."

"Hence the idea for your own bereavement," she murmured.

"Silly of me to prevaricate." He sighed. "If only he'd died sooner. I grew to hate that distillery. Much of the output went into Pa's stomach, making him more and more distant as time passed. Ma was complaining worse each year, flying into rages when he refused to move back to a city. By the time I was sixteen, it was too much. I left for Baltimore and got a job in a shipyard."

"So you do know something about the shipping business," she said when he paused. "Does your knowledge extend beyond building the vessels?"

"Yes. Building was never my strength. Within the year I had transferred to the office of one of the top Baltimore importers. I know the business well and have plenty of contacts, though this is not the ideal time to start my own company. If this contretemps over impressment does not resolve soon, I don't see how I can succeed."

"That is a problem, of course." She shook her head, knowing that the problem was already out of control. It would be two and a half years before he could do anything. "But why did you lie about your family?"

"I returned to the farm a couple times a year to check on the crops and make sure the kids weren't starving. Pa had taken in a wanderer to help with the fields, but the fellow wasn't all that bright. My last visit was in March—to make sure all was ready for the spring planting. And I figured to stretch their supplies by taking Raymond back to Baltimore with me. He hated the farm and hated what Pa and Ma were putting the kids through. With what I had saved, he could have set himself up to learn a trade."

"He was the next brother?"

He nodded. "There was a gap behind me, so while he was the second son, he was barely seventeen." He struggled with grief before continuing. "I met up with Josh Norton in Washington. He lived half a day west of us and was also headed home, so we rode together, arriving just before dusk. I invited him to spend the night."

"Just being neighborly," she suggested softly.

"In part. He'd been showing some interest in Katy, who'd just turned sixteen. . . . I should have known something was wrong the moment we rode into the yard." His voice grated.

"There wasn't a sound. But I didn't suspect a thing until I opened the door. Katy was lying in the hall, her fingers still dug into the floor from trying to crawl outside. She'd been stabbed a dozen times. I followed the blood trail upstairs. They were all there. Raymond, Thad, Marcus, Milly. All stabbed in their beds. All dead. Blood was everywhere. Ma was on the floor of the room she shared with Pa. She had the end of Pa's dueling pistol stuck in her mouth, with the top of her head blown off. Pa was still alive."

She jumped. "Alive? Had he done it?"

"No." Fury speeded his pacing. "He'd been stabbed six times, and was too weak from blood loss to move. But he was sober enough to tell the tale. Ma had been getting odder and odder, exploding in fury over little things, yet not seeming to care about serious problems. Pa was doing nothing by then—except drinking himself insensible every day. The hired hand left at Christmas after Ma threatened to kill him. Raymond took over running the farm, but his heart wasn't in it, and last year's crops were so poor, they did not even have enough food to survive the winter. If anyone had thought to mention it to me—" He paused to regain his composure as grief again cracked his voice. "Whatever the reason for their silence, the situation was beyond desperate. They'd eaten all the seed grain and even the potato and onion sets. With no way to replace them, there would be no new crops. The final straw must have been my last letter to Raymond. Since I found it in Ma's room, I doubt he even saw it."

"Is that where you mentioned setting him up in Baltimore?"

He nodded. "She'd always had a bee in her bonnet about her aristocratic breeding—which amounted to being a squire's daughter and sister-in-law to a baron. She yearned to be a society hostess in New York or Philadelphia, but we had neither the money nor the connections to meet the leading families. Pa's move to Virginia was the death knell for her dreams. That's when she started getting irrational. I think she ran mad when she found that letter. She couldn't stand the thought that her children might return to civilization, leaving her to rot with Pa. So she grabbed a butcher knife and started slashing."

She glared at him. The scene he had described didn't jibe with his explanation. "Why would she kill herself then?"

"She didn't. Pa wasn't as drunk as usual that night. He not only woke up, but managed to turn on her. He killed her, then staged a suicide to avoid any questions. But by then, he didn't have enough energy to get to the neighbor's. He collapsed on the bed and all but passed out. I got there two days later. Pa was too far gone to save. He died the next morning."

"Tragic, but why cover it up?" she asked.

He shrugged. "How can you tell someone you haven't seen in twenty years that his wife's sister killed six people and his cousin killed her? What purpose does that serve?" He sighed. "And now he's suffered an apoplexy. Even if he recovers, I dare not tell him for fear of bringing on another attack."

She didn't agree, but she could see his point. Any hint of madness could taint an entire family. People in this era didn't understand mental illness, and few would risk contaminating their own lines. A twentieth-century psychiatrist could have a field day figuring out what had driven Mrs. Raeburn to murder, but as Frederick had said, it was over. What purpose did revealing the truth serve? "Had there been any other unbalanced people in her family?" she asked.

"Not that I know of, but I wouldn't know. Ma turned her back on them the moment she married into the aristocracy. So did Aunt Faith. But I suppose I should check."

She heard his sudden realization that he might carry a stain in his blood, but also noted his determination to do what was necessary. Nodding, she turned the conversation to America and some of his interests. He was determined to start a shipping company in England. She saw no reason to dissuade him. He would learn of the war soon enough. If she was successful in preventing Drew's wedding, he would have an estate on which to live in the interim. And she suspected that his interest in Anne would grow. Anne had looked radiant enough lately to guess that she fully returned his attraction. Hopefully, the madness that had seized his mother would not prove to be hereditary. It may have been born solely from stress.

The butterfly's wings were hardening. It wouldn't be long before it was ready to take flight. She was about to excuse herself when Anne arrived in the clearing. Her blush was proof enough that Frederick was here by appointment. But Cherlynn let it go. Frederick would not take advantage of Anne, especially now. As soon as they were engrossed in watching the butterfly, she quietly returned to the house.

Too bad Fay's behavior did not qualify as mad. Or perhaps not. She quite liked Frederick and didn't want his life complicated by the fear of madness. Nor would she wish any of the hereditary mental problems onto her worst enemy. If only Fay understood that living with someone who despised her was hell. Power and fortune couldn't compensate for it. Cherlynn should know.

She had hoped that divorce would finally put her life with Willard behind her, but it hadn't. What a naïve idiot she had been.

They had met at Georgetown in a summer school political science class. That summer had been the only period of her life when she'd felt good about herself. For the first time since childhood, her weight was under control. Her success at derailing the marsh bill had triggered an interest in politics. And she'd just finished her first novel and sent it out to publishers.

Snorting at her own stupidity, she retreated to her room and stared at the gardens. Willard had been a classmate. A Harvard law student, he was serving a summer internship with a senator. Neither luck nor ability had secured his appointment. As the only son of a big-name lawyer and long-time lobbyist, Willard had merely expressed an interest. The senator created a job for him on the spot. Willard was accustomed to getting exactly what he wanted. When he met Cherlynn, he had wanted her.

Foolish, foolish girl! She had done little dating over the years so had no defense against his practiced wiles. He was handsome, charming, sophisticated, and wealthy. Despite her initial skepticism, he had swept her off her feet and boosted her self-esteem, then introduced her to the world of money, power, and privilege. It was no wonder she had fallen in love. She tried to hide her feelings, distrusting their different backgrounds, but it was impossible. By the time he took her home to meet his parents, she was a firm believer in fairy-tale endings.

Idiot! Her soul-searching during the divorce had revealed every mistake. At least half of her attraction was the excitement of actually moving into the high society that she had read about for so many years, but she hadn't realized that until later. His attentions had flattered her, catering to needs she had not previously recognized. Even his overbearing mother and hard-nosed father had failed to dim her euphoria. They were cool but polite. If only she had known about the tirades they had directed at Willard. The son of old-money, New England aristocracy did not marry the daughter of a Virginia shopkeeper. She lacked beauty, breeding, fortune, and any claim to social status. They derided him for poor judgment, claiming that he'd fallen for the wiles of a scheming gold digger. It was the wrong approach. In a fit of youthful defiance, he married her within the week and took her back to Harvard for his final year of study.

It hadn't taken him long to regret his decision. His parents canceled his allowance. She couldn't find a job, so she filled her hours with reading and writing. Willard belittled the romances she loved and derided her desire to write what he considered trash. His own income barely covered a tiny apartment, food, and school expenses, worsening his temper. And her depression over a sheaf of rejection letters made it hard to care about mundane chores like cooking and cleaning, which further infuriated him.

Law school was stressful enough without adding financial pressure and a dysfunctional marriage. Daily arguments soon revealed his parents' continuing tirades. They stayed in touch, reminding him regularly that he need only rectify his error to get his allowance reinstated. The arguments also revealed his arrogance, stripping away his facade of caring tolerance to reveal a shallow, selfish snob, whose initial attraction arose from pique that she hadn't fallen worshipfully at his feet. Knowing that she had misjudged him from the start killed her last vestige of self-confidence, convincing her that she was doomed to failure.

The final betrayal occurred when she got pregnant. He

was furious, convinced that she had deliberately conceived. Vowing that he never wanted children, he ordered her to get rid of it. She refused. Even after her doctor explained that the antibiotics she had taken for a strep infection had reduced the effectiveness of her birth control pills—a known interaction that no one had thought to mention earlier—he didn't believe her protestations of innocence.

She thrust further images aside. It did no good to remember those days. She had more important things to consider—like saving Drew from a similar fate. He wouldn't have the luxury of divorcing Fay. Once the vicar pronounced them man and wife, he would be stuck for life—which in his case was a barren three years.

Chapter Eleven

Fay seethed. Drew needed a reminder of his duties, but she hadn't been able to deliver it. While heading for Broadbanks, she'd spotted him half a mile away, riding with Emily Fairfield. The scheming chit was too prostrated to accompany Anne on calls, yet possessed the energy for a cross-country gallop.

"Harlot!" She was becoming a serious threat. And not only because Drew fancied himself in love with her. Emily herself was a problem. An unexpected core of steel lay beneath her surface innocence. And considerable independence. Why then had Drew responded so positively, when he derided those same traits in her?

She would never forget that humiliating confrontation five years earlier. She had followed him to one of the follies, demanding tales of the recently concluded London Season and making the perfectly natural statement that she could hardly wait until he took her with him.

"Why should I?" he had demanded.

"Surely you'll take your wife to town!" she'd sputtered in surprise.

"Of course, but that has nothing to do with you."

She'd nearly swooned at the cruel words. "You know very well that we're betrothed," she had shouted at him. "Our fathers arranged the match years ago."

He had laughed. "Surely you're not naïve enough to believe the foolish prattle of two old men. They've tossed the idea around, of course, but it was always left up to us to decide our own futures. And mine doesn't include you."

"But you can't jilt me! I've counted on this match all my life."

"Forget it, Fay," he'd said coldly. "I'm not responsible for your delusions. I've never given you any cause to expect an offer from me. My wife must be sweet-tempered, quiet, and conformable. I'll not be saddled with a pest. You could never qualify."

Her father had verified that no settlements were yet signed, but assured her that Broadbanks considered the match settled. He had passed off Drew's comments as the usual spoutings of a man just down from his first Season, but she wasn't convinced. For months she had worked to become his ideal wife, but when she pointed out her progress, he had coldly dismissed her and moved to Thurston Park.

She hadn't spoken to him again until he returned to announce that he would wed the insipid Lady Emily. At least she'd thought the girl insipid when they'd spoken briefly at the ball. But she wasn't. And that was dangerous. So independent a chit might even accept a position as live-in mistress.

She cursed, not bothering to lower her voice. Beyond choosing a wife with backbone, Drew must have confessed his crimes to her. Jaime had reported seeing the pair on the cliffs one day, with Drew apparently pantomiming his fight with Randolph—which eliminated her best method for forcing Lady Emily out of Broadbanks. Threatening to expose his misdeeds should have made Drew send her away. Whatever possessed the girl to remain with an admitted killer?

More curses filled the air as she rode back to Raeburn House. Lady Emily could easily convince her brother to leave. She need only claim that society would misconstrue her continued stay at Broadbanks. Lady Clifford was already anxious to be gone, spurred by a suggestion that Emily's reputation had been besmirched by Drew's hovering in the sickroom and would only recover with a prompt marriage. She considered repeating the insinuations to Lord Clifford, but reluctantly set the idea aside. Gentlemen had rather odd ideas about honor. If Clifford thought Drew's attentions had injured his sister, he might feel compelled to challenge him.

She sighed.

Lady Emily wasn't her only problem. Frederick was another thorn in her side. The moment he had learned of her father's attack, he had taken charge of the estate. No one questioned his right, but he was making the most of the situation, ordering her to remain at home and threatening to replace Miss Testmark with a stricter companion if she disobeyed. Somehow, she needed to get rid of him. He ignored her age and impending marriage. He disregarded the fact that ownership of the estate would transfer to Thurston in another month. His demeanor had been even more unsettling since his two-day absence last week. He now stared at her, pursing his lips like a disapproving spinster. And he treated her like a wayward child.

A solution sprang to mind, bringing a smile to her face. She could remove both of her problems with one stroke. Frederick must marry Lady Emily. It would be to his advantage. The girl had a considerable dowry, and Frederick must be destitute if he was willing to demean himself by turning to trade. Even inheriting the barony would not overcome that taint. He would have to return to America, where Emily's dowry could buy an estate.

She immediately tracked him down in the stable and broached the subject.

"You are all about in the head, Cousin," he exclaimed, breaking into laughter. "I have no interest in Lady Emily, nor she in me. Forget it."

"Why not? She's nice enough to look at. Her training is all that is proper. And her dowry will set you up very nicely."

"I don't need to marry for money," he countered, surprising her. "Besides, I've already got my eye on a wife."

"Some tavern wench you met in town?" she scoffed. "Or is it the squire's daughter?"

"Watch it, Fay. Your mother was a squire's daughter—or have you forgotten? Not that it matters. I'm looking at Lady Anne. We will suit quite nicely."

She glared at him. "What fustian is this? No marquess's daughter is going to look at a landless baron's heir, especially one from the wilds of America who has little choice but to return there."

"It is a closer match than a marquess with a baron's daughter," he taunted her. "And I have no intention of returning to America. Broadbanks will include Raeburn House in her dowry. Thurston has already expressed regret that your father did not keep it for his heir."

Shaking with rage, she left him. He would not scuttle her plans. Raeburn House was hers! And he must move far away. Something about Frederick disturbed her. Perhaps his incessant stare. His eyes were too perceptive. She could not allow him to live close by.

Whatever his thinking, he had not yet acted. Rumor would have reported if he were paying court to Anne, so she had time to counter this threat. Talking to Drew was her best option. He would counsel Broadbanks to turn down any suit. And Raeburn House must be put in her name before the wedding. But that would not be enough. Frederick must take Emily off her hands. Since he wouldn't do it willingly, she had to maneuver him into compromising the chit.

Anne was at home to visitors, finally giving Cherlynn a chance to question the local gossips.

As Grace helped her into an afternoon gown and arranged her hair, Cherlynn set aside her nervousness. "Have you heard any new tales of Miss Raeburn?"

"It ain't right to pry," protested the maid. "Accept that he won't ever be yours."

"We've been over this too many times, Grace. Blame that horrid messenger if you must, but I have to do this. If Drew truly prefers Fay, I can live with that, but I won't drop my investigation until I know he will be happy with her. Now what did you learn?"

"She's a bad one to cross, Lady Emily," said the maid with a resigned sigh. "Few people will discuss her at all. She turned off one of the housemaids last spring. The girl had a broken arm, but refused to say how it happened. I don't doubt Miss Raeburn was responsible, but nobody will say it right out."

That fit her image of Fay, but without evidence, it didn't do her much good.

"Does she have any friends?"

"Not that I can find. I saw her talking to one of the Broadbanks tenants yesterday, but like as not they was only exchanging greetings."

Cherlynn couldn't picture Fay being friendly with inferiors. "Who was it?"

"Jaime Potts. He's a big man, all dark and broody. But he just mumbled a few words and took hisself off. I was too far away to hear what he said."

Jaime Potts. She'd heard the name before. The gamester whose luck had turned. A man had been lurking in the woods just beyond the gardens that morning. Jaime? The description fit well enough.

Ridiculous. She had spotted that man several times, so he was probably a groundskeeper. Between farming and gaming, Potts wouldn't have time to hang around Broadbanks.

Setting her questions about Fay aside, she focused on Regency decorum. Attending a gossip session would provide invaluable research. But she must be careful how she probed Fay's activities, and not just because Fay would retaliate for any perceived threat. Lady Travis would be one of the visitors. Every word Emily said would be disseminated to the *ton*, which would affect the girl's reputation.

Cherlynn vowed to be the shyest, most retiring maiden in history, and not just on her own account. Even Emily would have had something to hide from the notorious snoop. She could not disclose Emily's love, Drew's proposal, or Fay's blackmail. Fay's reputation didn't count, of course, but any mistakes would redound on Drew. And on Emily herself.

Fortunately, by the time Lady Travis arrived, half a dozen other callers graced the drawing room. Cherlynn had quietly accepted felicitations on her recovery, though more than one voice was tinged with censure for her having fallen to begin with.

Lady Travis's arrival was like letting a hurricane into the room, interrupting new speculation on Jaime Potts's sudden solvency. "I see you have recovered from your fall, Lady Emily," she observed after the most perfunctory of greetings to Anne.

"Quite," said Cherlynn.

"She is still weak, however," said Anne. "Dr. McClarren believes full recovery will take until autumn."

"What fustian," said Lady Clifford, pursing her lips in disapproval. The woman had never believed in Emily's amnesia, declaring that the girl was simply making herself interesting and that once Emily decided to recover, she would. "Has the Regent retired to Brighton yet?"

"Last week," confirmed Lady Travis. "Will you be going there yourself?"

"Lady Ledbetter requested that we visit. A few weeks in Brighton will be excellent preparation for the Little Season."

Cherlynn tried to keep her face calm, but inwardly she grimaced. Emily's memory wasn't all that Lady Clifford expected to control. By announcing plans Charles had not yet accepted, she believed that he would have to comply. And he might. She couldn't figure out Emily's brother. He vacillated between genuine concern for her condition and rigid propriety that disapproved of her behavior, especially her calf love for Thurston. He had not put the infatuation into words since he had accepted her amnesia, but it lurked beneath his restrictions—she was to avoid the library, never leave the house without a maid, and pass the time with either Lady Clifford or Lady Anne. Fortunately, he trusted her to obey, so he hadn't actually watched her. She had twice ridden alone with Drew, something Charles would never condone.

So Charles was an enigma. She could do nothing to counter Lady Clifford's manipulation except feign continued weakness. Any protests would send Charles for the carriage. If she admitted she must stay near Drew, he would drag her away instantly. But she had no other valid reason for remaining at Broadbanks.

She had missed considerable gossip. Woolgathering would hardly accomplish her research. But even as she pulled her mind back to the drawing room, the discussion of Mrs. Monroe's niece ceased as Fay arrived. That covetous gaze raked the room while Hardwick announced her. Fury briefly glinted in her eyes to find Emily part of the group, but she turned to Anne for the usual polite greetings.

Cherlynn effaced herself even further. She had no desire to speak to Fay. Instead, she set her mind to discovering how the various women interacted. The callers included both gentry and aristocracy, ranging from the vicar's wife to Lady Anne. But rank wasn't everything. Lady Travis, a baronet's widow, wielded more power than Viscountess Portrill, and even the vicar's wife was more respected than Fay, a baron's daughter.

Lady Travis quizzed Fay on her wedding plans. The girl's triumphant smirk turned to cold determination when the gossip cut her short.

"Your father's condition will postpone the happy event, of course," Lady Travis said firmly.

Fay jumped. "I doubt it. He is holding his own at present."

"I am surprised that you chose to call this afternoon rather than see after his welfare," said Mrs. Monroe primly. "Rumor places him at death's door."

"Or beyond it," murmured Lady Portrill.

The undercurrents in the room raised goose bumps on Cherlynn's arms. Every lady present despised Fay, but she retained enough credit to be received. Yet it was odd that she had come today. With her father reportedly unconscious and barely breathing, Fay courted censure by her careless disregard. Had she come because of Emily? But that made little sense.

"An exaggeration," said Fay coolly. "While he remains confined to bed, he has recovered much of his movement. His valet is sitting with him at present. And my cousin."

Introducing Frederick succeeded in diverting attention to his background and plans. Miss Langley recalled the romantic summer during which Lord Raeburn and Frederick's father had fallen in love with the Ryder twins, marrying them in a double ceremony after a whirlwind courtship. That led to speculation on how Hope had adapted to the wilds of America. Cherlynn kept her mouth shut, watching the interplay of personalities and the adept way Anne kept tempers under control.

The afternoon added new questions to her list. Talking about Lord Raeburn had displeased Fay. Or perhaps his illness enraged her. The man's death would affect her plans—unless she was willing to flout convention by marrying during deep mourning. Would she take such a chance? It could ostracize her from local society. But postponing the wedding would give Drew time to investigate her activities. And Broadbanks's death would remove the sword she was holding over Drew's head. Would his credit cloak her once they were wed? Not a woman in the room approved of her—which meant Drew's own reputation should survive when he jilted her.

At least locally. She hid a frown. Logic did not always count in the Regency period. Anyone who did not know Fay—and that included most of the *ton*—would hear only that he had broken off the betrothal. Thus she had to find proof of something so heinous that no one would question his action. Mistreating servants wouldn't do it. Even her affair with Randolph might not.

Once the last caller left, Lady Clifford accompanied Cherlynn upstairs. It was hardly unexpected. She had been staring daggers ever since Cherlynn had refused to back up her summer plans. Thus it was no surprise when she launched into a tirade.

"Enough of wallowing in weakness," she snapped the moment they reached Emily's room. "No lady reveals her inadequacies to the world. Nor does she allow bad manners to show in public. I was most displeased with your performance today."

"Why?"

"Why! You shook your head when I spoke of moving to Brighton. How dare you contradict your own mother?"

"I will not lie," Cherlynn stated coldly. "You know very well that Charles plans to remain until Lord Thurston's wedding, and that Dr. McClarren refuses to authorize any travel. He fears the jostling will make this memory loss permanent."

"Ingrate. You would accept the word of a charlatan who cannot explain the very condition he claims you suffer. I have known you since birth! The only thing wrong with your memory is a missish refusal to cooperate. Obstreperous girl! You know your duty, yet you pretend ailments to avoid it."

"Would you care to state that in plain English?" she retorted, furious at the woman's antagonism. She had put up with similar determination in her youth. Her mother had always wanted to be an actress and had tried to live that fantasy through her daughter, forcing her into dance classes, music lessons, and countless theatrical auditions. But at least she had eventually accepted that Cherlynn lacked the looks, the talent, and the interest that were necessary for success. She finally quit pushing, though she never fully approved of her daughter's real interests. But Lady Clifford didn't even give her a chance to protest—something she had never thanked her own mother for—instead, planning everything for Emily, right down to the identity of the girl's husband. Poor Emily. After years under this woman's thumb, she would have no idea how to take charge of her life.

"You must find a husband," declared Lady Clifford, confirming her suspicions. "Already you are eighteen. Charles should have insisted you come out last Season. I yielded to your pleading then, but no more. I will not tolerate this unnatural desire to avoid town."

She said nothing. Arguing could only make matters worse. Lady Clifford's mind was as tightly closed as Fort Knox. Emily had probably refused a Season because she had not yet caught Drew's attention. But she could hardly defend the girl without revealing her relationship with Drew.

"There is more at stake here than your supposed memory loss," continued Lady Clifford firmly. "We must escape this accursed place before you are ruined. Your reputation is already tarnished. In another month it will be in shreds."

"Why? Surely you, Charles, and Anne are sufficient to lend me countenance."

"That's just what I mean. This house is exerting a vulgar influence on you. Never before have you countered my direction, yet you now dispute every word I say. You will never find a husband if you put yourself forward to such a degree."

Damn! What was she to say to that? She paced the floor trying to decide how to respond without giving either Emily or herself away. If her quest succeeded, Emily would wed Drew. If it failed, she doubted Emily would wed anyone.

"Sit still," ordered Lady Clifford. "Ladies do not display agitation. It is quite apparent that Lords Broadbanks and Thurston have exerted an unbecoming influence on you. They cannot be the gentlemen I presumed—in fact, Charles should sever the connection, and will when he understands how precarious your reputation now is."

"What horrid thing have I done now?" she muttered, perching uncomfortably on the couch, knees together and back straight. Sprawling was her preferred pose.

"Miss Raeburn saw you riding with Lord Thurston the other day—without a groom!"

"And how did she decide we were unaccompanied?" she countered, though it was the truth. "She never approached us, never even came near enough that we spotted her." So that was why Fay had called—to apply more pressure on Lady Clifford. The woman was too easy to manipulate, at least for Fay's purposes.

"Are you saying she lied?" demanded Lady Clifford. "So amiable a lady would never dream of it."

"I would rather suggest that she was mistaken, catching only a fleeting glimpse when the groom was hidden by trees or lost in a fold of land. She does not know me well enough to rule out unconventional behavior."

"Nor can I, if your performance downstairs is any indication." She dabbed at a nonexistent tear with a scrap of lace. "How could you reveal such unbecoming knowledge to Mrs. Monroe just now. Lady Travis was sitting next to me and could not have missed it."

"We were discussing *Hamlet*," she protested, fighting to rein in her temper. "You can hardly object to a play that every person in London has seen."

"But you have not yet come out and should know nothing of such subjects. Do you wish people to call you a bluestocking? I can't imagine where you learned such nonsense. Not from your governess! She was most proper, restricting her instruction to manners and feminine accomplishments, though after your ridiculous performance the other evening, I cannot believe that you learned much."

The tirade continued, but she was no longer listening. The woman reminded her too much of the Cardingtons, with her rigid views and quick condemnation of any deviation. They had rejected her even before meeting her because she lacked the breeding they demanded. Their friends were the same.

Now she occupied a body that had all the breeding society could want. Yet Lady Clifford was berating her for unacceptable behavior. This despite knowing that her standards were more rigid than many in society expected. But as far as Emily's mother was concerned, any lady with more than one brain cell or who actually used the one she was allowed was doomed to ostracism. Could no one judge her for herself?

Chapter Twelve

Drew swore fluently. He had paid little attention to the estate since Randolph's death beyond checking the books each month. Stevens was a competent steward who had long since agreed that modernizing was desirable and that Broadbanks was hopelessly old-fashioned, but this wasn't the year for making changes. His father's condition might have deteriorated until the man was no longer capable of discussing business, but someone was bound to tell him if Drew modified any of his orders. Fury could kill him. Even mentioning Randolph threatened to bring on a new attack.

Not that he had wanted to discuss Randolph or anything else. Guilt, grief, and horror had left him in a stupor for months. He felt like an interloper in his own home. The servants were sullen, the tenants suspicious. Even the villagers viewed him warily, as if he threatened their livelihoods. Fear for Emily's recovery had finished the job of isolating him. But no longer. She had already given him gifts beyond price, freeing him from guilt and offering hope that he need not endure Fay for the rest of his days. And she had suggested the investigation that was rapidly mitigating his grief. God, he loved her!

In the weeks since their talk on the cliffs, he had scoured the records of all the Broadbanks properties, starting two full years before Randolph had begun helping with the bookkeeping. Now he stared at his notes in fury.

His father had long kept all estate records himself, using his stewards only as supervisors to see that tasks were completed as ordered. It was a long-standing arrangement. After encountering a dishonest steward in his youth, he had decided never to allow the book into other hands. The exception was his beloved and trusted son.

Again Drew swore.

Randolph had begun siphoning cash four years earlier by padding merchant accounts and occasionally adding fictitious ones. The amounts were minor—ten pounds here, twenty there. Sums that probably paid gaming vowels. But when he had taken over the day-to-day management, the amounts had exploded. Thousands of pounds had disappeared. And those were just the obvious frauds. It would take an on-site investigation of every property before he would know the true extent of the damage.

How had Randolph hoped to get away with it? Broadbanks would not live much longer, a fact he must have known. Once Drew acceded to the title, Randolph's oversight would have ended. Drew had never kept his determination to adopt Coke's innovations a secret. Randolph had disapproved of the changes Drew proposed. So why were the thefts so blatant? Broadbanks would have turned the money over to him merely for the asking. Did he revel in danger? Or did he live so thoroughly for pleasure that he never considered even the next hour, let alone future months and years?

He sighed. He had already disbursed thousands of pounds to pay Randolph's unexpected debts to tailors, bootmakers, and other vendors of gentlemen's apparel. Randolph's wardrobe had been expensively extensive. Then there were horses, carriages, jewelers' bills for baubles that could only have gone to mistresses. And the vowels. Randolph had caroused through London—though never when Drew was in town—as well as Brighton. Even when at Broadbanks Hall, he had spent his time drinking, gaming, whoring, and devising new ways to cover his defalcations. He was a wastrel.

And Emily had been right, though it hurt to admit his own blindness. The fight on the cliffs went beyond drunken pique over his spurning of Fay. His unexpected appearance threatened Randolph's finances. Whether or not Randolph cared for Fay, killing his brother would have solved all his problems.

He closed the books, returning them to the study shelves.

He had always felt guilty over Randolph. It had been drummed into his head since birth that he would one day be head of the family, bearing the ultimate responsibility for family honor, power, and welfare. Since the Villiers clan was enormous, the duties had always seemed daunting, but he had done his best—starting with his younger siblings. Yet his early efforts were often heavy handed and doomed to failure. He could not replace the mother his sisters had needed after Lady Broadbanks died of a chill ten years earlier. He could not make friends with the rebellious Randolph, who had always resented being the second son. Then there was William, who had reluctantly bought colors as Drew so fervently longed to do. After William's death, guilt had gnawed at his conscience. Had he tried to live vicariously through his brother, pushing him into buying a commission he had not wanted?

But whatever he had contributed to William's demise, Randolph was his biggest failure. Only two years apart, they had unconsciously competed for most of their lives. Drew was older, stronger, and more athletic—facts Randolph had resented—but Randolph was sneakier. He had wormed his way into Broadbanks's affections by mimicking his attitudes and parroting his ideas, then used his position to inflame their father's passions whenever Drew disagreed on even innocuous subjects.

"Devil take him!" he exploded as he slammed out of the house.

Randolph had manipulated them all, knowingly and deliberately. Drew was interested in reform, so Randolph had described the reformist arguments in terms that guaranteed angry antagonism. When Drew asked if Randolph planned to follow the custom for second sons by buying colors, he had twisted the innocent question into a plot to separate Broadbanks from the only child who understood him. In like manner, he had scuttled Drew's interest in assuming one of the marquessate's seats in Commons, deflected Elizabeth's interest in one of Drew's friends—though her marriage to Lindleigh had ripened into love, so there was no lasting damage—and kept Anne from attending school. The strife had ultimately driven Drew to Thurston Park, giving Randolph the opportunity to wreak havoc with his inheritance. Would Randolph have given himself over to indiscriminate gaming if he had not envied him so much?

He groaned, turning down the path that led to the Grecian folly. He needed a quiet place to think. The Broadbanks fortune could absorb the losses, but that did little to mitigate either his fury or his guilt. Yet he was powerless to retaliate. Randolph was beyond justice. Exposing his misdeeds would only hasten his father's death and destroy the last vestige of respect between them.

But this explained the lack of welcome he had received since returning home. Randolph must have poisoned the estate dependents against him, convincing them that his reckless ideas would destroy them. So he had his work cut out for him. Somehow, he must persuade them that progress was in their own best interests.

Rubbing his temples, he emerged from the forest to find the folly occupied. Had he come this way because Emily so often spent her afternoons here?

"Have you a headache?" she asked when he appeared in the entrance.

"The beginnings of one," he admitted. "I've been studying estate records all day."

"Not exactly restful," she agreed, but her eyes sharpened as she studied his face. "It's more than too much reading, though, isn't it? You found something wrong."

He nodded, surprised that he was willing to share the family shame with her. "Randolph had been siphoning funds for years."

"How much?"

"I've no idea. The obvious sums total more than forty thousand pounds."

She looked shocked, as well she might. He thought she murmured something about a million bucks, but that made no sense. "Why would he need to?" she asked. "Surely he had money of his own."

"A considerable sum, actually. But he was a gamester, among other vices, and lost everything."

"Then you're lucky he didn't do more damage. Will the estate be all right?"

"Yes, though I'll have to sell shares to handle the maintenance that he neglected. I should never have let him drive me away."

"What tale is this? I thought your retreat to Thurston was to escape your father and Fay."

"I hadn't realized how much I let Randolph manipulate me," he admitted, sitting next to her as he explained his new understanding of his brother's behavior.

"Iago. One meets the type in all times and places."

"Iago?"

"Shakespeare's *Othello,* as I'm sure you know." She grinned at him.

"Of course. It is only that your education continues to surprise me. You never showed it off before your accident."

"Is that a problem?"

Fear flared in her eyes, making him wonder what was going on. "Of course not. It is quite pleasant to conduct an intelligent discussion with a beautiful lady."

"I wish you'd tell my mother that. She raked me over the coals yesterday for mentioning *Hamlet* to one of Anne's callers."

He hesitated, searching for the right words. Emily must understand the standards that would be expected of her in society, but at the same time he could hardly condemn her for something that he found so enjoyable. The task was harder because most of his mind was occupied with kissing those rosy lips, removing her sprigged muslin gown, and taking her to bed. His fantasies were growing bolder by the day, which would spell trouble if he didn't keep them under control. Until he got rid of Fay, he could not afford to touch her.

"I know how difficult it has been for you these past weeks," he began slowly. "I cannot imagine how I would function if all knowledge of manners and expectations were suddenly wiped from my head. Society includes many educated ladies, but those who control the marriage mart are not. Thus one must avoid intellectual discussions in some company. Once you are established in the *ton,* you may choose friends who share your interests, but even well-known bluestockings adapt their conversation to their audience. This is a lesson you knew well before the accident, for you never allowed anyone to glimpse your learning. It is a pleasant surprise to discover that I can hold a rational conversation with you. But not everyone is so enlightened. You must be careful, for your mother is correct that disclosure can damage your reputation."

She sighed. "Just once in my life I would like to live with people who accept me for myself and don't force me to mimic their own prejudices."

"It sounds lovely, but civilization demands rules if it is to succeed, so we all must conform to expectations."

"Which only makes it easier for unscrupulous schemers like your brother to manipulate people." She sat up straighter, apparently shelving her melancholy thoughts. "Have you learned anything that might expose Fay's lies about Randolph's death?"

He paced the folly. "Nothing I can use, though Mason overheard two of the footmen whispering about her yesterday. But they refused to repeat their conversation—hardly surprising if it was derogatory. No one would dare report such gossip to me."

"True. Or to any of your servants, which means your groom likewise is useless. How about your father's servants?"

"Same problem. They are loyal to him and would follow his wishes. He has been pushing an alliance with Fay since I was eight years old, so they would hardly repeat anything that might endanger it. Their duty requires obedience to my orders, but they clearly resent my return, so I can only assume that Randolph poisoned them against me. If I cannot gain their respect, I will have to let them go, though it galls me to do so. Many are local and will be unable to find another position nearby. Randolph's venality has hurt more than just me."

"Don't blame yourself for his enmity," she said softly, rising to place a hand on his arm.

"How did you know I did?"

She shrugged. "You take on everyone's troubles, but being heir to Broadbanks does not mean you are infallible. Nor does it make you responsible for other people's quirks and bad decisions. Randolph willfully chose to ignore both legal and moral bounds. You had nothing to do with it."

"I'll try to believe that." He grimaced.

"Do that. In the meantime, my maid has heard several rumors suggesting that some of Fay's activities wouldn't pass close inspection. Not one lady who called yesterday likes her. Not one approves of her. I could hardly raise the issue with so many gathered together—especially since my mother and Fay were taking in every word I said—but perhaps Miss Langley or Mrs. Rumfrey might be willing to talk in private. If her transgressions call her veracity into question, no one will believe her word over yours should she raise the subject of Randolph's death."

He was touched by her determination to free him, but he was beginning to wonder why she tried so hard. Did she remember more than she claimed? "Em, did someone tell you about our friendship?" The words were out before he could stop them.

She hesitated. "Charles is your best friend. You were often at our estate, according to my maid. Both she and Charles agree that you were kind to me and rarely treated me as the bratty little sister I must have been."

He lifted her chin to look into her eyes. She was lying. He could see the truth in those blue depths. And the pain. He should never have asked. Prudence demanded he leave her here and not see her again until he was free.

Prudence be damned. His head bent until his lips lightly brushed hers. Desire washed over him, tearing words from his throat that he had never before uttered. "Dear God, Em, I love you." Crushing her to his chest, he kissed her.

Heat engulfed him. This kiss was nothing like those they had shared in the past. Whatever door had opened to expose her mind had also released her passion. She opened her mouth to his kiss, drawing his tongue deep inside and caressing it. Her hands slid deliciously up his chest to circle his neck and thread his hair. She arched into his embrace as though she were starving for his touch.

Happiness bubbled to the surface, the first he had known in months. Convention no longer mattered. He cared nothing for his father's antagonism or society's outrage. He must have Emily for the rest of his life.

But even as his fingers slipped beneath her bodice to tease her excited breasts, the last vestige of conscience urged patience. *Wait! Do it right! Protect her reputation until you can expose Fay.* Yes, he must expose Fay, though he needn't do it publicly. All he needed was a sword he could hold over her neck that was equal to the one she had suspended above his.

Emily moaned, reminding him that unless he stopped immediately, they would both be dishonored. He pulled his hand away from her soft flesh, seizing one last kiss. So rapturous was her response that his thudding heart drowned the soft sound of approaching feet.

Fay listened to a boring discourse by Lady Clifford as they wandered toward the folly. Or pretended to listen. She was bursting with excitement, her plans on the brink of fruition.

Jaime Potts had noted that Lady Emily retired to the Grecian folly every afternoon without her maid. It had been no trick to lure Frederick here. The rustic American was so untutored that he didn't even realize Lady Anne would never have sent a missive requesting that he meet her in the folly at four o'clock. He should have arrived about three minutes ago. Politeness would force him to converse with Emily long enough for Lady Clifford to find them *sans* chaperon and demand that he do the honorable thing.

She allowed a smile onto her face as they rounded the last corner. It was even better than she had planned. The couple in the shadowed depths of the folly was engaged in a passionate embrace.

"My goodness!" gasped Lady Clifford. "Emily!" The man lifted his head and turned, instinctively protecting the girl from view.

Fay heard nothing else as she teetered on the verge of swooning. Damn Drew! He couldn't even wait until after the wedding to establish that bitch as his mistress.

* * *

Drew turned at the sound of Lady Clifford's voice, fury and guilt driving passion into hiding. The audience couldn't have been worse. Lady Clifford was already hysterical over Emily's indiscretion. And Fay seemed on the verge of murder. Whatever rumors Emily had heard must be true. Rage twisted Fay's face. Beyond being unscrupulous, she was evil.

"Horrid, spiteful girl," sobbed Lady Clifford. "What have I done to deserve so vulgar a daughter? No gentleman will offer for you now."

"Quiet," he ordered, glaring into her face. "Are you so unnatural a mother that you would condemn your own daughter without a hearing?"

"Unnatural!" she sputtered wildly.

"Exactly. You ignore anything you don't wish to hear and readily manipulate her to achieve your own ends. I found her crying because you had unjustly accused her of improprieties she had not committed and had criticized behavior accepted by much of society. I admit that in comforting her distress I overstepped the bounds myself, and I must apologize for that. You can be sure that no one will hear of the incident from my lips. Or from those of Miss Raeburn," he added, turning such a savage look on Fay that she whitened.

"I won't let you take the blame for this, Drew," swore Emily, straightening to face her mother. She had managed to smooth her gown—at least to a casual eye—but her hair was tumbling down on one side. Yet her obvious embarrassment couldn't hold a candle to the glare she directed at Fay, furious that the woman would look askance at anything she and Drew might do. "That kiss was hardly one-sided. And I can't consider it a crime."

Damnation! He nearly cringed. Emily's words made things worse—as she would have known if she'd stopped to think. Society expected both ignorance and absolute innocence of its daughters. Not even amnesia had driven that knowledge from her mind, but his attentions must have scrambled her wits.

Lady Clifford abandoned hysterics, reading such a lecture that Emily appeared ready to lash back. He felt the same urge, but he couldn't intervene again. Fay grabbed his arm and jerked him aside.

He deliberately removed her claws from his sleeve and smoothed the fabric, flicking aside a mote of dust. It was time she learned that he was in charge. Once she accepted that his desire was all that mattered, jilting her would be easier.

"That girl leaves now," she hissed, further inflamed by his disdain. "You won't make me a laughingstock by entertaining your whore in your home."

"Your vulgarity worsens every day," he growled in return. "I've an urge to end this farce this minute."

"Farce?" she squeaked.

"Quite. I find the prospect of acquiring a Billingsgate fishwife more onerous than distressing a man who will be dead before many months have passed."

"Try it and I'll see you disinherited," she vowed, curling her hands into fists. "Or under sentence of death for murder."

Before he could respond, Frederick emerged from the trees and glared. "What is the meaning of this contretemps?" he demanded of Fay.

"Nothing that need concern you," she replied. "Lady Emily has merely shown her true colors to the world."

"Your doing, I suppose." His anger was obvious.

"What does that mean?" demanded Drew.

"She tried to talk me into eloping with Lady Emily two days ago. I should have suspected some plot when she accepted my refusal without argument. Today I received a note, purportedly from Lady Anne, asking that I meet her here at four o'clock. Knowing that she had not sent it, I stopped at the Hall to warn you of Fay's schemes. Not until I was sure the trap no longer awaited me, did I come here to confront her."

Lady Clifford abandoned Emily and began berating Fay for her lack of breeding.

Drew smiled, then turned back to Frederick. "I will settle with her in a moment. Perhaps you can arrange for someone to accompany her from now on. Someone besides Miss Testmark," he added.

Frederick nodded, then joined Lady Clifford in denouncing his cousin.

As soon as their attention was fully engaged, he slipped to the back of the folly where Emily had all but collapsed. "Buck up, my love," he whispered, reaching back to fasten her gown. She had been unable to manage one of the tapes. "I wish I could spare you the scolding you're in for, but this certainly settles the question of my betrothal. I'll search for evidence that will keep her quiet, but regardless of my success, nothing will induce me to wed the witch."

She nodded. "You'd best consider how to break the news to your father."

"If I can't silence her, I will let my word stand against hers. I'll not drag Randolph's character through the mud."

"Of course you won't. But you haven't much time. The wedding is less than a month off. You must notify the guests before they set out."

"I know."

The argument was winding down, making further conversation impossible. Frederick was soothing Lady Clifford, giving Drew a chance to again draw Fay aside.

"I'll not tolerate any more of your mischief," he said coldly. "If you do or say anything, no matter how insignificant, that calls Lady Emily's character or behavior into question, you can consider our betrothal at an end. No more chances, Fay."

"But—"

"I mean it, Fay," he interrupted. "Father's life is near an end. When I compare a few months of disillusion for him to a lifetime of having to endure your spite, disillusion seems the better bargain. Don't force the choice on me. You'll lose. And as to criminal charges, living in seclusion has distorted your understanding of society. There isn't a court in the land that would accept your word over mine."

She opened her mouth to respond, but Frederick grabbed her arm and dragged her away. Lady Clifford and Emily had already departed.

Drew sat down and dropped his head into his hands. Why had he kissed her? It had happened less than five minutes after his self-reminder to stay in control. The fact that it was far from their first kiss was irrelevant. He was morally tied to another. Future intent could not excuse ignoring his betrothal. And even if he could twist logic far enough to condone the kiss, making love in the folly was idiotic. The place was far too public, as events had proved. Her reputation would suffer.

Only a cad would lose his control so thoroughly. But beyond that, he had handed Fay a powerful weapon. Neither his threats nor Frederick's watchdogs could keep her under control. She had always been vindictive—and very creative about it. He need look no further than this plot to get rid of Emily. What would she do now that it had failed?

He shuddered. Charles would have to stay close to Emily for a few days—provided he would listen long enough to grasp the problem. Once Lady Clifford got hold of him, he could well end up facing his closest friend at dawn.

Cherlynn locked herself in her room with a sigh of relief at finally escaping Emily's family. Lady Clifford had ranted on for nearly an hour about honor and duty, swearing that if word ever got out, Emily would die a spinster, ostracized by society. Charles had then taken over the scolding. She had managed to talk him out of challenging Drew, but he had already left for London to fetch Dr. McClarren. The moment the man declared her recovered, they would leave Broadbanks.

She feared that this day had irreparably damaged Drew's friendship with Charles. Only a full explanation of Emily's efforts to save Drew's family might repair it, but that was impossible. Charles would never condone her intentions. If he had any idea of her plans, he would whisk her all the way to Yorkshire without bothering to consult the doctor. Even explaining after Drew broke with Fay might not reinstate the relationship.

McClarren would find her healthy, of course. She could have left a month ago. Nothing could divert Charles at this point, so she had only two days to complete her mission. Her first step was to call on the village gossips, though that would have to wait for morning. It was already past visiting hours. And she needed time to work out her approach.

Would they wish to help Drew, or had Randolph's vitriol poisoned their minds?

Grimly focusing on that question, she shoved all memory of Drew's kiss aside. She would think of it only after returning to her own time.

Chapter Thirteen

"You sent for me?" asked Cherlynn from the library doorway. She hadn't planned to see anyone before dinner—she needed the time to get her emotions under control—but Drew's summons had changed her mind. Had he learned something new about Fay? *Please be true!* If she didn't get back to her own time soon, she was going to commit a worse folly than kissing him.

Her vow had lasted barely an hour. All the feelings she'd been studiously suppressing rushed back the moment she saw him. His arms had felt so good! It had been too long since she had been crushed against a man's body, and longer yet since she had enjoyed it. But this was not the time to think about Drew's well-muscled chest or hungry lips. Not if she wanted to survive this encounter with both her sanity and Emily's virginity intact.

Drew set aside the *Times*. "Close the door."

He was sitting in one of the chairs before the fireplace. She silently complied, then took the other.

"I must apologize for my behavior in the folly," he began softly. "It was inexcusable."

"Are you sorry you kissed me?"

"Of course not!"

"Then I refuse to accept your apology. We both enjoyed it and would have changed nothing except the audience. We won't discuss it again."

"But I should not have forgotten my training as a gentleman," he protested.

"So chalk it up to my amnesia. If I'd remembered my manners, I would have protested in a most maidenly fashion and you would have stopped. Thus the fault is all mine."

He started to protest, but the twitch of her lips gave her

away. He suddenly grinned. "You're roasting me, aren't you."

"Of course. There is nothing wrong with sharing a kiss with someone you care for." His grin turned her stomach on end, distracting her until she hardly knew what she was saying.

His head shook. "Em, you're going to have a devilish time if you keep that attitude. But we'll leave that for now. I've been thinking about Fay's scheming ever since we left the folly. She hates you—which is another sin you can lay at my door. Overhearing my argument with Randolph would have told her how much I love you. Try to remember the night you fell. Do you have any idea who was nearby?"

"It's a waste of time. My first memory is of you picking me up from the hearth."

His eyes widened. "You were conscious?"

"Only for a moment. When your arms closed around me, I knew I was safe, so I let it go."

"Safe." Excitement filled his voice. "It's an odd word to use—unless you were in danger. In one of your deliriums you claimed to have been pushed. Try to remember, Em. Who pushed you?"

"I don't even know that I *was* pushed," she said crossly. "It's no use, Drew. The memories aren't there."

"Think, sweetheart," he urged. "Please?"

Damn you, Emily! Can't you at least give me this one piece of information. How did you fall? But it was useless. Poor Drew, who loved Emily so totally. It must be hell to watch her turn into a stranger.

"Let's approach it from a different direction," said Drew. "You remember so many things—tales about America, like that expedition to explore the French territories. I had heard of it, but know few details. I doubt Charles even knows that much, so where did you learn about it? And the war. You can't have gotten all your information from the newspapers because you know facts I've never read. Try to recall how you learned things. Books? Newspapers? Was there a neighbor who taught you? Though I can't imagine who. Even Sir Harold isn't that informed."

"I suppose I must read widely," she suggested desperately, keeping her face turned toward the fire so he couldn't see her consternation at his questions. Drew might be an idle aristocrat, but he had a formidable intelligence. Now that he'd turned it on her, she was in big trouble. Why hadn't she guarded her tongue more closely? *Because you didn't want to.* And it was true. Talking to him, even verbally sparring with him, was too stimulating.

"That won't wash," he insisted, pulling her out of her thoughts. "Charles might occasionally leave the *Times* on his desk, but much of your information can only be found in publications like *The Edinburgh Review* or *Cobbett's Weekly Political Review,* neither of which he reads. His interests are neither literary nor political."

"But yours are," she said softly, grasping the chance to deflect him. "Why then are you friends?"

"Friendships arise from many causes. It is not necessary to share every interest in order to feel comfortable with someone. Think, Emily," he urged, refusing to follow her lead. "Even without a memory, you should know by now that I am insatiably curious. Where did you learn so much? And why did you hide it from me?"

"How can I answer such questions when I remember nothing?" she countered.

"Think! Have you been leading a double life all these years? I've often seen you reading Elizabeth's novels since your accident. Yet you used to deride novels as works of the devil—quoting your mother, no doubt, but very convincingly. You took charge of your own recovery, forcing me to find all manner of herbs—some of which are nearly impossible to get—and provide foods that should have harmed you. Yet you have always fainted at even the mention of blood." He moved behind her, resting his hands on her shoulders. His virility beat against her, scrambling her wits so she couldn't think. "Why, Emily? Why have you hidden so much? You knew that I would welcome an intellectual challenge. Yet you continued to play the hen-witted fool. Why?"

"How should I know?" His touch was making her weak. He leaned over the chair back, his breath hot on her neck.

She fought the urge to lose herself in his arms. There was no safety there now.

"How did you come to fall, Emily? Who pushed you? Was Fay there? Did she try to kill you, my love?"

He wasn't angry or even loud. The words beat against her ears, burrowing into her head to search out the truth. The heat from his hands ignited fires all over her body, raising the insidious desire to just once have him look at Cherlynn Cardington and know her. She broke from his grasp, fleeing to the window in a futile attempt to escape that mesmerizing voice.

"Think," he urged, following her to again grasp her shoulders from behind. "You were standing by the fireplace. I caught your eye and let you see how much I cared. Perhaps I made you careless, but after today I don't believe it. Ten minutes later, you fell. Who did it, Emily? Who pushed you?"

"I don't know! I don't know! I don't even know if she *was* pushed." She froze in shock, both hands over her mouth.

"What?" Drew whirled her around to face him.

"I—nothing. My head is so fuzzy, I don't know what I'm saying these days." She tried to pull away, but his hands tightened.

"No, Emily! No more evasions. I want the truth."

"Truth?" She laughed humorlessly. "Are you ready for the truth?"

He nodded.

"Very well, my lord. There is nothing wrong with my memory. I recall none of Emily's past because I am not Lady Emily Fairfield. She shoved me into a fireplace, abducted my essence, and installed it in her body without even the courtesy of telling me who she was or what she wanted. If she were here right now, I'd wring her neck."

Drew released his hold and staggered back to his chair. "You are mad."

"Not in the least. She died four days after your betrothal ball. I read about it when I was researching the Broadbanks history while trying to learn more about the—" Her throat froze, stopping her words. No matter how hard she tried, she could not mention the curse. Shaking her head, she resumed her seat near the fire. "She had died of the injuries she suffered during your ball. Lady Travis was quite scandalized that you announced your betrothal clad in bloodstained clothes, by the way—at least that's what she wrote to Lady Debenham. Anyway, Emily had haunted the great hall ever since. She shoved me into that same fireplace while I was touring Broadbanks on June 15, 1998. I woke up in her body."

Drew cringed into the wingback chair, staring at the woman sitting calmly in its mate. She looked the same, her ebony hair glinting in the shafts of late-afternoon sunlight that filtered through the leaded windows, her blue eyes as bottomless as usual, her slender body crying to be caressed. Yet her movements were jerky. Her voice had assumed an unfamiliar rhythm. And her words made no sense at all.

"W-who are you?" he stammered.

She sighed. "I was born Cherlynn Edwards. Until recently I lived in the United States. But at the time of my accident, I was the Marchioness of Broadbanks."

"You are married?" His face turned stark white.

"No. I bought the title at Christie's for ten pounds."

"Preposterous! No Broadbanks would ever sink so low."

She opened her mouth, but no words emerged. "Damn!" she muttered to herself. "I can't talk."

"What?"

"I wish Emily had at least told me the rules of this game she's playing. Obviously, there are topics I am not permitted to mention. The words refuse to form. I suppose disclosing them would break some cosmic regulation I don't understand." She shrugged.

"You belong in Bedlam."

"It must sound like that. In fact, I did not fully accept it myself for quite a while. I have no idea what happened, except that I woke up in Emily's body fully four days before she died. The obvious conclusion is that she stepped aside early so that I could save her life. The only reason she would have for doing so is that she plans to return. In fact, I expected to be gone as soon as the fever broke. When she didn't come back, I figured that she also wanted me to take care of Fay for her—Grace knows about your arrangement, by the way. Since Emily believes I can do this, there must be something that will prevent Fay from making your life miserable once you jilt her. I just haven't found it yet. Emily must love you very much to have waited all these years to save you."

He recoiled in shock. "That blow to the head did more damage than I had supposed."

She glared, but it was a reasonable conclusion. "Skepticism is inevitable. Let's see what I can come up with to convince you." She paced the library for several minutes deep in thought. Fortunately, Emily's afternoon gown had a full skirt so she didn't need to shorten her stride. "Frederick is lucky he sailed for England when he did. Shortly after he left, the United States declared war, in part because of impressment and England's intransigence over trade."

"Impossible. We repealed the Orders in Council in April, and the treaty negotiations are nearly complete."

"Nice try, but too little, too late. Americans didn't have that much patience. Still don't, for that matter. In your time, they were brash from the newness of freedom. In mine, they're a world power used to controlling their own destiny. But enough of that. Let's see. . . . 1812. . . . On July 27, Wellington won a victory at Salamanca, capturing two French eagles. Word of both events should reach London this week."

His face turned even whiter. He glanced at the newspaper, but it was on the floor, its folds obscuring the headlines.

"What's wrong?"

"You can't have seen the paper. I was in the hall when it arrived and have been reading it ever since."

"And?"

He held it up. The report of Salamanca was on the first page. His head shook. "You look so normal."

"How would you expect a time traveler to look? Like some alien monster with three heads and a tail? I just wish Emily had left me with a few of her own thoughts. Research doesn't begin to cover everything I need to know to live in this period."

He pounced on the admission. "If Emily brought you

back here without warning, why had you researched this period?"

"I write novels set in Regency England. I need to make the stories believable."

"Coming here must be the ultimate research tool," he growled. "Have you enjoyed dipping into our lives?"

She didn't miss the spark of anger. It was inevitable. Emily had perpetrated an enormous hoax on him with this escapade. Drew was not a man to enjoy being a victim, however loving the motives. But her own emotions were also close to the surface. Scorn on top of everything else was too much.

"I didn't ask to be wafted back nearly two hundred years," she spat furiously. "And I sure as hell could have done without Lady Clifford or that bloody quack! God, what I wouldn't give for an aspirin right now! Or my computer. Or a Twinkie!" She strode around the library, arms waving in frustration.

"What—"

"Never mind. I doubt they will allow me to explain." She cast her eyes to the heavens, fighting to regain her composure. "Look, I'm sorry you got stuck in the middle of this mess. I've been thinking about what you said earlier. Since Emily pushed me into the fireplace, perhaps she was giving me a clue after all. Someone may have deliberately pushed her at the ball. In one of Lady Clifford's tirades over my clumsiness, she mentioned that Fay had stalked away from the scene because I made such a cake of myself. So she might have tried to get rid of a rival. As you pointed out, she knew that you had planned to marry Emily."

Drew stared at her wordlessly. His head was spinning, but despite all logic, he believed her. Shy, hen-witted Emily had managed to reach into the future and bring back a woman who could save them both. But he was having trouble sorting out his thoughts. He had just gotten used to the idea that Emily was intelligent, and now he discovered that she wasn't Emily after all. His head shook.

"Sit down," he said wearily. "Can we start at the beginning? I haven't quite taken all this in yet."

She smiled with understanding, resting her hand briefly on his shoulder before resuming her own seat.

"My name is Cherlynn Edwards Cardington," she began.

"I thought you said you weren't married."

"I'm divorced. It's quite common in my time," she added as he flinched. "Believe me, I'm much better off without the creep."

His head was again shaking.

"Drew, my own life really isn't relevant to this discussion."

"But I'd like to know." Curiosity was pushing all else aside. Or perhaps he needed extra time to assimilate her claims. "Tell me a little about yourself."

She shrugged. "I was born in 1972 in Virginia—only a couple of miles from Frederick's farm, if I understand his descriptions. The area has completely changed since he lived there, of course. I never got along with my family, so wasn't much disturbed when the last of them died. I already had degrees in English literature and European history and had moved on to my own life."

"Degrees?"

"College degrees. From the University of Virginia. Awards for finishing a course of study, like you probably got from Oxford."

"Women in college." His head was spinning.

She laughed. "Women have full equality in my day. They vote, get equal educations, serve as judges, senators, governors, doctors, soldiers, sailors, and everything else. They work construction crews, run corporations, and fly the space shuttle. England's prime minister during most of my youth was a woman. Anyway, I worked for a Congressional committee until I met Willard and stupidly married the jerk. What a disaster!"

"Did he beat you?"

"Not physically. But my breeding didn't match his—something you should understand. America doesn't have the kind of class system England still does, but you'd never know it in some circles. His parents hated me on sight. He married me anyway in a burst of rebellion, but regretted it the moment they cut off his allowance. We toughed it out for a while, but after my miscarriage, I gave up and walked out on him. The divorce decree came through just before I left for London."

"Where you bought a title." Pain ripped his chest at the thought of something so precious being offered up like the cheapest bauble.

"That was an accident," she said with a shrug. "And it is one of those topics I can't find the words to explain. Perhaps when this is over, I'll be able to tell you about it. It was after I came into possession of the title that I visited Broadbanks Hall—though I would have done that anyway. It's one of the best Regency houses in the country; you did a marvelous job of redecorating."

"Oh, God!" he moaned softly.

"I shouldn't have said that, I suppose."

"It's just so hard to take in."

"I know. It took me weeks to accept it—though I was out of my mind for much of that time. At any rate, I toured the house. When I got to the great hall, Emily attacked. I guess I was the first one she found who could help her."

"Does she want to be a marchioness that badly?"

"No, Drew. I believe it was you she wanted to save more than herself. At least that's the impression I've gotten from Grace."

"Where is she now?" he asked suddenly.

She shrugged. "Who knows? Perhaps she's occupying my body. Her lack of medical knowledge wouldn't matter since everyone else knows how to keep it alive. Or she may be watching me—she needs to know when to return. If she had let me know a little more, perhaps I wouldn't have blown my cover so badly. But at least I've nearly finished. You won't be marrying Fay."

"Nothing could force me into it."

"I believe you, because my head isn't freezing up. If you'd gone through with it, you would have died in September of 1815."

He recoiled. "Wh— How?" he stammered.

"I don't know all the details, though Lady Travis claims you found Fay playing around with a groom. After revising your will to banish her to Scotland, you walked in here and blew your brains out."

"Oh, my God!" He was shaking.

"But you won't do that now, will you, Drew?"

He shook his head.

"Good. Nothing is worth killing yourself for, especially a bitch like Fay."

He stared.

"Sorry. I forgot where I was again. Women do occasionally swear in my day, particularly when the subject is so venal."

He laughed. "So how do you know what Lady Travis has been writing?"

"I bought fifteen of her letters to Lady Debenham in an antique shop shortly after I arrived in London. Old letters are a great research source for those interested in the culture of a time period rather than the dry facts of war and politics."

"I'd better burn all my correspondence," he muttered. Then another of her odd comments returned to mind. "You mentioned Napoleon's Russian campaign."

"Right."

"The winter?"

"Of the six hundred thousand troops that started the campaign, seventeen thousand will return. The horrors they encounter will be remembered well beyond even my time."

"Dear Lord! Where did he find that many men?"

"Many of them come from conquered countries, but he also pulled some troops out of Spain."

"Leaving the armies more evenly matched," he breathed, hope and wonder flooding his body. "Is this the end of the war, then? Is Salamanca Wellington's final push into Spain?"

"Almost." She was surprised that the words came, but relaxed and continued. "He has split the army by now, half to take Madrid, the rest to hold off the French at Burgos. But Burgos is better defended than he thinks. He hasn't the troops to take it by force, and he left his siege equipment elsewhere, so he'll pull back to Ciudad Rodrigo and Badajoz for the winter."

"I thought you couldn't talk about future events."

"I can't, at least not about anything that matters. Think about it. Even if you went to London to warn the government that Wellington needs more men and equipment to take Burgos, and even supposing they believed you and didn't lock you in Bedlam, by the time anyone could act, Wellington would have discovered the information for himself." She shrugged.

"Will he win?"

She managed to nod.

The last of his tension relaxed. "Enough of war. I agree that Fay probably pushed Emily at the ball. All I need is to find a witness and I'll be able to keep her quiet about Randolph. I'll start with Lady Clifford." He paused as another thought hit him. "Do you recall how long my father will live? How long do I have to keep Fay quiet?"

Her mouth worked silently for a moment. She finally managed two words. "Not long."

He bowed his head in a moment of grief, but in truth the marquess suffered considerable pain. "Thank you, Cherlynn. Or should I call you, my lady?"

"It would be better to stick to Emily."

He nodded, then smiled and relaxed. The unreality of this conversation would catch up to him later, but for now he intended to satisfy his curiosity.

"Enough about my time. Tell me about yours. What was that you said about women and space?"

"You would home in on that one," she complained with a grimace. "Describing the space program requires briefings on dozens of subjects."

"So what are you waiting for?"

Sighing, she launched an explanation. Images floated through his head—of cars, airplanes, and rockets traveling at unimaginable speeds; of tall buildings filling cities that held enough people to dwarf even London; of organ transplants, wonder drugs, and artificial body parts; of photographs, moving pictures, and satellite surveys of earth and the universe; of telephones, computers, and an information network connecting the world.

"It sounds like Eden," he murmured in awe.

"Technologically, perhaps. But there is much to be said for your time, Drew. Why do you think so many people read stories set in the past?" And she went on to describe the pressures exerted by technology, from the push to always be doing something to the need for acquiring ever bigger, faster, and better technology; the search for relief from that pressure that led so many people into drug addiction; the crime that grew from addiction and from packing people so closely together; the destruction of the environment; the wars that were still fought; the diseases that even advanced medicine couldn't cure; the lack of respect that pervaded every level of society.

The dressing bell sounded. "And just as well," she said with a sigh. "I've been talking too much. You live in a wonderful age, Drew. Enjoy it. Hungering for another life will prevent appreciation of what you have."

"Very true. But before I can start living, I need to defang a serpent. There are still a few tenants who might be willing to answer questions about Fay's activities."

She nodded. "I will chat with the village gossips tomorrow—individually—in hopes of learning something useful. The sooner we get this over with, the sooner Emily will return."

He watched her leave the library, confusion again filling his mind. Did he want Emily back?

The question shocked him, but it wouldn't retreat. Even as he went upstairs to change, it hammered at his head.

Emily had seemed the perfect bride only five months ago. She was beautiful, and her kisses raised a hunger for more. She was a model of propriety otherwise, versed in the accomplishments that would make her a delight in the drawing room, trained in the niceties of entertaining and of supervising a household, and with both the breeding and the manners to charm society.

Cherlynn had none of that. Yet she challenged and excited him in ways he had never considered. Her intelligence was formidable; debating with her left him glowing with pleasure. She was determined, forthright, and independent, all traits that should have made him shudder, though they didn't. But his greatest confusion arose from the kiss they had shared in the folly. It had been the most shattering experience of his life, inciting more passion than the most accomplished courtesan. He had attributed his response to love, but now he wondered. Emily—Cherlynn—had participated as never before. Was that what had made the difference? Or had his fascination with Cherlynn's mind affected his emotions? Did Emily share that passion, or was it all Cherlynn's? Did it matter?

Probably not, he admitted ruefully as Mason helped him into his jacket. Cherlynn would be gone soon, taking her intelligence and independence with her. If he was lucky, the passion was Emily's and had been suppressed by custom. But whatever the truth, he owed Emily too much to allow a momentary infatuation with a woman from another time to interfere with his marriage.

And marriage there would be. On the fifteenth of September, as scheduled. He had already dispatched his secretary to London to acquire a special license in Emily's name. She had saved his life and his sanity. A century of devotion wouldn't begin to repay that debt.

A wave of guilt washed over him. Why had God gifted him with such extraordinary intervention? He had done nothing to deserve it. Even innocence in Randolph's death didn't make him a candidate for sainthood. Others were certainly more worthy.

Or was Emily the true recipient of celestial favor? She was caring enough, as her recent actions proved. Whatever the truth, his marriage would be quite different than he had envisioned. He could no longer consider his own needs. Her efforts deserved both recognition and reward. And part of that reward would be fulfillment of her every wish. He would have to work hard every day to make sure she never regretted her decision. The prospect was daunting.

Chapter Fourteen

As dawn filtered through the window, Cherlynn gave up trying to sleep. Too much had happened the day before.

"Damn it, Drew!" she muttered, pulling on a dressing gown to combat the chill that permeated English nights even in August. "Why the hell did you have to kiss me?"

Her feet paced faster, but couldn't out-race her memories. His hand tracing her cheek, moving across her hip, sliding under her bodice to cup her breast. His fingers unpinning her hair, whispering down her throat, peaking her nipple. His lips and tongue hot and wild as they plundered her mouth. Never had she encountered such a carnal kiss. Heat pooled in her womb, as it had been doing all night.

"Okay, so you want him," she chastised herself, trying to force the images away with logic. "Who wouldn't? The man positively radiates sex. But it wasn't you he was kissing, girl. It's Emily he wants and Emily he loves. Don't ever forget it." Not that she would have the opportunity. Now that he knew who she was, she needn't fear a repeat.

Fear?

Who was she trying to kid? Even the most naïve Regency miss would want more of Drew Villiers. That hunk of blazing manhood could warm the coldest night, fill the loneliest heart.

And more. He had an interesting mind. Intelligent and educated, of course, but that wasn't unusual, even for a Regency aristocrat. It was his curiosity, his tolerance, and his almost-twentieth-century willingness to embrace change that had surprised her. He cared about the people of his estate and wanted to improve their lives. Those who accepted jobs in the new industries worried him, for he anticipated the problems that Dickens would describe so eloquently. He was open to new ideas, even accepting, though with understandable reluctance, her appearance from the future. And his respect for others transcended both gender and class boundaries.

Intelligent, sexy, caring, tolerant. The perfect male. Too bad he lived in the wrong time period. She sprawled onto the couch and frowned. Surely the combination wasn't *that* rare. There must be any number of men in her own time who were equally enticing. She just hadn't noticed them yet. And that was hardly surprising. After walking out on Willard, she'd wanted nothing to do with men. A very acrimonious divorce hadn't changed that. So what had?

She frowned, trying to pin down when the numbness of the last two years had worn off. Pain, grief, and despair had piled up, layer upon layer, until she could barely drag herself out of bed—fights about her worthiness to be a Cardington, arguments over her pregnancy, the accident that had nearly killed her and *had* killed her son, months of recovery, the dingy room she'd called home during the divorce proceedings, six new rejection letters, this last-ditch effort to do enough research so that her next book might have a chance, the unvoiced admission that she would never be a writer and should abandon this dream, too.... When had despair turned to hope?

When Drew had lifted her from the hearth and cradled her close. The safety and security had overwhelmed her, answering a need she had not recognized, but that had gnawed at her all of her life. The need for warmth, unconditional acceptance, and love.

"Damn it, you've fallen in love with the man," she scolded herself furiously. "What a fine mess you've gotten yourself into this time!" And what utter stupidity! Buying a death sentence couldn't hold a candle to loving a man who had perished more than a century before she was born.

Hadn't she learned anything from the disasters she had already survived? This jaunt to the Regency was temporary, so forming an attachment was just plain dumb—worse even than marrying Willard. She and Drew could never be together. Even discovering a way to return to 1812 in her own guise wouldn't help. He was off limits. He loved Emily, and

Emily was everything she wasn't—beautiful, adoring, and conformable; the kind of wife who would devote herself to serving her husband and would never dream of arguing with him. He frankly hated Fay, whose independence and determination matched Cherlynn's own.

This was yet another reason to get this job over with. She needed to leave before Drew discovered her idiocy. He would pity her, and that was the last thing she wanted. Visiting the local gossips would keep her out of his way for now. With Dr. McClarren due back as early as tomorrow, there was no further need to pretend weakness. Only if she learned something useful would she see Drew. Or perhaps she would write him a note with all the specifics. Another *tête-à-tête* in the library would risk both exposure and a broken heart.

By late morning Cherlynn was sitting in Miss Langley's sitting room, drinking a cup of tea. Grace had disappeared into the nether regions to interview Miss Langley's maid.

Somehow, the conversation had moved onto the topic of flighty young girls—the spinster hurriedly disclaiming that Emily was included among their numbers. "Like that silly Maude Gardner," she said with a snort. "She'd caught the eye of a prosperous farmer, and seemed quite puffed up with her prize. But two days after the first of the banns were called, she ran off without a word."

"Where to?"

"No one knows. She disappeared last spring and hasn't been heard from since."

"That *is* odd. But perhaps she changed her mind about the match."

"It's possible," conceded Miss Langley. "She was the one who did most of the chasing, becoming scandalously forward at times, but perhaps she had merely meant to flirt. Some claimed she was taken aback when her father accepted the offer without consulting her. Or they may have had a disagreement. But we'll never know. Both her father and her betrothed died not long after she left."

Cherlynn shivered, but couldn't for the moment think why. It didn't matter anyway. She needed to move the conversation to Fay. "So many people have died this year. Mr. Raeburn mentioned that his entire family succumbed."

"Tragic," agreed Miss Langley, "but hardly surprising. If people will insist on moving to such uncouth places, they must expect it. Why anyone would choose to live among savages, I do not know. Poor Mrs. Raeburn must have been terrified. She was always such a sensitive girl."

"Were she and Miss Raeburn's mother really twins?" she asked, hoping to find a place to start. There must be something in Fay's background that Drew could use against her.

"My, yes," twittered Miss Langley. "Identical as two peas in a pod. The marriages shocked the neighbors something awful, but who could blame the boys? Despite their breeding, the Ryder twins had long attracted the eye of every gentleman in the area. They were beautiful—blonde hair, blue eyes, lovely figures—and they exuded an aura that attracted men like bees to honey. Dangerous, of course. Even my late brother, who was happily married, felt their allure."

"Circe," Cherlynn murmured, sipping her tea. "So they caught the Raeburns?"

Miss Langley nodded. "Lord Raeburn's heir—that would be Master Jonathan—was staying with him that summer. The Ryder girls enslaved them within days despite being so far beneath them."

"I understood they were gentry." As a baron, Lord Raeburn was at the bottom of the aristocracy.

"Barely. Their father was Squire Ryder of Wychurch, who had married a yeoman's daughter. But the Raeburns didn't care. They seemed almost bewitched."

"Surely not!" She put enough disbelief into her tone to elicit further information.

"I wouldn't be surprised," confided Miss Langley. "There have always been strange doings in that line—whispers, secrecy, and who knows what else. Faith and Hope the girls were named, in hopes they would avoid the curse."

"Curse?"

"Madness."

Memories of Frederick's story twitched shivers across her shoulders. "Is all the family mad, then?"

"No," the gossip admitted, helping herself to a biscuit.

"No one has confirmed a single case, but rumor is rife—and has been since I was a child. Where there is smoke, one usually finds fire."

"Is rumor specific?" What would this mean to Frederick and Anne?

"At times. The ill health that prevented Mrs. Ryder from attending the weddings was madness—or so the story goes. And my own mother recalled how Mrs. Ryder's mother killed her son's pet dog, though to be fair, the animal had destroyed a good part of her wardrobe. But 'tis also rumored that an aunt was locked away for crimes too awful to discuss in decent company."

"How about the twins themselves?" She accepted a second cup of tea.

"They seemed quite all right. Both doted on young Frederick—now there was a bonny babe, full of mischief and inquisitive as a cat. I best remember finding him in Jeb Perkins's fishing boat—he would have been about two—trying to untie a rope so he could float out for a closer look at a schooner in the Channel. Always loved boats, he did. His nurse wasn't able to keep up with him from the day he took his first step."

"Poor woman. But you were mentioning the twins."

"Yes, I was. His mother was perfectly normal during the time she lived here," she admitted. "Except for hiring that nurse. The smartest move she made was leaving the woman behind when they left for America. Nothing odd there. Of course, she's been gone a good many years. Lady Raeburn was a bit eccentric, but did nothing that could be construed as mad, unless you count hiring the same nurse for the infant Fay. Miss Testmark is still at Raeburn House and no more able to keep up with Fay now than she was twenty years ago with Frederick."

True, but she was a family connection so keeping her around was not exactly mad. "When did Lady Raeburn die?" she asked, trying to recall everything she knew about genetic mental illness, which unfortunately wasn't much.

"Six years ago. She got lost during a snowstorm—it rarely snows here, so she must have become confused—and died of exposure."

"How sad. Miss Raeburn must have hated losing her mother."

"She ran quite wild afterward."

Further probing yielded nothing she could use. Fay may have run wild at age fourteen, but she had carefully covered any misdeeds in the years since. Her return to apparent decorum coincided with Drew's declaration that he wasn't interested in marriage and probably arose from it. The change was too profound to be coincidence. Fay's fifteenth year passed normally. Only after Drew moved to Thurston Park did she begin to backslide.

But Miss Langley knew nothing beyond an abrasive personality. Or did she? A note of unease simmered deep in her eyes. Was it Fay herself who kept gossip quiet? Grace had heard rumors of witchcraft—not that Cherlynn believed in such a thing. But a common thread connected tales of the family madness. Murder—of a dog, of a husband and children, of . . . what? Was that behind the crimes too awful to mention? Did Miss Langley fear for her safety if she enraged Fay? It seemed preposterous, but then her entire life of late had been preposterous.

She collected Grace and bade her hostess farewell. The vicar's wife was out, as was Lady Travis, so she could do nothing but return to Broadbanks. Hardwick informed her that Drew would like to see her, but she was still too shaken by her morning revelation to seek him out. Instead, she headed for the garden where she might be able to think.

Lord Broadbanks was on the terrace.

"Good afternoon, Lady Emily," he said slowly, gesturing for her to join him. His color was slightly better this day, but he was still a visibly ill man. By her calculation, he had less than a month to live.

"My lord."

She accepted yet another cup of tea, exchanging pleasantries. His mind was apparently troubled, for his conversation wandered without purpose for several minutes. Not until he began talking about Randolph did she concentrate on what he was saying.

"Such a loving son," he murmured, half to himself. "His death was tragic."

"Tell me about him," she suggested, suspecting that he wanted to talk, but that Drew could never have listened. And she was suddenly overwhelmed by the feeling that Randolph was more important than she had suspected. Was he the key to neutralizing Fay? Not because of their affair. Something teased her mind, but she couldn't quite bring it into focus.

"Such a loving son," he repeated with a shake of his head. "Yet there was that in his eyes that sometimes made me wonder. He was too much like me."

"I would think that was good."

His brows lifted. "In a way. I often wished that he had been first-born. Drew holds too many ideas I cannot accept. Yet I fear I did Randolph a disservice by favoring him. It widened the rift that had already existed between them."

"Brothers do not always get along," she agreed.

"Perhaps not, but encouraging Randolph to manage the estate was wrong. I had no unentailed estate to give him and knew well that Drew would never appoint him as steward. Their ideas were too different, and Randolph would never accept subservience. Yet I prevented him from pursuing an acceptable career. Military, church, government. He was trained for none of them."

"Perhaps, but that is not entirely your fault. He could have chosen differently."

"With me demanding his assistance and playing on his affections? I think not. As I said, he was much like myself—weak, following always the easiest path. I recognized it. Keeping him by my side was a misguided attempt to protect him from the dangers of London, but I failed. He sowed his oats with as much abandon as any young man, overindulging in wine, debauchery, gaming, and pranks without understanding that forgiveness is less forthcoming when one is not heir to a title. Society often condemns younger sons for deeds it ignores in their older brothers."

She nodded. "Did he get into trouble then?"

"Some. Enough to underscore his status as second son. I should have controlled him better, but he was ever my favorite. I should have taught him moderation, but exposing my own heedless youth risked losing his regard. Ah, vanity!

If he had indulged less in wine, he would not have died. Guilt has weighed heavily on me ever since."

"Don't, my lord," she begged. "Every parent since Adam has faced the specter of an imperfect child and tormented himself with guilt. But there is no need. You made the best decisions possible. He was well past his majority at the time of his death and thus responsible for his own actions. A man of four-and-twenty is capable of reason. If he chooses to imbibe more than is seemly, then he must bear the consequences. It is tragic that he died so young, but you can only accept it and move on. Your health will not recover until you can put this behind you. Remember his good qualities without dwelling on the mistake he made at the end."

"But I should have taught him more," murmured the marquess. "I knew—who better?—where wanton self-indulgence can lead. Perhaps he would have lived if I had shared my experiences with him."

"Perhaps, but children are rebellious by nature. Would he have listened? Or would he have ignored your warning, assuming that you were prosing on about situations that he would never face? He might even have done worse just to prove that he was better or smarter than you had been."

"You have a grasp of human nature that belies your years," he said with a tremulous smile. "That is precisely what he would have done, for he never balked at a challenge. And he could find challenge in situations that most people would ignore."

"A common trait in younger sons. They must constantly prove themselves to be the equal—or better—of their older brothers. Did not your own brothers do as much?"

He smiled. "Ah, yes. In riding, in flirtation . . ." His head nodded in fond memory even as his voice died away.

"Set your fears aside, my lord," she urged as Hardwick approached. "The past is gone and cannot be changed. Accept it and move on to the future."

"Mr. Raeburn requests a word with you, my lord," said Hardwick.

"I will leave you, then," she said, slipping into the gardens.

Half an hour later she was returning to the house when that elusive memory jumped to the fore. Why had Randolph been walking home? She must send Grace into the village to ask a few questions.

But that action had to be postponed. Broadbanks was still on the terrace, his face looking several years older. Fearing that he was on the brink of another attack, she was turning toward the door when he beckoned her.

"Are you all right, my lord?" she asked.

He nodded. "I have received several shocks. May I intrude upon your time to make use of your uncommon sense?"

"Of course." She waited patiently while he sifted his thoughts for a place to begin. But her mind was less than patient. What had Frederick said that had upset Lord Broadbanks so badly? It was too much to hope that he had denounced Fay and broken off the betrothal. She examined the marquess's gray face. Had he learned of Fay's charges against Drew? That would put an end to the connection, but it would also widen the chasm between Drew and his father, creating ill will that would plague Drew's mind long after Broadbanks died.

He sighed. "Mr. Raeburn has requested leave to pay his addresses to Anne."

"I know that he cares deeply for her, and I believe she returns his regard," she said carefully, wondering why this turn would shock him.

"That is not the problem. In making this request, he felt it necessary to air all his family skeletons. His mother ran mad not long ago, and he has learned since his return that the problem is common in her family."

"I hard heard hints of this," she admitted as her mind slipped into high gear. Would Frederick have investigated his family if Emily had died on schedule? The news had obviously shocked the marquess. She didn't want to precipitate an early death, but Frederick may have discovered something that Drew could use. "Our discussion of his mother may have prompted his probe of her family. But I do not know any details. Lady Langley mentioned the twins' eccentric mother, grandmother, and aunt. Are there others?"

"He spent two days in his mother's home village and questioned several people. Nearly a third of the family members are afflicted."

"Are any men included in that number?"

His gaze sharpened. "An odd question."

"Not at all. Many inherited traits affect only sons or only daughters. For example, I have met several men who are blind to color. When I questioned Dr. McClarren, he admitted that it is a deficiency found only in men. In like manner, he recounted skeletal problems that occur only in women and an odd bleeding disease confined to men. Perhaps this form of madness is similar."

"Perhaps. The people that he mentioned were all female."

"How many cases did he discover? If it is a female problem, then it must move from family to family."

"Fourteen, though once he retreated past three generations, the evidence becomes apocryphal. As you say, the families involved kept changing, and the lower classes keep few records."

"Were daughters of male offspring also afflicted?"

"No."

"Then you need not fear that either he or his children will suffer." She bit her tongue to keep from mentioning Fay. Let him raise that issue on his own. It sounded as though he was already leery of the match. "Did you approve Mr. Raeburn's courtship?" she asked instead.

"I will discuss it with Drew, and possibly Anne."

"A good place to start. I doubt Anne is in any danger, but she should be informed."

"Quite. Would you summon my valet, Lady Emily? I must rest before facing my son."

She nodded and returned to the house.

Was this the break that would free Drew? Probably not. Publicly disclosing the family madness would harm Frederick and Anne. Jilting Fay without mentioning the madness would destroy his own reputation. And she doubted that Fay would end the betrothal to avoid disclosure.

Her head swirled. Why couldn't common sense prevail? Fay would make a lousy wife by any standard. There was no reason to condemn him for dumping her!

Chapter Fifteen

Cherlynn avoided Drew for the rest of the day, but she could not escape him after dinner. With Charles in London, he declined the port, following her upstairs when she bypassed the drawing room.

"You are ignoring me, Cherlynn," he said softly. "Why?"

She shrugged as he led the way back to the library. "After that fiasco in the folly yesterday, I can't chance being caught alone with you again. Emily's reputation would never recover." It wasn't the entire truth, but he accepted it.

"No one will disturb us here. Father described your conversation. I cannot believe that he discussed such a delicate issue with anyone unrelated, let alone a female."

"He claims I have uncommon sense. We've spoken on several occasions, so he realizes that he can trust me—though the main reason for that has escaped his notice, thank heaven. Since I have none of Emily's memories, I doubt she will retain any of mine."

"Do you really believe that Frederick is untainted by madness?"

She nodded. "By my time, scientists have learned much about inheritance. Certain disorders are passed to the offspring through the male and female seed. A small number of these are gender specific. Since the afflicted members of Fay's family are all female, and since no child of a male suffers, we can safely assume that such is the case here. Which means Frederick is no more likely to harbor madness than you or I."

"You are sure?" His eyes begged for a guarantee.

"I can't swear that he will never do anything you would describe as mad, Drew. Events can drive people to extremes regardless of heredity. Given the right circumstances, you are capable of suicide," she reminded him. "I consider that mad. But Frederick is strong, rational, and willing to face trouble head-on. That makes him an unlikely candidate."

"You relieve my mind. And I now have adequate cause to terminate this ill-conceived betrothal."

"You can't cite madness, Drew!"

"Why?"

"For God's sake! Must I explain your own era to you? Everyone knows Frederick is Fay's cousin. If you dump her because of family madness, he will be branded as well. Anne is the one who would suffer. No matter how willing you are to believe, most people would not accept your word that Frederick is untainted. It would take twentieth-century genetics to prove it."

"Gen-etics?" he asked, stumbling over the word.

"Damn," she muttered. "I wasn't going to get technical. Traits are passed from parent to child via tiny bits of matter called genes. We all have thousands of them. One gives you chocolate-brown eyes. Another makes your hair curl—" *Bad examples,* she realized as heat pooled in her womb. Wrenching her eyes from his face, she forced a businesslike tone into her voice. "The study of genes is called genetics. Abnormalities in genes cause many diseases in humans, some with symptoms that your era collectively refers to as madness."

"It is a disease then?"

"Some madness arises from genetic mistakes that affect behavior. Other forms come from emotional problems or stress that the person cannot deal with—like your suicide. Both kinds can be treated in my time so victims live normal lives."

"So madness is not a pestilence caused by the devil," he murmured.

"Not at all. I have not studied the subject in depth, but there are two types of genetic mental illness that I do know of. One is porphyria, which is the disease afflicting George III. I saw a movie about it a few years ago. Unfortunately, the remedies that his physicians prescribed actually made him worse, until he is now beyond help of even my own time's doctors. Another disease is called schizophrenia, in which a person hears voices that urge him to criminal or destructive behavior. It can be controlled with medication."

"Amazing," he breathed. "But I thought you could not discuss future events."

"I don't know the rules of time travel," she said on a sigh. "Some things I cannot talk about. Others are not a problem. Perhaps psychiatric advances are so far in the future that mentioning them now will mean nothing. After all, the science of psychiatry itself was not developed until the 1860s. But let's stick to the subject. Citing madness to jilt Fay will only get you off the hook by hurting Anne. Have you discovered anything else?"

"Not about Fay. But Father related a tragic tale that explains how I came to be in this fix." He restlessly paced the room.

She raised her brows, but said nothing as she settled into a chair. Though her curiosity was high, she could not force him to betray family secrets unless he wanted to. But he seemed to be in the mood to do so. Perhaps knowing that she would soon be gone, leaving no memories behind to trouble Emily, made speaking easier.

"Father claims he was not a sober, dutiful, and very proper figure when he was a young man. In fact, to hear him describe it this afternoon, he must have been wilder even than Lord Devereaux."

"Who is one of your more incorrigible rakehells, as I recall." She nearly laughed at his expression. "Don't forget that I've studied this period. His foibles have not mellowed through two centuries of retelling, believe me. Nor have Brummell's or Prinny's or anyone else's." She almost included Byron, recalling just in time that his most appalling behavior lay in the future. In 1812, he was newly published and idolized by society.

"Of course. Anyway, Father and his friends enjoyed life to the fullest—gaming, drinking heavily. . . ." He hesitated.

"Wenching? I would expect no less. Don't try to spare my delicate sensibilities, Drew. Where I come from, women don't have any."

"A pity. He and his particular friends were a wild bunch.

They might easily have joined the Hellfire Club if that group had not already been disbanded."

"Yes, I'm familiar with it," she answered his unspoken question. "Quit stalling. What did he do thirty years ago that would bind you to Fay?"

"He and Lord Raeburn were very close, having grown up together. They often wagered with each other—betting on people's behavior, the gender of the unborn bastards sired by various royal dukes, their own sexual prowess...."

He paused, turning to the window to hide his face. She shook her head. Men hadn't changed much in two hundred years. They still bragged about their conquests—and often exaggerated them.

Drew sighed. "One night after a profitable session at a gaming hell, Father and Lord Raeburn got to wondering if they had consumed enough wine to incapacitate them sexually. They finally wagered on which of them could better pleasure a young lady—obviously they would have to choose the same young lady so she could compare their performances. The chosen judge was an opera dancer fresh up from the country."

Horror filled his voice, despite his efforts to remain calm. "Unfortunately, they had consumed the wrong amount of wine. There is a stage of drunkenness when frustration converts to anger. When neither could perform as expected, they lashed out at the girl. With a prize of a thousand guineas riding on the outcome, both went a little mad. By the time sanity returned, she was dead."

"No wonder he became so rigidly proper. Guilt must have driven all enjoyment from his life."

"True. But it was worse than that. Father had consumed more wine than Lord Raeburn and could think of nothing beyond escape. Raeburn was the one who took care of hiding the deed. Father knows no details, and Raeburn has never mentioned it, but the knowledge was always there, hanging in the air between them whenever a question of cooperation arose. Father felt more vulnerable because the marquessate gave him farther to fall if the truth ever came out." He sucked in a shuddering breath. "And because it was he who struck the fatal blow. So he often agreed to proposals he might otherwise have scorned—like matching me and Fay in marriage."

"Poor man," Cherlynn said. "He told me he kept Randolph close to prevent him from becoming too wild. Now I see what he meant. He must have recognized his own failings in Randolph. And if he hadn't harped on duty and honor every minute of your life, you might have been less inclined to buckle under Fay's coercion."

"Can you see any way I can use this against Fay?"

"Not without blackening his reputation," she said, shaking her head. "If Lord Raeburn were healthy, perhaps he could do something, but he is not."

"Devil take it!" he muttered. "This is too frustrating. She's blackmailing me, but I can't reveal the blackmail without exposing her lies, which half the *ton* will accept as truth, including my father. She harbors seeds of madness, but I can't use that without hurting my sister. And I can't jilt her without destroying my own credit, which will hurt Emily."

She nodded. "Don't give up hope, Drew. I think our best course is to find out whom she's sleeping with at the moment."

He stared.

"Surely you didn't think she was innocent."

"I never really thought about it," he admitted, running his fingers through his hair. "But now that you mention it, she does have a very knowing look in her eye. How did you recognize it?"

"I'm not Emily. Remember? Besides, I know about one of her affairs. Unfortunately, it's not one we can use."

"Oh, God. Randolph?"

She nodded.

"I should have expected that. He has always envied me everything."

"I suspect his feelings went far beyond envy. Hating you would explain the way he looted your inheritance."

"Where did you hear about him and Fay?" he asked, resignation and pain threading his voice.

"From a witness, but it does no good."

"Why? After Father's confession, I doubt it would shock

him. And hearing about it would set the stage for me to jilt Fay."

She sighed. "Not this time, Drew. The only witness is Anne. You can't put her through the agony of describing what she saw."

"No." His eyes squeezed shut as he shuddered. "The attention would destroy her. But perhaps my groom can learn something. Surely someone on the estate knows of their affair. Or about some other liaison."

"Let's hope."

"So when should I schedule Anne's wedding?" he asked, abruptly changing the subject.

She stared into the fire, unable to move or respond. He was fishing for his father's death date. But he wouldn't get it. She no longer worried about doing irreversible damage to the fabric of time. Her own acting might be abominable, but there was indeed a power in charge that would prevent her from revealing anything that mattered. Besides, considering all of Broadbanks's recent shocks, she could no longer count on him living until the wedding.

"At least I can rest easier knowing I tried," he said with a shrug. "Let's find something you *can* talk about. What do you miss most about your own time?"

"Surprisingly little. Reeboks, I suppose. At one time I would have added jeans, but I'm getting used to wearing skirts."

"And what are Reeboks?" he asked, taking the other chair.

"Truly comfortable shoes." She laughed. "Why has no one yet noticed that left and right feet are shaped differently? But leave the future for now, Drew. I would rather talk of your time. I need more insight into how Regency gentlemen think and act. It is difficult to create believable characters unless I can crawl inside their heads. How do you and your friends view sex, for example?"

"You can't possibly write about that!"

She was surprised to see a flush on his cheeks. "Surely you're not embarrassed! Or maybe you are. In my day no topic is off limits. Women discuss sex quite freely, even with men. It is such a natural part of life that it should not be hidden and secretive. Many novels follow a loving couple into the bedchamber and enjoy their pleasure. From both points of view."

"Is nothing sacred? It sounds like men have lost most of their power," he grumbled. "And all of their wits."

"Not at all. Admitting that women are intelligent and capable does not demote men to a lesser role. Relationships are based on honesty, mutual affection, and respect, creating true partnerships where each strives to help the other. It does put pressure on the men, of course, for they can no longer use braggadocio and intimidation to mask incompetence. But then, women can no longer indulge in weakness and vapors to avoid dealing with problems."

He nodded. "So you want to learn more about relationships between the sexes in this era?" She could hear the effort that kept his voice steady. He had obviously never conducted so strange a conversation.

"We might as well start with the worst subject. Then all the others will be easier." She grinned. "Tell me about young men going to London for the first time. How many girls are they likely to encounter? Where do they find them? And where do they conduct these meetings?"

"Good God! You don't want much, do you?" His face was brick red.

"I'm sure you know enough braggarts to give me a general picture. If not, you're welcome to describe your own experiences." The interview was necessary research that only Drew could help with, and it would provide a unique glimpse she could get nowhere else, but she was having trouble remaining aloof. Even thinking about Drew's sexual experiences filled her with both heat and fury.

After shifting uncomfortably for a minute, he abandoned his seat and wandered over to gaze out the window. Not being able to see Emily's body must have helped, for he produced a clipped description of the typical young man's first year on the town. Her fascination grew as he spoke of gaming hells and card sharps, brothels and opera dancers, men's clubs and society gatherings. Very young men rarely set up mistresses, preferring to taste as many ladies as possible. Not until the constant variety began to pall and fears of contracting disease increased did they become more discriminating. The wealthy often established a permanent mistress. Others limited their encounters to the most reputable houses. Still others preferred to dally with society wives.

She wanted to ask him in which category he belonged, but that was one piece of information she didn't think she could handle. So she turned the conversation to society gatherings and the best places to shop in London, carefully committing his words to memory since she would take nothing home but her mind.

As the evening lengthened, conversation grew easier, in part because they had moved away from the intensely personal. They again compared their worlds, her fascination with the past echoed by his curiosity over the future. But his enthusiasm was rapidly eroding her common sense. The more relaxed she became, the harder it was to suppress desire. She wanted to explore his body as well as his mind. When her choices had been reduced to fleeing or tearing his clothes off, she terminated the discussion. But leaving was the hardest thing she had ever done. Only the need to protect Emily's virginity made it possible.

Charles and Dr. McClarren returned the following afternoon. By dinner Emily had been pronounced fit to travel. Charles would have immediately removed to Brighton, but Drew begged him to stay for one more week. Anne had accepted Frederick's offer. The formal betrothal announcement would be made during the house party preceding his wedding, but he scheduled a smaller gathering for the neighbors five days hence so he'd have an excuse to delay Charles's departure. Cherlynn had to remain at Broadbanks.

Drew invited his other sister's family to come for this celebration and stay until his wedding. The Lindleighs arrived while he was interviewing tenants, but he lost no time hunting Elizabeth down on his return.

"Did you come to visit Oscar?" she asked. He'd caught her as she left the nursery. "He still gabbles about you playing horsey with him. You made quite an impression."

He smiled. Oscar was three years old and promised to be

full of mischief. "I'll visit him later, but at the moment I wish to speak with you."

"Oh, Lord. What have I done now?" she asked with an exaggerated sigh, as she had done so often in her youth.

"Did I cut up too stiff after Mama died?" he asked suddenly, recognizing her expression.

She hesitated.

"Don't mince words with me, Lizzy. I've made plenty of mistakes, but I'm trying to identify them so I can avoid repeating them."

"I wouldn't describe it as a mistake exactly, but you were rather rigid in your expectations, and you *did* take on more duties than necessary at times."

"That's a diplomatic way of saying I was an overbearing prig, I suppose. No, don't deny it," he added, stopping her protest with a raised hand. "Mama was gone, and Father was too grief-stricken to care about us. As eldest, I assumed both of their roles, undoubtedly increasing your misery. My efforts certainly did Randolph no good."

Surprise blossomed in her eyes. "You had nothing to do with Randolph's problems, Drew," she said firmly. "They were apparent long before Mama died."

"Why did I not know?"

She sighed, leading him into an empty sitting room. "He was always crafty, having learned early on that you would report any wildness and that Father would punish his misdeeds. So he buried his nature beneath a facade of amiability that fooled even me."

"*Even* you?"

"I was his first target, but by age eight, I'd learned to fight back. After I bloodied his nose, he left me alone, so I thought he had outgrown his meanness. Unfortunately, he had merely turned his malice on William—and probably Anne, though we've never discussed it. They were too much younger to stand up to him. I've berated myself often for not recognizing his tactics, but you know how charming he could be. I didn't learn about William until shortly before he bought colors."

"What had Randolph done?" His heart was sinking. How had he remained blind for so many years? Allowing Randolph to manipulate him into leaving Broadbanks had brought misery to more people than he had imagined. He had left shortly after Lizzy's wedding, leaving both William and Anne in Randolph's care.

"I don't begin to know the details, but William got blamed for many of Randolph's escapades—like Sir Walter's dead cattle and the fire in the stable."

Dear God! One of the reasons he had pushed William to buy colors was the hope that military life would steady him. Had it been Randolph who was responsible for that long string of pranks and vandalism? What coercion had sealed William's lips?

"Don't blame yourself, Drew," she begged, correctly interpreting his horrified expression. "I am more at fault than you, for I knew how much pleasure he took from hurting others, yet I allowed him to lull my suspicions. But enough of Randolph. Tell me of Anne's betrothed. Does she truly love him? Since we are being honest, I have never liked the Raeburn family, begging your pardon."

"No insult taken. I'm not fond of them myself and am looking for an excuse to end my betrothal so I won't have to jilt her at the altar."

"You would?"

"If necessary, but we'll speak of that later. Frederick is a different matter entirely." He described the man and his background, finishing with, "And Anne loves him."

"Excellent." She turned to go.

"Not yet, Lizzy. What I really wanted to discuss was Lady Emily's fall. Did you witness it?"

"I should have, of course, for I was right next to her, but I was talking to Lady Redtree and only realized something was amiss when her head thwacked the fireplace." She grimaced at the remembered sound.

Damnation! "You were my last hope."

"Does she refuse to discuss it?"

"She remembers nothing before she awoke," he explained. "But don't repeat that." A missing memory would tarnish Emily's reputation. "I suspect Fay pushed her, but I can't prove it."

"Why?"

"Of the three hundred people in the great hall, not one seems to have witnessed the fall itself," he said, deliberately misinterpreting the question. His eyes bore into hers, forbidding her to pursue Fay's animosity.

"It is possible," she agreed. "She had been talking with us a short while before."

He sighed, taking her through the events of the evening. But her recollection of who was in the immediate vicinity turned up no one he had not already questioned. He could only hope that someone across the room had been looking in Emily's direction. But surely they would have come forward at the time.

Cherlynn was well aware of Drew's reason for scheduling the extra betrothal party. And she was grateful that he had stepped in. Once Charles removed her from Broadbanks, Emily would have no reason to keep her around. She wasn't ready to leave, dangerous though it was to stay near Drew. Yet the extra time mocked her continuing impotence. Calls on Lady Travis and Mrs. Rumfrey produced nothing about Fay. Even Mrs. Monroe added no new information.

Drew was turning up similar blanks. "I'd like to hit something," he growled, pacing the library like a caged lion. They had fallen into the habit of meeting there each night after everyone else was in bed.

"What a masculine response to frustration," she muttered.

"The only reason you're not bothered is that this gives you more time to comb my brain for embarrassing memories!"

"Come now! You're only upset because the wrong girl caught you skinny-dipping at the Enderfields' house party."

"Nothing is going to turn up, Cherlynn," he said firmly, refusing to be sidetracked. She wished he would go back to calling her Emily. He was courting disaster by vocalizing her real identity. What if the servants overheard, or he slipped when in company? "I might as well call it off and be done with it."

"No, Drew." She caught his gaze and held it. "Don't ruin Anne's party. Give it until the end of the week. That's only three more days. I can't explain it, but I know we'll find something by then. What did you learn today?"

"Nothing helpful. The tenants won't talk about Fay. I thought it was due to the betrothal, but their nervousness makes me think they fear her."

"I've gotten the same impression in the village, even from Miss Langley and Lady Travis. But I have no evidence you can use."

He nodded. "Both Elizabeth and Lady Clifford saw Fay near Emily after I stepped out of the ballroom that night. But by the time they realized Emily was injured, Fay was gone. Neither saw her leave or saw Em fall."

"Lady Clifford must be protecting your feelings then," she said. "She told me that Fay whisked herself away the moment I fell. But she didn't actually see anything incriminating."

"There were three hundred people in that room. Surely *somebody* saw something!"

"Not necessarily," she said soothingly. "People see what they expect to see."

"I suppose," Drew agreed with a sigh. "Damnation! Why am I so sure I'm missing something important?"

"So you feel it, too?"

He nodded. "Any ideas?"

"Not really. The feeling is strongest when I hear about Randolph, but I can't figure how that can help you. I've found no new information about his affair with Fay. How about you?"

He shook his head. "His embezzlement doesn't count."

"And none of his other crimes are relevant." She shrugged, ignoring the question blazing in his eyes.

"Don't do this to me, Cherlynn," he said with a scowl. "He was my brother. If you're not going to share the information, why did you bring it up?"

He had a point. Why had she brought it up? She hadn't meant to, but something had forced the words out. "I found out why he was so short-tempered that night on the cliff," she said with a long sigh.

He stared at her. When she said no more, he wandered to the window and gazed out at the darkness. "I'm waiting."

"Jack Gardner's daughter Maude was betrothed to Ben Lockyard. When Jack woke up the morning of March 15, Maude was missing. Grace heard that she was in the family way, but not by Ben."

"Randolph?" he asked.

"Nobody really knows. The innkeeper's daughter is the only one who knew of her condition. Maude never named her lover, but there had been rumors that Randolph was dallying with her. By evening, Jack and Ben were looking for him. Two hours later, Jack was found unconscious from a beating. He died of his wounds, but not before urging someone to run. Ben's body turned up two miles away—and only half a mile from the cliff. Randolph's horse came home without him that night. I'd wondered why he was walking back from the Blue Parrot. The image didn't fit my understanding of the Regency aristocracy. It's all of three miles."

"Devil take it!" He strode back to his chair. "I hadn't thought of that. Randolph never walked anywhere. But why didn't the grooms say anything?"

"The head groom knew the horse would never have gone near the edge of the cliff, so when Randolph's body turned up, he assumed suicide. But mentioning it would have distressed your father."

"And affected the burial," he finished, dropping his head into his hands. "At least we know his death was an accident. I wonder if he meant to kill them."

"Probably not Jack. I suspect they jumped him, but once Jack went down—Randolph must have thought him already dead—he would have gone after Ben to hide his involvement. Having just killed twice, he had no qualms about attacking you. Perhaps because he hated you, or maybe he wanted the added protection of being Broadbanks's heir."

"He was too drunk to think that clearly. He may have thought I had seen him. The fight would have concluded only minutes earlier. I must have passed Ben's body, but missed it in the dark."

She nodded. "When you hit that rock, he probably thought you were dead. His confusion from all that fighting would explain why he fell over the cliff."

He frowned. "You're forgetting Fay. Why didn't she

calm Randolph down and help him roll me over the edge? That way she could get a husband who loved her, as well as the position and wealth she has always coveted."

"She may not have had a choice. Since you didn't see her, she was probably in the trees. Randolph may have fallen before she realized he was in danger. At that point, she had no choice but to force you into marriage if she hoped to realize her dreams. But I can't see any way to use Randolph's crimes against her."

"Nor I." He sighed. "And we've only three days to find something we *can* use. I don't know if I can survive acting her host at dinner tomorrow."

"Of course you can. I thought Regency gentlemen had stoic masks that could hide their innermost feelings despite the most awful provocation."

"I wish that were true." His eyes raked her from head to toe, setting fires alight in every part of her body.

"Don't, Drew," she whispered.

"I'm going to miss you, Cherlynn."

"It's only the novelty," she said, turning toward the door. "That would fade if I stayed longer."

His hand stopped her progress. A finger tilted her chin so she had to meet his eyes. "Tell me you'll miss me."

"You know I will. Writing will be terribly frustrating. I'll kick myself every time a question arises that I forgot to ask." She was fighting to keep her voice light and her face calm. This must be the last time they met like this.

"You care," he breathed, and she knew she'd failed.

"Don't, Drew," she repeated. "Win, lose, or draw, I'll be gone soon. I've accepted that. I can live with it." Her eyes squeezed shut so she wouldn't see that beloved face hovering so close to her own. But the unwanted admission tore from her lips. "I'll never love another." Bidding him farewell, she forced her feet upstairs, wishing she had left ten minutes earlier. He was too perceptive. The last thing she wanted was his pity.

Chapter Sixteen

A sleepless night left Cherlynn on edge. Time was rapidly running out. Charles was still determined to leave, despite Drew's imminent wedding and his vow to stand up for his friend. Rumors that Emily was questioning Fay's background had led to a furious exchange in which he accused her of meddling. She could hardly deny the charge, so she'd fallen back on swearing her behavior was unexceptionable.

That argument had immediately been followed by an altercation with Lady Clifford in which Cherlynn had condemned the woman's selfish manipulation and refused to consider wedding Rupert. Emily's mother left in hysterics, but Cherlynn no longer cared. Too many other problems pressed close.

By the time the last guest arrived for the betrothal party, her tension had multiplied a hundredfold. The undercurrents sweeping the drawing room made her want to scream. Charles watched her like a hawk. Lady Clifford glared, especially when Drew pulled her aside to report on his latest interviews. No one had seen anything untoward. They were no closer to finding proof of Fay's transgressions, though he had talked to a dozen more guests from the ball. And their investigation of Emily's fall was now common knowledge, raising speculative glints in more than one eye.

Lord Broadbanks had suffered yet another attack after confessing his sins to Drew. He would not join them this evening, though he had spoken to Frederick that afternoon. No one knew what had passed between them, but Frederick's eyes often strayed to Fay, who was noticeably irritated. Might Frederick cancel Fay's betrothal? Cherlynn didn't know if he had the authority to do so. Lord Raeburn still lived, though in a coma.

She exchanged pleasantries with Miss Langley and Mrs. Monroe as questions simmered in her mind. Frederick's increasing hostility toward Fay might warn the girl that her betrothal was in danger, giving her a new reason to harm Emily. Would Fay confront her in the drawing room or lure her away from company?

Cherlynn tried to keep one eye on Fay as she spoke with other guests, but she soon lost sight of her. The crowd was larger than she had expected. Sixty people were attending this neighborhood betrothal dinner. Not until she was laughing with Drew, Frederick, and Anne did she again spot Fay. Their eyes clashed, sending a shiver of fear down her back. The girl was furious. And even more so when Drew steered Cherlynn away to meet a distant cousin, one hand resting lightly on the small of her back. Did Fay realize, as she did, that he was paving the way for a change of fiancées?

Fay planted another poisonous seed in the fertile ground of Lady Travis's mind, determined to destroy every last vestige of Lady Emily's reputation. The girl was a whore who should not be inflicted on respectable people. Drew was a high stickler whose infatuation would never survive rumors of Emily's infidelity.

"I saw them with my own eyes," she continued. "Writhing, without a stitch of clothing between them."

"With her groom?" demanded Lady Travis.

She nodded, a smile tugging the corners of her mouth. Let the slut try to get out of that one!

But her good humor vanished moments later. Drew was sticking so close to Emily's side that no one could cut her without also cutting him. And his frown when Fay had earlier tried to claim his attention boded ill.

Her irritation rose when she discovered the seating arrangements at dinner. Lady Emily was placed at Drew's right, while she, the future Marchioness of Broadbanks, languished halfway down the table between the vicar and Lord Clifford. Mr. Rumfrey was such a dithery man that he rarely understood what anyone was saying, usually responding with placating absurdities that urged forgiveness for any sin. She doubted he understood even her most blatant hints. And

Lord Clifford would never accept calumnies against his sister. He even ignored truths.

Irritation changed to fury during the betrothal announcement.

Drew rose to present the happy couple. "I propose a toast. To my sister Anne and Mr. Frederick Raeburn, who will wed in December, God willing. Unfortunately, the health of both Lord Broadbanks and Lord Raeburn is too frail for them to join us on this joyful occasion. But my father has expressed delight with Lady Anne's choice."

"Where will you be living?" asked Lord Lindleigh once the company had drunk to the couple's future.

Frederick smiled. "At Lord Thurston's suggestion, Broadbanks will include Raeburn House in Lady Anne's dowry."

Several more toasts were offered, but Fay refused to participate. How dared Broadbanks give away her estate? Everything was going wrong. She had demanded that Drew put Raeburn House in her name, threatening to tell his father about Randolph's death if he did not. Instead of complying, he had smiled and told her to go ahead.

Lady Emily had bewitched him until he no longer cared what others thought. What if he no longer cared whether Broadbanks lived or died? It was a frightening thought, for if true, he might jilt her.

Her mind twisted frantically. How could she prevent it? The steps she had taken to destroy Emily's reputation wouldn't suffice. If he was besotted enough, he wouldn't believe them. He might even cite them as just cause to end their betrothal, and if he could disprove even one of her charges, these arrogant cats would tear her to shreds. Emily would become the toast of the neighborhood.

Such an insult couldn't be borne. It was too late to look for alternatives to Drew. She had played fair from the start. He was the one who had thrown over the arrangement their fathers had made all those years ago. He was the one who had tried to discard her like an old coat he no longer wished to wear. And he would do it again. No matter how dishonorable the action, he was going to leave her standing at the altar. This insulting position at the table confirmed it.

Servants cleared her untouched plate, offering her a choice of sweets. She chose a tart, methodically tearing it to shreds. By the time the pastry had been reduced to crumbs, she knew what she must do.

Kill Lady Emily.

Only by destroying the girl could she control Drew. Once his inamorata was gone, he wouldn't care whom he wed. Duty demanded a wife, so he would accept the one already poised to assume that role. She had already tried once, but that had been a sudden whim triggered by the intimate look they had exchanged. This time she would take no chances.

Decision made, she watched Emily circulate in the drawing room after dinner, laughing with Drew, joking with Frederick—she would have to do something about him as well, or Raeburn House would be lost—and charming several ladies who had earlier lapped up all her spite. Emily must die. And it must be soon.

"How dare you show your face in respectable society," hissed Lady Travis as Cherlynn joined her and Miss Langley after dinner. The gentlemen remained ensconced over port, so she was on her own.

She raised her brows. "Would you care to enlighten me on my supposed transgression?" Who had spilled the beans about Drew's kiss in the folly? Fay? Or had the servants overheard Lady Clifford's ranting?

"You were seen, my fine lady, disporting yourself with your groom!"

Fay must be spreading spite. "How odd! I have no groom, nor have I had dealings with anyone else's."

"Your sins will never be forgiven," said Lady Travis firmly, beginning to turn away in a deliberate cut.

"Will you condemn me without a hearing?" she demanded, glaring at the gossip. "When did this indiscretion take place? Where? With whom?"

"Tuesday last at eleven in the morning," snapped Lady Travis.

"As I thought. It could not have been me," she said. "I was taking tea with Miss Langley at that time."

"Quite right, my dear," confirmed Miss Langley, realization blossoming in her eyes. "We had such a comfortable coze."

Lady Travis's glare changed to speculation.

"Someone mistook the identities of the participants," said Cherlynn firmly, thanking fate that Fay had made the mistake of including specifics so the tale would sound more authentic. The first rule of successful lying was to avoid details that could be checked. "Or is someone deliberately piling calumny onto my name?"

"No lady would do such a thing," exclaimed a shocked Miss Langley.

"Was this tale mentioned by a lady?" Cherlynn asked slyly.

"She considers herself so," stated Lady Travis, "though I've had my doubts. And this proves them."

"Miss Raeburn fears your friendship with Lord Thurston," said Miss Langley, abandoning circumspection in light of this condemnation.

"It is true that his lordship treats me with kindness, but he is my brother's friend," protested Cherlynn. "I am merely Charles's little sister."

The ladies accepted her statement. And Fay's attempt to smear an innocent young girl breached a dam, allowing all manner of memories to spill out. Cherlynn learned more in ten minutes than she had in all her previous probing. The witchcraft rumors had arisen because Fay dabbled in potions, not all of which were beneficial. A tenant who had gone to her for help with spots had found herself with a painful rash that left her face permanently pitted. She had angered Fay some days earlier by attracting the attention of a young man with whom Fay had been flirting.

Which led to tales of Fay's effect on gentlemen. Like her mother, she was a beautiful woman with a fey charm that attracted men in droves. And she welcomed their interest. No one knew details, but all suspected that she was no longer chaste. Yet no one would dare mention the possibility to her face. Fay Raeburn was not a person to cross.

Cherlynn sighed. None of the tales were first-hand accounts, and none of Fay's paramours were named, so she *still* lacked proof.

She moved through the rest of the evening deep in calculation. Their departure had been delayed one more day, thanks to Drew. One of Charles's horses had mysteriously gone lame, but she had twenty-four hours at most. Identifying any of Fay's liaisons would take too long. Rumors of witchcraft wouldn't suffice even in this superstitious age. Her best chance was to lure Fay into attacking her. The assault itself would be enough, but if she could also get the girl to admit any of her transgressions, it would assure her future silence.

But how could she guarantee the attack would fail? Emily would be irritated if she sacrificed her life in order to free Drew. And Drew wouldn't be pleased, either. Would he go along with the idea if he was there to guard her safety? That would also ensure that any confession called down instant penalties.

Yet she needed more than just Drew's guard. Fay harbored the seeds of insanity. Watching her dreams crumble might push her into harming them both.

Who else could she involve in this plot? Not Charles, she decided instantly. He would never condone her plan. But Frederick might. As soon as she worked out the details, she would meet with the men to make arrangements. They would have to lure Fay into the trap tomorrow. A second accident would raise Charles's suspicions.

Fay crouched behind a hedge, peering nervously at the cottage. Damn Frederick for assigning his groom to watch her whenever she left the house. He was treating her like a child. A second look in all directions verified that she had escaped his scrutiny.

Why was everyone so determined to oppose her? She had been trained to be Marchioness of Broadbanks. Drew had grown up knowing that their future was together. And though he had bowed to the inevitable, he still looked to others for companionship. Frederick was no better. Not only was he watching her every move, but he had stepped in to steal *her* estate. Even worse, his diatribe last night had not only denounced her efforts to drive Lady Emily away—

somehow he had discovered her lie about Emily and the groom—but had hinted that he might break off her betrothal.

Never! she vowed, making a final scan of the area to make sure that no one was in sight. She would see Frederick in hell before she'd forego her destiny. It was a fitting place for the interfering American.

Jaime's summons claimed that he had new information for her, but she would have come today in any case. One day soon, she would take care of the arrogant farmer, but not yet. He was too useful. It was Jaime who had noticed that Lady Emily spent most afternoons alone in the Grecian folly. But now she had a more serious job for him. Or perhaps two. The blackmailer was about to be blackmailed. He would take care of her problems—all of them—after which she would take care of him. Once she was Marchioness of Broadbanks, she would arrange an accident for her nemesis. In the meantime, he was useful. And he did such deliciously wicked things to her body. Her eyes closed on a wave of heat.

"What did you learn?" she asked an hour later, her voice throaty from the lingering dregs of passion. One hand skimmed lightly over his sweaty chest. The first time, he had been reluctant—but only because of her exalted station. Now he couldn't get enough of her. His shaft was already lengthening under her palm. Lusty. The way she liked all her men. Even the controlled, disdainful Drew would go mad with desire once she got her hands on him. She smiled at the image, teasing Jaime into wild need, then holding him off while she questioned him.

"What has Lady Emily been up to?"

"Social calls," he panted, lunging for her.

She danced lightly away. "I know that. I saw her last night. I'm paying you to watch her meetings with Thurston." She ran her fingers lightly over her bare breasts, smiling coyly at the lust that exploded in his eyes. His manhood swelled, raising an answering heat in her belly. Lifting one heavy breast, she licked the nipple, then again sprang out of reach. "What have they been doing, Jaime?" she managed to gasp through her own need.

"Talking. Just talking. Every night in the library."

Fury paralyzed her so that his next lunge pinned her to the bed. Flipping her onto her stomach, he pounded into her from behind. But his attention was not wholly focused on her body. "He lives for those meetings," he taunted as his hands painfully squeezed her breasts. "But he treats her with the respect a gentleman accords a *lady*. And she *is* a lady, my wanton slut. You won't find *her* rutting with the grooms or throwing herself at the tenants. And that's the real reason you hate her, isn't it? You may incite lust in males and fear in females, but you'll never command respect."

Fury exploded, quashing all trace of her passion. "Get off me, you lout!" she grunted, trying to twist free. But he effortlessly held her beneath him, dominating her, riding her until he'd had his fill. Then he cast her scornfully aside.

She flew across the room to jerk on her clothes. "I won't be coming again," she spat.

"Reckon not," he said comfortably. "But I 'spect Thurston will be right grateful to see me."

"You wouldn't dare!" she hissed. "You'd lose your farm if he found out you'd raped his fiancée."

He frowned, but she didn't care. The man was getting above himself after a fortnight of rubbing shoulders—and other body parts—with the quality. It was time to remind him who was in charge. She reached into her reticule.

"Lady Emily has outstayed her welcome," she said coldly. "I no longer need you to follow her. But I do have one last job for you. The fee is a thousand pounds."

His eyes narrowed. "I doubt I can do any work that pays so much."

"You'll do it or live out your days in Botany Bay for blackmail and rape. I want Lady Emily dead." She pulled out a pistol. "This can't be traced to you, so you're safe enough."

"No."

The implacable voice raised her temper another notch. "You don't have a choice, Potts. Either you kill Lady Emily or I will swear out a complaint with the magistrate."

"You'll swear out nothing, my little slut," he drawled. "I will claim that you are retaliating because I refused to service you. I can name enough of your partners to guarantee that folks will believe me, not you. I'm not the only one you had to pay to climb into bed with you."

The cruel, mocking words were the last straw. "You despicable bastard!" she shrieked, growing angrier when he laughed. But he didn't laugh long. Raising her hand toward the muscular chest she had been stroking only minutes before, she pulled the trigger. "We'll see who laughs last, Jaime Potts," she said, her voice now deadly calm. "I should have known better than to trust a blackmailing coward. I'll take care of Lady Emily myself. And Frederick. Nobody crosses me with impunity."

Casting a last look around the bedroom, she collected her reticule and hat, then stopped in the kitchen long enough to reload the pistol before slipping out of the cottage.

Where was Emily likely to be? Fay circled Broadbanks Hall, keeping her horse in the trees so she wouldn't be seen. Her luck was in. Emily was riding away from the stables. Alone.

Smiling, she followed, surprised to see the girl stop in the exact place where Randolph had died. Dear Randolph. So eager to take what should have been his brother's. So drunk that he didn't realize he was far from the first. He had wanted her badly and had even begged her to marry him, but she had known his passion was only part of his lifelong campaign to destroy his brother. What he hadn't known was that Drew had already repudiated her. Randolph had been stupid about many things. Had he actually believed that she would give up Broadbanks after waiting her entire life to become its mistress?

Tethering her horse to the same tree she had used the night she'd pushed the wastrel over the cliff, she waited until Emily's back was turned, then calmly left the cover of the forest. A dead stick cracked under her foot. Emily jumped, whipping around to freeze a scant yard from the edge.

Needing to inflict as much pain as possible before the denouement, Fay stopped a dozen feet away. "Good morning, Lady Emily." She smiled. "What a lovely day to die."

Emily gasped as Fay drew out the pistol and aimed.

* * *

Jaime lay where he had fallen, unable to stanch the blood that flowed from the bullet hole. Taunting her had been stupid, he admitted grimly. She was mad. He should never have taunted a madwoman.

And now he would pay with his life.

A whisper of sound echoed from the other room. "Ben?" he called as loudly as he could, but the word barely made it past his lips. Groaning, he slowly mustered the strength to try again, but the first effort had been enough.

"Cor!" exclaimed the orphan he'd taken in to help around the place. "What 'appened?"

"Find Lord Thurston," he gasped. "Tell him . . ." The spots swirling before his eyes merged into a sheet of black.

Drew was leading his horse from the stables when a panic-eyed child collided with him.

"Lor' Thurston?" the boy gasped.

He nodded. "And who are you?"

"Ben. Jaime needs help. 'E's bleedin' somethin' awful."

"Jaime Potts?"

Ben managed to nod. The boy was all but unconscious—hardly surprising if he had run the two miles from the Potts farm.

"Where's Jaime now?" he demanded.

"In bed."

"Ted! Find Dr. McClarren and take him to Jaime Potts's cottage at once," he shouted to a groom. "Let's go." Mounting his horse, he jerked Ben up in front of him and galloped down the drive. "What happened?"

Ben was cringing in fright. "I dunno. 'E said ta get you, then blinked out."

"Did he fall?"

The boy's head shook. "Looked like 'e was shot."

Shot? Drew's head swirled. Who would shoot a tenant farmer? On the other hand, the man had suddenly come into considerable money. Had he run afoul of the local smuggling gang or double-crossed a partner in crime?

Five minutes later, he reached the cottage and turned his horse over to Ben.

Jaime's blood soaked the quilt. But he still lived. Though

weak, a pulse throbbed in his neck. The bullet had entered just below the rib cage on the left side, exiting the back. But it had somehow missed everything vital. Drew found a towel and set about trying to stop the bleeding. Every move revived memories of Emily's near-fatal fall. Thank God Charles had fetched McClarren back from London. Dr. Harvey would never do in this crisis.

As he shifted Jaime to reach his back, the man's eyes cracked open.

"Who shot you, Potts?"

"Fay."

The voice was so weak that he wasn't sure he had heard correctly. "Fay Raeburn?"

Jaime nodded.

"Why?"

"I refused to kill somebody."

His hands tightened, pulling a groan from Jaime's throat. "Start at the beginning, Potts. And take your time. I don't think this wound is fatal." McClarren wouldn't bleed the man. And perhaps Cherlynn could suggest further remedies to assure a full return to health.

Relief relaxed Jaime's muscles. Anger and a need for revenge strengthened his voice.

"Started last spring when I was walkin' home from the Blue Parrot. I come to the edge of the trees up on the cliffs and saw you and Lord Randolph knockin' each other about."

"You saw us? Why the devil didn't you tell me sooner?" But his anger died when Jaime cringed, the motion forcing another yelp of pain from his mouth. "Sorry, Potts. Tell it your way."

"I thought it was a unfair fight since I knew your brother was three sheets to the wind, but before I could step out and stop it, he knocked you into a rock. Then he grabbed ahold and tugged you toward the cliff. I was startin' after him when Fay slipped out of the woods. I figured he wouldn't toss you over with a witness, so I left. But I looked back once to make sure everything was all right. That's when I seen her rush up and shove Lord Randolph over the edge."

"My God!" In all his agonizing over that night, he had never once considered that Fay had murdered Randolph. But now that Potts had jogged his memory, he realized that the fight had been considerably farther from the edge than where he had awakened. He had actually been staggering toward the cliff when he went down.

"I stayed long enough to make sure she didn't do the same to you, then I left. She's a chancy one to cross. So was your brother, beggin' your pardon. His death lightened a lot of hearts."

"Then you didn't know that Fay claimed it was I who pushed Randolph over?"

"Bitch!" muttered Jaime. "I'm sorry, my lord. It weren't none of my business, so I forgot it. Until I fell into debt. Then I went to Lord Raeburn to see if he would loan me a bit."

"The truth, Potts." He stared into the man's eyes.

Jaime winced. "So I put the black on Raeburn. I'd a come to you, but I didn't know you had cause to wish her elsewhere, and she *did* save your life. I figured Raeburn might want to keep Fay's actions quiet. Only he weren't inclined to pay. Went off in a huff to have it out with Fay. A few minutes later, she brung me the money. Well, I weren't about to question nothin', especially when she paid me more than I'd asked."

"Why would she do that?"

Jaime closed his eyes, wheezing in pain for several minutes. "She made me work for her, claimin' all the money was for that. It didn't seem like much, just keepin' a eye on Lady Emily. She said she wanted to know how the girl's recovery was comin'."

"That's all?" he asked derisively. "You've gone through at least two hundred pounds in the last fortnight. Quite generous pay for watching an invalid. You aren't stupid enough to think Fay's requests were legitimate."

"Okay, that weren't everything. I was also servicin' her," he added belligerently. "She's a lusty wench."

"Thank you. That's all I need to jilt her."

Jaime stared. "Good man. But you'd best find 'er soon. The chit's gone mad. She shot me when I refused to kill Lady Emily. I think she's goin' after 'er 'erself."

Drew's heart stopped. "Thank you, Potts. I'll take care of her." Sounds outside proved to be McClarren.

"Do everything possible for him, George," he urged as he let the doctor in. "He's a valued tenant."

Where was Cherlynn? Galloping back to the house gave fear time to ripen into terror. He hadn't seen her since Anne's betrothal party the night before. Fay had tried to destroy Emily's reputation, but she'd been so heavy-handed about it that even the normally obtuse Vicar Rumfrey had seen through her efforts and warned him. Drew had already hinted to Lady Travis and others that he would never wed a scheming liar. The support for severing his connection to Fay had allowed him to sleep easier than he had in months.

Now he felt worse than in his blackest hours of believing himself a killer. Cherlynn was in deadly danger, and he didn't even know where she was. If anything happened to her, he'd never forgive himself. It was his fault that she was in danger. He hadn't told Charles to stay with her because he'd been afraid that any hint of the truth would drive them from Broadbanks. He should at least have assigned his groom to accompany her whenever she left the Hall. *Please let her be inside!*

"Lady Emily left some time ago," Hardwick informed him when he reached the house. He was turning back to his horse when a footman spoke up.

"Begging your pardon, my lord, but I seen her riding away from the stables just now."

"Thank you, Will." His heart was back in his throat. Fay was somewhere in the area. Had she seen Cherlynn leave?

Voices in the drawing room erupted in laughter— Charles, Frederick, Anne, and Lady Clifford. If Fay had truly run mad, he would need help. "My apologies for intruding, Anne," he said, stopping in the doorway, "but a small problem has arisen. May I borrow the gentlemen for a moment?"

Charles raised a brow, but excused himself, as did Frederick. They joined him in the morning room.

"I fear that your cousin may have lost her reason." Drew addressed Frederick.

"It wouldn't surprise me," he replied calmly.

Charles raised both brows.

"Insanity runs in the female line of our mothers' family," he admitted. "My mother ran mad some months ago." He turned to Drew. "What is she doing?"

"She has a gun. After shooting one of my tenants, she vowed to kill Lady Emily."

"Where is she?" growled Charles, already heading for the door. "Damn that horse! We should have been gone by now."

Drew cringed as a wave of guilt engulfed him.

"How is the tenant?" asked Frederick, following.

"He'll live."

They strode toward the stables while he related what he'd learned about Emily's whereabouts. Conflicting stories awaited them. One groom claimed he'd seen her ride toward the village. Another thought she had headed for the Roman folly.

He bit his lip. She had no real reason to go to the village, having spoken to everyone last night. Nor was she likely to spend this day enjoying the view. They both knew that Charles would not compromise on leaving in the morning. He would walk if that was what it took. But she might have learned something new about Randolph.

"The cliffs," he said, then thanked the grooms. Mounting his horse, he led the way to the shortcut.

Chapter Seventeen

Cherlynn gasped as Fay aimed the pistol straight at her heart. This was not how she had expected to spend her day.

Fay's blatant lies at the party had earned the wrath of the local gossips. It didn't take a brain surgeon to figure that Fay would retaliate. Cherlynn had planned to use that desire to bait her trap. The cliffs seemed a perfect site for the confrontation, allowing Drew to catch Fay in the act. She had come out here hoping for inspiration on how to lure Fay into attacking, but hadn't counted on Fay following her. Nor had she expected to face a gun. Now she was on her own with no weapons and no witnesses.

Light glittered in Fay's eyes, a fanatical light that could only mean madness, but the gun remained steady, without the slightest tremor. Was this really what fate had in store? Perhaps Emily's death was ordained so nothing could prevent it. Would they both perish, or would she return to 1998?

Poor Drew. Emily had saved him from Fay's clutches, but he would not live happily ever after. Would he flee into the army as he had done before? At least she knew he would survive the war. When he returned, perhaps he could find someone congenial who would provide him an heir.

Defeatist! Haven't you learned anything? You'll never succeed if you don't try! Her eyes sharpened, driving away her mental fog. She had to at least make an effort to survive. She frantically tried to recall the tactics that hostage specialists used. There had been a nasty confrontation just a week before she'd left for England. One of the newspaper stories had commented on the negotiator's approach. Keep the culprit talking. Get him to explain his reasoning so you can appeal to it. Play for time. The longer a perpetrator waits to act, the less likely he is to carry through.

She carefully inhaled, then let the air out slowly to relax her muscles. Too much tension would paralyze her if an opportunity for action arose. Sparing one thought for Willard—he'd often predicted a sorry end for her; how smug he would be at his prescience—she focused on Fay and smiled.

"I can't say I'm ready to depart this world, but if I must, this is indeed a lovely day for it. Are you going to shoot me?"

"Not unless I have to." Fay seemed shaken by the calm response. Good. Keeping her off balance might give Cherlynn enough time to think of an escape. The gun jerked toward the edge. "All you have to do is walk a little. Three steps ought to do it. How tragic that you ventured too close."

"Honestly, Fay," she said with a snort, "no one will believe that! Charles knows I avoid cliffs. I'm terrified of heights. If you need to stage an accident, you'll have to think of something else."

Fay frowned. "No. This will have to do. There isn't time to go elsewhere. I will describe how you panicked."

"Perhaps that would work," she agreed, unwilling to push too hard. "But you'd best set it up over there. That clump of flowers could explain why I stepped too close." In the guise of moving to a new location, she took three steps toward Fay.

"Stop!" Fay's voice was panicked enough that she complied. "We'll do it here. Now!" Again the gun jerked.

Cherlynn took a cautious step toward the cliff. "Would you mind telling me why I am dying?"

"Drew cares too much for you."

"Absurd. He offered for you."

"Don't deny it. I saw you in the folly!" Her voice scraped harshly through the air.

"Of course you saw us, but what did you see? If you hadn't startled me enough that I allowed him to escape, you'd know that he was unwilling. I attacked him, hoping to change his mind about wedding you. He read me a lecture even stronger than my brother's afterward."

"You lie!" growled Fay furiously.

Cherlynn took advantage of the wavering gun hand to regain the lost step. She hadn't been lying about being afraid of heights—the beach was fifty feet below at this point—but that was the least of her worries at the moment. Fay was out of reach, but was too close to miss the shot. A light breeze swirled past, momentarily pressing her skirt against her legs. She shivered. "Believe what you will."

"I believe what he told Randolph in this very spot," spat Fay. "He loves you and wants to wed you. But nobody takes what is mine!"

"If he belonged to you, why did he claim otherwise?" she asked, hoping to move Fay into a calmer discussion. Too much fury might jerk the finger on that trigger. Her knowledge of Regency weapons was slight, but some dueling pistols had hair triggers. Hopefully, this wasn't one of them. A gull shrieked, making Fay jump. The gun didn't fire.

Relief sagged through Cherlynn's muscles until she had to lock her knees to keep from falling.

"He has always been contrary," Fay said with a sigh, as if discussing a little boy who disliked eating turnips. "My father negotiated the betrothal agreement eighteen years ago. Drew knew from childhood that we would wed. But he tried to throw over the agreement, refusing to accept that betrothals are binding. A gentleman cannot back out." Her eyes were growing more fanatical. "Broadbanks is mine. I've trained for the position all of my life. Nobody is going to take it away."

The gun again wavered as Fay's histrionics threw her arm wide. Cherlynn gained another foot. How much of her self-defense class could she recall? It had been three years since she had taken it, and she hadn't been that good to begin with.

"But it will be yours in less than two weeks," she pointed out reasonably. "I can't do anything about it now. Drew has publicly announced the betrothal. What more do you want?"

"I want you dead. You should have been long ago—I pushed you hard enough at the ball. But I won't take chances this time. Nobody can survive a fall over this cliff.

Drew is mine. I won't tolerate a cheap little whore sharing his favors."

"I wouldn't dream of it," she countered. "I can't believe you would think the daughter of an earl would stoop so low. I'm no threat to you. Not only does Lord Thurston care nothing for me, I will be gone by tomorrow." All of which was true in a way.

"Hah! Anyone who wants something bad enough will reach out and take it."

"Is that how you caught Drew?"

Fay frowned, then shrugged. "Of course. The stupid man thinks he killed his brother. All I have to do is threaten to tell his father and he does anything I ask."

"Does he? It would be more like him to tell you to go ahead. He knows that he wasn't responsible."

"He couldn't. He was dead to the world when I shoved Randolph over the side."

"You did?" She couldn't keep the surprise out of her voice, but it proved to be beneficial.

Fay gloated. "Of course. He was getting utterly dreary with his pleading that I wed him—as if I would; all that wine sapped any trace of passion. But he served a noble purpose by forcing Drew into living up to his responsibilities. So don't doubt I'll kill you."

"I doubt nothing." She caught a movement at the edge of the trees behind Fay. Drew. Her knees nearly collapsed in relief, but she quickly pulled herself together. "He believed you at the time, but he knows better now. You made the mistake of leaving him where he fell."

Fay was frowning. "What—?"

"It doesn't matter, Fay. We all makes mistakes now and then."

"Not me!"

"Really? You must be the only perfect person in the world. What else have you done that's so clever?"

"Don't think I won't shoot you if that's the only way to get you over the edge," Fay warned.

"I believe you, though cold-blooded killing is a trifle harder than shoving a drunkard who is already incoherent with rage." By shifting her weight to one foot, she managed to slide the other three inches forward under the cover of her skirts. Already she had gained six inches that way. The breeze covered her movements.

"Don't believe it. I shot a man no more than two hours ago for daring to threaten me. Everyone will assume that smugglers killed him."

Not likely. Drew was in the trees twenty yards beyond Fay. Charles and Frederick joined him, then fanned out to either side.

"You look skeptical," gloated Fay, pulling her mind back to the conversation.

"Why did you shoot him?" She gained another three inches.

"He tried to blackmail me. The idiot even told my father about Randolph. I had to drug Pa to keep him quiet. It's been irritating keeping him alive but unconscious all this time. At least I can let him die after the wedding."

A muffled groan from Frederick whipped Fay's head around. Cherlynn swore under her breath, but picked up another foot before Fay's attention swung back.

"Damn you!" shouted Frederick, striding into the open. "You are no better than your mad mother. What have you been feeding Uncle Toby?"

"Stop, or I'll shoot her right now," said Fay coldly. "My luck is really in today. You were next in line anyway. You should have stayed in America. I'll not let you steal my estate."

"Stubble it!" hissed Drew as Frederick opened his mouth.

Fay cast a quick glance over her shoulder. "One more step, my love, and your mistress dies."

"She's not, of course. And she was telling the truth about leaving tomorrow," he said levelly. But he froze in place. "This exercise is pointless, you know. I will not wed you. I would have told you yesterday, but did not want to spoil Anne's party."

"It's too late," said Frederick softly, having regained control of his temper. "Lord Broadbanks and I already agreed to terminate your betrothal. He does not want to stain his bloodlines. He would have informed Thurston this afternoon."

Cherlynn saw the shock in Drew's face. Was Frederick lying? She wasn't sure what game he was playing, but it was a dangerous one. All she could do was hope that he understood Fay's insanity. What she really needed was a diversion to distract Fay's attention. None of the men was close enough to disarm her, so the job was hers.

She exchanged a long glance with Drew, shocked into near immobility that she could read his mind. He was furious that he hadn't brought a dueling pistol with him. And he was nearly as furious at Frederick for revealing their presence. But once he read her intentions, he set about providing the needed diversion. She relaxed and began inching up her skirt in the back.

"You've finally received your just deserts, Fay," he said lightly. "Never has anyone been in such need of Bedlam. I wouldn't have met you in church, by the way. I had long ago planned to jilt you at the altar. You would have been a laughingstock, especially after I disclosed my reasons to society. How many men have you seduced this year alone, my little slut?"

"How dare you!" she spat. "You've doubtless bedded half of London."

"Now, now. No need to be upset. As a matter of fact, I've been quite true to the woman I love. As have you, of course. You love only yourself. But I have no intention of tying myself to a light-skirt."

"I'm no light-skirt!" she fumed.

Cherlynn had her hem above the knees.

"Good point. Even the most elegant courtesan accepts money for the use of her body. But you were the one paying for services rendered, weren't you? What's the matter? Couldn't you find a willing partner?"

"Randolph was willing!"

"Only to spite me," he said with a laugh. "He'd have bedded Satan's own handmaiden if he thought I'd disapprove. And it appears that he did. Your aim is terrible, by the way. Jaime is quite all right and insisted on describing every minute you spent in his bed. In graphic detail. I'm tempted to send the tale to the *Tattler's* society column. It would make quite edifying reading."

"How dare you!" she screamed, jerking the gun toward him.

It was the move Cherlynn had been waiting for. Whisking her skirt aside, she launched a kick that would have made Radio City's chorus line proud. Fay screamed as a foot connected with her wrist. The gun landed ten feet away.

Men raced from all sides. Cherlynn flung herself away from the cliff, staggering into Drew's arms, which folded around her, holding her safe. She savored his heat. The sandalwood scent he favored filled her nostrils, driving back her terror. His chest was solid muscle. Emily's head fit perfectly against his shoulder. She burrowed closer, wrapping her arms around his waist. This embrace was all she would have for a lifetime. But one eye remained on Fay, who was still dangerous.

Fay's head twisted from side to side as the men charged. She sidestepped Frederick and tripped him, shoving him toward the cliff, but he rolled aside.

"Grab her!" he yelled as Charles closed in.

Fay danced out of reach. As Charles's momentum carried him past her, she dove for the pistol.

"Don't move," she shouted, springing to her feet, her eyes again gleaming with madness.

"Give it up, Fay," said Frederick, warily standing up. Charles edged away to spread out her targets. "You can't kill all of us."

"Bastard!" she hissed, aiming the gun at Frederick. She backed up a few feet so she could keep everyone in view, freezing Charles with a glance. "You've ruined my life, Cousin."

"I've done nothing to you," he said soothingly. "Just put the gun down so we can talk."

"Never. You'll rot in hell for stealing my estate, but you're not worth killing. Nor are you," she added to Charles. "So which one will it be?" Her lips parted in an evil grin. "Satan or his whore?" The gun wavered between them, coming to rest pointed at Cherlynn. "You bit—" But her voice died in mid-epithet.

Cherlynn gasped.

Drew had tensed to throw her to the ground, but he froze

when a wavering mist appeared next to Fay, rapidly coalescing into a man. It boxed her in so she had no place to run.

"Randolph!" he choked.

"The ghost on the cliff," Cherlynn whispered, recalling Mabel Hardesty's words. Randolph had lived and died in violence. He must have been condemned to walk.

Fay blanched as she back-pedaled. "No, Randolph. Don't blame me! It wasn't personal. If you hadn't been trying to kill him, I never would have touched you. But I had to stop you. . . ." The gun slipped from her hand when she stumbled over a tuft of grass.

Drew surreptitiously pulled Cherlynn toward the trees, but Randolph paid them no attention. His battered face twisted in fury as he stalked Fay. His form seethed, bubbling over the ground and growing larger by the second. He loomed over her, shading her from the sun. Clawed fingers stretched out.

She whimpered, eyes wide with terror. Before anyone could shout a warning, her retreat stepped into space. With a shout of triumphant laughter, Randolph's image dissolved.

"Dear God!" gasped Frederick, closing his eyes in shock.

"A fitting revenge," murmured Drew into Cherlynn's ear as his arms tightened around her. "And I forgive him everything. He saved your life."

"Anne claimed he always paid back every insult," she recalled shakily. "Fay had pushed him off the cliff."

"I know." He pulled her face against his shoulder.

Charles and Frederick said nothing. The silence stretched as they stared at the spot where Randolph had stood. Not until a gull settled, screeching, at the foot of the cliff, did Charles shake himself. "Are you up to retrieving the body?" he asked Frederick, ignoring the fact that his sister was again in the arms of his best friend.

Frederick glanced at Drew, who nodded toward the far end of the clearing, where it was possible to pick a way down to the beach. The two set off on their grisly quest.

"You're free, Drew." Cherlynn pulled back, looking into his eyes for the last time. One hand caressed his cheek.

Dizziness was already assailing her. "Be happy." Even as he lowered his lips, she was gone.

Emily's body collapsed.

Drew stared into the blank eyes. "Cherlynn?" He shook her, praying that she had merely fainted from shock. *When I finish my task, Emily will return.* Her voice mocked him. "Cherlynn! Come back!"

Tears streamed down his face as he laid her on the ground and listened to her heart. Nothing. "Cherlynn! Don't leave me. I love you." Thrusting his hands into his hair, he scanned the heavens. "I can't live without you, Cherlynn! Who will debate with me and laugh with me?"

Nothing.

Burying his face in her breast, he succumbed to wrenching sobs. "Em," he managed at last, "I always cared for you, but you must know that my love was never as deep as yours. I'm awed by your devotion and owe you an incalculable debt for what you did, but if you have watched over us these past weeks, you must know that my love for Cherlynn exceeds anything I have ever known. Please?"

Still nothing.

Conscious this time, Cherlynn was sucked into a vortex of light, feeling like a dust mite caught by a vacuum cleaner. Far below, Drew was weeping over Emily's body. Was this his fate? Had he lost Emily anyway? She twisted to see her destination and spotted her own body sprawled against the Broadbanks fireplace. The tour guide and half the tour members clustered around it as others raced from the gift shop to see what had happened. Drew's ravaged face still looked down from above the mantel. She slowed, hanging in space. Had nothing changed? But he would not really be happy until Emily returned, and so far her body remained dead.

"Thank you for saving him," said a shy voice.

She started, then realized that another spirit drifted in the void with her own. It wasn't hard to guess whose. "Emily? So nice to meet you at last. You will take care of him, won't you?"

"Of course."

"Keep him happy. He's been through so much."

"I know. You will still have a title, by the way, though only Lady Thurston, and only by courtesy. And your books will attract a wide readership from now on."

She nodded, though getting published no longer mattered. Grief already overwhelmed her. But at least she would have something of Drew's. "Just out of curiosity, why did you choose me?"

"You were the first one who would do." A sigh filled the void. "The vehicle had to be connected to Broadbanks and had to know enough to survive Dr. Harvey's bloodletting. But that proved nearly impossible. I was tied to the house. That crazy gypsy prevented me from reaching a candidate some years ago—the sixty-eighth marchioness, if I remember correctly. She came incognito, and the guides never spotted her. I suspect it was the title transfer that finally gave me an opportunity. It confused the gypsy long enough for me to reach you. Or perhaps her power waned once the title was no longer tied to the blood."

"You took quite a chance," she observed. "I might have bungled it badly. You knew nothing about me."

"Not true. You looked at Drew and recognized his pain. I could see that you longed to help him. That made success almost certain."

Drew raised his face to the sky and shouted.

"Oh, no!" Sobs choked Emily's voice as it sank into a despairing whisper. "They warned me of the risks, but I refused to believe!"

"What's the matter?" Cherlynn grabbed Emily's arm, amazed that it seemed to have substance. As did hers. Within moments, the girl's face also appeared, twisted in grief.

"He does not want me to return."

"Of course he does," she scoffed. "He loves you."

Emily cocked her head as though listening. Tears trickled down her face. "Can't you hear him?"

She shook her head. "I hear only you."

"He is begging me to send you back."

"That can't be!"

"It's true. He loves you."

"He's merely confused, Emily. Give him time to catch his

breath. It's only been a few days since he learned who I was."

"No. He wants you." Emily stared into her eyes. "Do you love him?"

She sighed. "How could I not? He is like no man I ever met."

"Enough to give up the conveniences you are accustomed to?"

"You mean I actually have a choice?" Her voice sang with hope.

Emily nodded. "I have loved him since I was fourteen. I devoted my life to him and postponed my eternal reward. But if he needs you to be happy, then go, with my blessing."

Cherlynn drew in a deep breath. "What a remarkable gift, Emily. But there is one thing I need to know. If I return, will I still have your body?"

"Why?"

"I was told after my miscarriage that I would conceive no more children. If that impediment comes with me, then I cannot accept. Drew needs an heir."

Emily nodded. "The true test of love. You would sacrifice yourself rather than bring him harm. Don't worry. It will be as before. You will bring your mind, your character, your personality. That is what he needs. The body is fully functional, and I offer it with pleasure."

"Thank you, Emily. You will always be first in my prayers."

"One more thing," added Emily with a last longing look at Drew. "I also bequeath you my memories. Love him well."

"I will," she promised even as the vortex reversed to spit her back into the clearing. She opened her eyes to find Drew weeping on her breast. One hand slid up to caress his hair.

"Emily?" he asked, raising his head to gaze uncertainly into her eyes.

She shook her head.

"Cherlynn?" The love that blazed on his face burned clear to her soul.

"She heard your plea and sent me back," she whispered, touching his cheek.

"Thank you, Em."

Arms closed around her. His kiss was even more shattering than the one they had shared in the folly—and nothing like the chaste exchanges he had dared with Emily in the Yorkshire woods. It went beyond lust, beyond passion, becoming an exchange of souls that united them as nothing else could have done. She felt his longing, his need, his wonder at the gift he had been given. In return, she basked in his love, his acceptance of every aspect of Cherlynn Cardington's character, his determination to make sure she never regretted her choice.

"It really is you," he said, pulling back to look her in the eyes. "I can't believe she sacrificed the rest of her life."

"She loves you, Drew. As do I. I would have done the same."

"I love you, Cherlynn. More than I thought possible."

"She sent us one last gift," she announced as he helped her to her feet. "Her memories. It will help me adjust to life here."

He grinned and kissed her lightly on the tip of her nose. "I'm scheduled to be married in twelve days. But I'm in need of a bride. Are you game?"

"Ready, willing, and able."

"For anything and everything," he agreed, pulling her into another embrace before leading her to the horses.

Epilogue

December 24, 1812

Andrew Villiers, Sixth Marquess of Broadbanks, held a glass of sherry up to the firelight and watched the sparks play through the amber liquid. "To our son," he said quietly, toasting with his wife.

"Or our daughter," replied Cherlynn, raising a cup of herbal tea as she rested her free hand on the swell that was barely detectable to her touch. The joys of pregnancy were countless now that she had a husband who shared them. She could hardly wait for that first fluttering kick. Any day now...

"Too bad Father died before we knew," he said with a sigh.

"He knew."

He raised a questioning brow.

"I told him that last night, though I wasn't quite sure. And even though he could no longer speak, he smiled, so I know he understood." Lord Broadbanks had lived nearly six weeks after their wedding, basking in his children's affection until the very end.

"You've a rare gift for love, Cherlynn."

"If so, it's something you brought out. No one else ever noticed." But she did not want to think of her past. "Guess what arrived today."

He unfolded the letter and held it up to the light. "Your book sold. Congratulations! Can even Christmas contain so many celebrations?"

She laughed, though he was right. Anne's wedding, Raeburn's recovery, Drew's anticipated heir, and now this. Only one cloud marred the horizon. She still had not been able to mention the curse, but she pushed the problem aside as another of those inexplicable cosmic rules. There were so many topics she couldn't discuss that she no longer tried to remember upcoming events. "Your critiques were right on target. Gothics are more my style. We'll leave the comedies of manners to Miss Austen."

Hardwick paused in the doorway. "Mr. Stevens requests a word, my lord."

"Send him in."

She suddenly had trouble breathing. She couldn't move, couldn't speak, couldn't see. So this was why she'd remained silent. Fay had not been solely responsible for calling down the curse. But surely Drew would do the right thing. The fluttering of her child's first kick went all but unnoticed, its life hanging in the balance as footsteps approached the room.

Mr. Stevens halted just inside the doorway, his expression softening as he took in the scene. "Excuse me, but Jeremy Fallon just returned from Dover. A woman and child have taken shelter in one of the caves on Chalk Down. It's no place to be just now, my lord. We'll have snow by morning if my knee is any prophet. She'll freeze out there. As will the babe."

Cherlynn quit fighting fate's paralyzing hand. She knew Drew, knew his mind, knew his compassion. There was nothing to fear.

"Of course it's no place for a woman, Stevens!" he exclaimed. "Why didn't Jeremy bring her to shelter? Fetch them in."

"At once, my lord."

By the time they returned from midnight services, the deed was done. Hardwick greeted them at the door.

"The lass is a gypsy, my lord," he said, his face carefully neutral. "But she carried this." He thrust a crumpled paper into Drew's hand.

"What is it?" Cherlynn asked as he smoothed the page.

"Damn him!"

Reading over his shoulder, she recognized the sheet as marriage lines. The groom was Randolph Villiers.

"Because he married beneath him?" She wished she could find the words to spell out their predicament, but they wouldn't come. Whatever the result of this encounter, Drew would carry the entire responsibility.

"Because the handwriting is his. I've seen half a dozen pages just like this. Randolph had a penchant for virgins. Whenever he couldn't seduce one, he married her—falsely, of course. How many others did he ruin and abandon?"

Expelling a sigh of frustration, he headed for the room where the gypsy and her child lay.

Cherlynn was appalled. Black eyes, black hair, and dusky skin had given the girl an exotic beauty that was still apparent, but she could not be more than sixteen, and she was very ill. Even untutored eyes could recognize the faint thread by which she clung to life. Her son rested in a cradle near the bed, looking little better. His eyes were dull and listless, but his parentage was obvious, matching sketches she'd seen of Randolph as a child.

"He's so thin," she murmured, gathering him into her arms.

The gypsy coughed long into a blood-spattered handkerchief.

Tuberculosis, Cherlynn diagnosed. Or consumption, as it was called in this time. They would have to keep the air moving to spare the staff.

"I can't breathe," gasped the girl, but Cherlynn was already opening the windows. Only when she saw the gypsy relax did she recall that the Rom hated being indoors.

"Where is my husband?" Another coughing spell claimed her.

Drew sat down on the bed, taking the thin hand into his own. "Randolph died on March 15. He stumbled over a cliff in the dark."

"So that is why he never returned. He had gone to break the news of our marriage to his father." A tear escaped to slide down her cheek.

"This is his son?" he asked softly.

She nodded. "Nicholas Randolph Villiers, after my father and my husband. He is three months old." Another cough wracked her. "I am dying, as I well know. But I had to bring Nicki home. My people would never accept him."

"He will be cared for." He exchanged a look with Cherlynn, who nodded. "We will raise him here, as is fitting for my nephew, but I will see that he learns of his mother's people. To which caravan do you belong?"

"Bless you," she murmured, adding a name before falling back against the pillow. In a moment she was asleep.

He summoned the housekeeper. "Find a wet nurse. At once, if possible. And assign someone to look after her."

"Keep those windows wide open," added Cherlynn as they headed upstairs.

"You do not mind taking in Randolph's son?" he asked when they reached their rooms.

"Of course not. All children deserve a good home."

"Even if he inherited Randolph's weaknesses?"

"We will love him and raise him to the best of our abilities," she said, sliding her fingers into his hair as he loosened his cravat.

"Thank you. That will relieve her mind. We'll learn more in the morning."

"She won't awaken. Her goal is achieved."

"How do you know?"

"That was the other reason Emily brought me here. To break the Broadbanks Curse." And with the uttering of the words, her frozen tongue unlocked, and she was at last able to explain the horror which his own generosity had averted.

"I can't believe it," he said at last, shaking his head one last time. "So much grief. Randolph and Fay between them destroyed an entire family."

"Fay must have started rumors that you killed Randolph. Why else would the girl have included you in her curse?"

He sighed. "My card case was missing the next morning. I never did find it."

"I knew Fay must have fabricated evidence against you. It was her ultimate threat, and one she would have acted on after marriage out of sheer perversity. She hated you. But that is past, my love. And we can now live our lives with no more inkling of what is in store for us than any other couple. It will be quite an adventure."

"Starting now," he murmured, sweeping her into his arms.

SIGNET REGENCY ROMANCE

TAKE A CHANCE ON LOVE WITH ALLISON LANE

- ☐ **THE PRODIGAL DAUGHTER** Amanda infuriated her father when she eloped with Jack Morrison. His untimely death in battle at Waterloo forced her to go home to a father who would not forget nor forgive her defiance. Now she was to live in seclusion, never to disgrace the family again. But she can not keep her eyes off the Duke of Norwood, the man her stepsister wants to marry. (186826—$5.50)

- ☐ **THE IMPOVERISHED VISCOUNT** Young and inexperienced Lady Melissa Stapleton was adrift in a world of deception and desire. Lord Heflin, the most rapacious rake in England, had her brother in his debt and Melissa at his mercy. She had to flee his odious advances—only to find herself in greater danger.... (186818—$4.99)

- ☐ **THE RAKE'S RAINBOW** Only the most bizarre of accidents could have made Miss Caroline Cummings, a vicar's daughter, the bride of Thomas Mannering, the most irresistible and infamous rake in the realm—but accidents do happen and did. Now Caroline's happiness was in the hands of this libertine lord who taught her the pleasures of love but who himself was besotted with another man's ravishing wife.
(186664—$4.50)

*Prices slightly higher in Canada

Buy them at your local bookstore or use this convenient coupon for ordering.

PENGUIN USA
P.O. Box 999 — Dept. #17109
Bergenfield, New Jersey 07621

Please send me the books I have checked above.
I am enclosing $_____ (please add $2.00 to cover postage and handling). Send check or money order (no cash or C.O.D.'s) or charge by Mastercard or VISA (with a $15.00 minimum). Prices and numbers are subject to change without notice.

Card #_____ Exp. Date _____
Signature_____
Name_____
Address_____
City _____ State _____ Zip Code _____

For faster service when ordering by credit card call **1-800-253-6476**

Allow a minimum of 4-6 weeks for delivery. This offer is subject to change without notice.

SIGNET REGENCY ROMANCE

DILEMMAS OF THE HEART

☐ **AN AFFAIR OF HONOR by Candice Hern.** The lovely Meg Ashburton finds herself in quite a dilemma when the dazzlilng Viscount Sedgewick is recovering from an accidental injury in her country manor. All too soon, though, he would be on his feet again, able to once more take Meg in his arms, and this time not to dance. . . . (186265—$4.99)

☐ **A TEMPORARY BETHROTHAL by Dorothy Mack.** Belinda Melville knew it was folly to be head-over-heels in love with Captain Anthony Wainright, who made it clear that he far preferred Belinda's heartbreakingly beautiful and calculating cousin, the newly married Lady Deidre Archer. Should Belinda hold out for a man who would be hers and hers only? Or was being second best to a man she adored at first sight better than nothing? (184696—$3.99)

☐ **LORD ASHFORD'S WAGER by Marjorie Farrell.** Lady Joanna Barrand knows all there is to know about Lord Tony Ashford—his gambling habits, his wooing a beautiful older widow to rescue him from ruin, and worst of all, his guilt in a crime that made all his other sins seem innocent. What she doesn't know is how she has lost her heart to him? (180496—$3.99)

☐ **LADY LEPRECHAUN by Melinda McRae.** When a lovely, young widow and a dashing duke are thrown together in a cross-country hunt for two schoolboy runaways, they are both faced with an unexpected pleasurable challenge. "One of the most exciting new voices in Regency fiction."—*Romantic Times* (175247—$3.99)

*Prices slightly higher in Canada **RA23X**

Buy them at your local bookstore or use this convenient coupon for ordering.

PENGUIN USA
P.O. Box 999 — Dept. #17109
Bergenfield, New Jersey 07621

Please send me the books I have checked above.
I am enclosing $_____ (please add $2.00 to cover postage and handling). Send check or money order (no cash or C.O.D.'s) or charge by Mastercard or VISA (with a $15.00 minimum). Prices and numbers are subject to change without notice.

Card #_____ Exp. Date _____
Signature_____
Name_____
Address_____
City _____ State _____ Zip Code _____

For faster service when ordering by credit card call **1-800-253-6476**

Allow a minimum of 4-6 weeks for delivery. This offer is subject to change without notice.